Song of Jamaica

by Hector Grant

LMH Publishing Limited

Published by: LMH Publishing Limited
7 Norman Road,
LOJ Industrial Complex
Building 10
Kingston C.S.O., Jamaica
Tel: 876-938-0005; 938-0712
Fax: 876-928-8036
Email: lmhpublishing@cwjamaica.com

Cover Design by: Errol Rhule (Jamaica)
Design & Typeset by: Michelle M.A. Mitchell (Jamaica)

Printed by Lightning Source Inc., U.S.A.   ISBN 976-818-405-1

Dedication

This book is dedicated to all those who have influenced my life beginning with my parents, John Amos and Adina Ethline Grant and through teachers R.G.A. Morris of Race Course, E.J. Whiteman of May Pen; Rev. E.B. Hinds and the members of Green's Temple AME Church, Palmers Cross; Revs.p S.U. Dunmoodie and A.S.D. Airall of the Methodist Church of the Caribbean and the Americas; Mr. H. McD. Messam of the Jamaica Boys Brigade.

In writing this book I was always reminded of the Jamaican proverb, *"If a man can't change his mind, he is not a man."* And so in my dedication I hope that the men and women of influence at every level of Jamaican society will find themselves reflected in the book and change their minds by whatever way necessary for the good of the "Land we Love."

CONTENTS

CHAPTER ONE

Four Paths, Clarendon, 1995

"Crown me!" Bigger Ferguson ordered. He flourished a crimson Red Stripe Beer bottle stopper over his head, then made three men jump, to land on the coveted eight check of the draughts board. Bigger could not know what his words would bring, and that forces were already in motion to alter the course of his life forever.

"Suh, wha' mek yuh suh sharp tenight?" asked Boysie Ellis. "Man, me can't even win one game. Wha' happen tuh yuh?" Boysie was despondent. He leaned forward as he studied the home made draughts board resting on a crude table, and pondered his next move. There seemed no way to avoid an obvious debacle. He was unusually thoughtful as he picked up a stopper from the pile beside his left arm, and placed it tentatively on the one Bigger had just deposited on the top line of the eight check. This game was proving to be far more challenging than he had expected.

"Yuh tink dis is luck? Dis is sciance, yuh kno'. Is sciance dis'." Crowed Bigger.

The shop in which they sat was adjacent to a rum bar which stood alone at a crossroads. From it's open door a broad swath of golden light cut through the darkness beyond the narrow asphalt road. The moist and windy chill moved like cold molasses through the folds of the north central Manchester mountains. It was enough to send sensible people home to snug blanketed beds. Or to the solace of the many rum bars and shops at every cross road throughout the parish. Bigger sat relishing his rout of the game. Boysie sat stunned at his utter defeat. Mr Errol Byrd, the proprietor, absent-mindedly rearranged bottles on the shelves behind the counter. None of them saw the tall man, dressed in black, who, avoiding the light, stealthily moved towards the entrance of the bar.

* * * * * * * * *

Walford Salmon was among those who had retired early. Lying beside his lovely wife, Enid, he looked up at the zinc roofing as he spoke. His worry echoed out through his words.

"Yuh kno', is night like dis I wonda weh Gad deh."

Enid looked at him in the dimly lit room. Her shock at his words was as strong as his expressed anger and frustration. This was not the Walford she knew. As she wondered what sort of response to make, a kaleidoscope of thoughts flashed across her mind; neither of them was deeply religious, although they held strong moral values.

True, they could be described as third generation Moravians and Anglicans , but poverty and lack of habit prevented them from being greatly involved in church activities. They had not even been officially married before a minister, although they had sometimes talked about doing so. None of their children attended church or had been baptized. Other than prayers learned in school, they knew no religious devotions.

So, she wondered, unless busybody evangelists had bothered Walford, he was not just talking about religion. Was it the continued theft of animals, fruits, and ground crops that was depressing him? Or, was it the money he owed to the bank that was now due but which he could not pay? The children needed money for lessons and books. Those would have to wait until the sow dropped another litter, or until the goat kids grew a little bigger. Yes, there was much on his mind, but she would not try to guess. Anyway, she welcomed his willingness to talk.

"Lawd, Massa, what mek yuh say a t'ing like dat?" she asked.

"Jus' look outside deh," he said gravely, pointing a thumb towards the shaded window.

"Walford, yuh kno' dat is Gad inna heav'n mek we last dis long in dis' wicked country. Yuh can't be serious fi seh such a t'ing as which part Gad deh. Suh, what's happen tuh yuh, man?"

He got out of bed, went to the window and drew back the curtain. The thick wall of darkness seemed to be pressing against the panes of glass, seeking to break through and envelop them; nothing was visible outside. He turned to face Enid while pointing at the window.

"Jus' tek a look outside deh."

Enid joined him at the window. She peered into the dark.

"Is night like dis t'ief love," he complained. "See me here, tired an' weary, tryin' fi catch a likkle sleep. An' I bet fifty dollars dat in de mawnin we gwine lose some goat, if not a cow."

"But Walford, we can't duh nutt'n 'bout dat."

"Das what ah mean," he said. "See me here, sick an' worried and in debt, an' I still haffi guh out in dis col' wedda with mi machete fi try an' protek mi dumb t'ings.

"Now, suppose me guh out deh and ketch a robba man? What me fi duh? Chop im up, or mek 'im shat me? Lawd have mercy! Is wat dis worl' comin' to, when a hard workin' man can't even tek him res' afta a lang backbreakin' day? Yes, is de trut' sometimes ah wonda weh Gad deh, an' on whose side 'im deh pon, on a night like dis!"

Enid had no reply. She too had on occasion thought like that, but had quickly stifled it. Walford had never held such a long conversation before, though, and one about God at that. Things had really come to a bump in Jamaica when a person like her husband was thinking so deeply about God. But she was worried too. Life seemed so unfair. They had tried so hard, yet it looked like all their work had gone only to support worthless hooligans. The government could do nothing to help. Politicians came around with loudspeakers at election time promising so much. But, once they got elected, did nothing to protect hard working people. It seemed the very ones who worked hardest to keep the country going, were the ones who had the fruits of their labours stolen. If politicians were not careful, there would soon be no one around to vote for them when gunmen wrecked the country.

She stared into the impenetrable blackness of the night. It seemed that their efforts to better themselves were blocked by forces as mysterious and densely stubborn as the darkness. Some knew that the problems facing the country, like those she and Walford faced, were far larger than mere praedial larceny. There was a sickness in the land that would not be cured by mere police work. For instance, she had never known her father. It's not that she needed anything like support from him. It was just that a piece of the puzzle of her life was missing. It would be terrible to die without knowing where a part of oneself was located. The bitter legacy of anonymous fatherhood was a sharp thorn that bored in the very heart of many young lives. Her burden might seem small to many people, but it hurt her deeply. She still had cousins who suffered because a sick mother had to raise half-starved children, without the benefit of a man's love and strength and helpful hand. Thank God, Walford was not like that.

Then, too, it worried her how the people who called themselves Christians could squander their wealth on themselves and not share with the helpless and the poor. That left the needy to do unlawful things to survive. She knew that God would be pleased if the ones with substance helped the needy. Yes, even though life was a bitter struggle for them, she and Walford still gave to the less fortunate. They always gave to the church at Harvest time. They never turned away a hungry person, and sometimes they made work for others which they could have done themselves and saved money. True, it was wrong for people to steal and wreck the lives of those who were trying to do something to help themselves and the country. Still, one couldn't always blame the thieves. So much had gone wrong in Jamaica, and the government just sat idly by, watching.

She turned away from the window. Walford was sitting on a chair and putting on his trousers. She watched as he put on a sweat stained shirt, a pair of socks, and a pair of old shoes. After dressing, he reached behind a door and picked up his machete which had been filed razor sharp.

"Yuh kno' Walford, we cyan blame Gad fi everything bad people duh. Accord'n to my thinkin' some people are just bad. I don' t'ink is because God nuh care, why t'hievin people t'ief. Is w'en dem see dat nobaddy nuh care 'bout dem an' dem haffi decide wedda fe t'ief or starve dat dem decide fi tek a chance. Dat don' mek it right, but when yuh tek stock of de situation, is hard time mek mos' t'ievin' people tief. Suh, wha' me a seh is, yuh have a right tuh get vex, but yuh don' haffi believe dat Gad is agains' we."

Walford looked at his wife. He tucked the long machete under his arm as he examined a flashlight. He removed the batteries, checked the bulb, then replaced the batteries. He flicked the switch. A bright light beamed across the room in response. He turned the light off with a satisfied nod, simultaneously thinking that he had never seen Enid more serious in all the years they had lived together. This night had touched both of them and pulled from them feelings of vulnerability as well as solidarity with the masses of suffering people. Beyond that, both he and Enid were sensing things they could not put into words. Breaking his wordless gaze, he reached for the latch on the door.

"Well, ah guess ah haffi guh try protek de animals dem. Ah will come back afta a while. Lack de door and don' open fi nobaddy till yuh hear me special knack," he said, as he stepped into the gloom.

A yellow streak of light from the doorway kept him company along the track, for a while. Enid watched him go, then closed the door. He merged with the dark shapes of the pitch-black night, following a well-known path. The pen with the animals was up a hill, some distance ahead.

The further he moved from the house, the more powerful became the sense of dread that overcame him. A cold sweat washed over him. A voice within urged him to turn back. After all, nothing he could do this night was worth the value of his 'safety' or that of Enid and the children. Suppose someone broke in on them while he was out trying to save a few goats. The night separating him from his loved ones became a heavy burden. Thoughts of his warm bed and the arms of his loving wife, battled with his will to move forward. Their tenderness to each other earlier in the evening came back to him with a surge that he found unusual. Yes, he loved his wife dearly. They were happy together. He shook off the feelings of fear, chiding himself for being foolish. After all, he had been out many nights to check on the livestock and nothing had ever happened. Thieves were as careful and as fearful as was he. They would watch and wait until he left before doing their dirty work. They neither wanted to go to jail, or to take a man's life. As a matter of fact, he thought he knew who the culprits were. It seemed suspicious that certain people were happy and suddenly wearing new clothes just after he had lost some livestock. Humph! he had lost too many animals. His property was being violated and he was being driven closer and closer to the almshouse. If this kept up he wouldn't be able to support his family. A man had to defend his domain or there would be nothing left to defend. He bowed his head against the cold wind.

* * * * * * * * *

The man seemed to materialize out of nowhere. One moment there was just the void of black roadway along which nothing moved, and then, there he was stepping up on the piazza and moving towards the counter.

He was dressed in blue jeans, black turtleneck sweater, and black tennis shoes with thick rubber soles. The hood of the sweater hugged the back of his neck and his head was covered with a skullcap matching the sweater.

"Mr Bartender, let me have a QQ of white rum," the man ordered softly. Turning to look around him, his casual glance appeared to take in nothing and everything all at once. His intelligent eyes missed nothing. Like a roving camera, his gaze swept the room. For a moment they locked on the two draught players, then moved on.

The two draught players looked up from their game wordlessly studying the tall man at the bar. The half-filled bottles of beverages before them indicated that they were drinking slowly, and that they intended to stay where they were for awhile. For them, the shop was an oasis, in the midst of the wide expanse of a stark and deserted landscape.

The shopkeeper measured the spirits and poured it into a glass, then placed another glass with water beside the first, and slid both before the customer. The quarter quart was one half pint of potent liquid. That was the equivalent of two robust snorts for a Jamaican drinking man. Often, a drinker would order a QQ, divide it, slowly drink one, then the other, chasing each away with generous drops of water. The macho drinker would often pour a sprinkle of water on the entire amount, gulp it all, place the empty glass on the bar counter, then grimace as he exclaimed, "Ah!" while the liquor burned its way down.

As he heard his order placed before him, the man turned, poured a few drops of water over the liquor, and lifted the potion to his lips. He took a long swallow and lowered the glass. Again he lifted the tumbler. This time he drained it before stopping. He gave the familiar grimace which suggested that swallowing liquid fire had taken an extra effort, but he made no sound. Reaching into his pocket, he took out a crisp five hundred dollar bill and placed it on the counter. He turned and left the bar without waiting for any change, disappearing as silently as he had entered. A pall of lingering sadness seemed to remain at the spot where he had stood.

Quiet reigned for long moments after the stranger left, then Bigger chuckled.

"Boysie, yuh believe inna duppy?"

"Massa, right now, I don' kno' what a believe," reflected Boysie. "All I can tell yuh seh is, dat I t'ink a man was in ya a while ago, but ef I evah see him again, ah don' believe seh a could reconnize 'im. Sump'n strange a gwan 'bout ya tenite. Maybe a betta stap drinkin' dis Red Stripe an' start drinkin' white rum, suh a can see wha' dat man who just lef' ya can see. Yuh look pon him eye dem?"

"Yes, man. 'im eye dem is de firs' t'ing ah see. Bway, dem look dead, enh? I don' haffi tell yuh nutt'n. Seems like seh we see de same t'ing. Mass Erral, yuh evah see nutt'n like dat deh man inna yuh life? Yuh kno' 'im, sah?"

"No, sah." replied the bartender. "Me nevah see 'im before. Him nuh come from 'roun' ya at all. Yuh see seh 'im left me one five hundred dolla bill, fi one twenty dolla drink?"

"Yes, Mass Erral, we see wha' 'im duh. Well, Boysie, seems like yuh an' me feel de same way. I t'ink is time we guh home an' ketch a piece a sleep."

Boysie stood and began to gather the bottle stoppers that had served as "men" for the game of checkers. He took the board and pieces to the shop counter and gave them to the proprietor, declaring: "Well, Mass Erral, I don' kno' ef yuh feel like me an' Bigga, but tenight we goin' home sooner than usual. See yuh tomorrow evenin', sah."

"I see what yuh mean, Boysie. A feel like going to bed meself. But mi gwine stay open a likkle while longa. Bway, t'ings feel strange roun' ya tenite! See yuh tomarra, Boysie. Yuh gawn tuh, Bigga?"

Yes, Mass Erral, mi a guh wid Boysie. See yuh tommarra, sah."

The friends left together. The proprietor stared after them. He moved thoughtfully as he gathered up empty glasses for washing, picking up and stacking empty bottles along the way. He arranged the stock on the shelves, and then he swept the place and wiped the counter and table.

An hour later, he was still haunted by a nagging uneasiness as he locked up his business for the night. That strange man in the all-black outfit was no ghost. He was up to something deadly.

And Bigger and Boysie. Something was funny with those boys. They had been hanging around his shop ever since they were children. They were like his own children. But how well did he know them? And they were acting strange tonight. Very strange. As Boysie had said, they were going home earlier than usual. Even though on occasions in the past, he had seen them leave earlier than usual, it just seemed they were in a hurry to go somewhere. He shook his head as if the effort to sort things out was too great for his tired brain. He had never remembered a night as dark, quiet, cold, and mysterious as this.

****

Bigga walked slightly ahead in his place as the leader. Boysie followed closely on his heels. Beyond the fading light of the shop, they turned up a track that branched from the road, and followed a narrow path which twisted its way against the steep grade of hillside. The two men headed further and further away from the darkened houses, with only an occasional glow of a traffic light marking the main road far below.

"Bigga, yuh t'ink we should tek a pass tenite?" asked Boysie tentatively.

"Man, wha' yuh a talk 'bout? Nuh yuh tell me seh yuh hungry an' me fi set up sum'thing?" retorted Boysie's friend and partner.

"Me know dat, man, but ah have a bad feelin' 'bout dis business tenite. Bout how much goat we tek from Walford a'ready? 'bout fifteen head?"

Bigga was silent awhile. Then he pursed his lips and hissed just above a whisper.

"Boysie, yuh memba dem man use to seh 'ef yuh keep yuh mout' shut, yuh keep yuh life? An' yuh memba dem use tuh seh' dark night have eyes, and walls have ears? Well, ef yuh memba, SHUT YUH MOUT'!"

Boysie opened his mouth to protest against his friend's outburst, but thought better of it. He sought re-assurance by patting the small of his back where the cold hard weapon rested snugly. He was now a veteran thief, but there was always a strong nervousness whenever he started out on a job. Tonight, however, his usual fear was being transformed to terror. He could not tell Bigga about it, because he did not understand it himself.

Poverty and desperation had driven Boysie to steal, but from time to time slim slivers of an ancient morality gnawed at his innards and stirred within him a sense of guilt at what he was doing. He had learned in school to "Do to others as you would have them do to you," and to:

"Speak the truth and speak it ever, cost it what it will. He who hides the wrong he did, does the wrong thing still." But that occasional urge to live an honest life was always eclipsed by the memory of his youth. Children at school had nicknamed him "One Shirt" because he had to wear the same stained khaki shirt for weeks. His poor mother had been ill for years, and he had never known his father. Often, he had to go to school without breakfast or lunch. He would watch other children eating hot patties or a delicious pudding, while he pretended not to be hungry. Occasionally, when fortune smiled on him, he would have a slice of bread and some sugar and water for supper, but the hunger pangs were always great.

No one missed him when he dropped out of school, for he had no real friends there. But staying at home did not help. It was depressing to watch his mother waste away day by day, so he began to walk the streets. He always wound up at the little shop at the crossroads, where Mass Errol allowed him to stay and often gave him odd jobs for which he would sometimes be rewarded with a spice bun or a few dollars. He would always proudly hurry home to share his earnings with his mother.

Then Bigga had recruited him. Bigga needed a partner whom he could trust, to join his operation. After weeks of playing draughts together, he concluded that Boysie was physically and emotionally fit enough, and hungry enough, to be taken into his confidence. So, Boysie had gone on his first expedition. He was shocked at the impersonal savagery with which Bigga shot and killed the angry farmer who had rushed at them as they were butchering that third goat. "Dead man tell no tales. Memba dat!" Bigga had said, as he calmly shoved the gun in his waist, and dragged the carcasses to the borrowed van waiting in the brush down the hill. "Come on, drag that goat, an hurry up before people start to come".

That first hundred dollars was the biggest payday be had ever had. The money soothed his screaming conscience and spurred him to ask when the next campaign would come. He felt good in the new shirt and the tennis shoes he had bought. He felt good about the steaming plate of rice and ackee he cooked for his mother..

"So, Bigga, when we a guh mek anodda payday, man?" he had asked softly over a game of draughts.

"Payshance, man. Yuh haffi cool it yuh kno', ef yuh hurry, hurry, yuh boun' fi mek mistakes. Here. See one money ya." Bigga had handed him a twenty dollar bill. "Trus' me man, ah wi' mek yuh kno' when we get anodda likkle action."

Boysie had learned patience, and had come to accept stealing as a way of life. Gradually he stopped seeing the small farmers as fellow strugglers against poverty. He buried all the remorse that used to well up in him when he saw one of his victims riding wearily home on a donkey, or walking the dusty track with a heavy burden on the head, or complaining to Mass Errol about another animal stolen, or a half acre of yam field which was plundered. The guilt had threatened to overwhelm him when a man had to plead for extended credit from the shopkeeper, and it took a great effort for him not to pull money from his pocket to pay for the man's groceries. But he steeled himself. If he didn't steal he would starve, and he chose to live. He accepted the truth of his situation and hardened his heart against those he was destroying. Although he knew very little about Bigga's past, he suspected that his friend's story was similar to his. Few would believe like him that the generous, laughing sport, who treated all the boys to bun and cheese, and cared for him like a brother, was a vicious and ruthless robber after dark.

So now, despite the hoarse whispering of an almost expired voice of conscience, Boysie stumbled on, just a few paces behind his best friend and hero. Their eyes, now adjusted on the dark, started to pick out familiar outlines of trees and jutting rocks along the track, as they neared their destination. The barbed wire fence of Walford Salmon's property came into view.

* * * * * * * * *

Walford tightened his grip on the machete, sensing a presence. Although he saw nothing move, he felt that he was not alone. It must be those good-for-nothing thieves, he thought, for he did not believe in such things as ghosts. Long ago, his father had said, "Wally, is not dead man yuh must 'fraid of; is live man will kill yuh." He never forgot the words.

He remembered the night he was going home from a dance. He had to pass the Swaby's graveyard where a man had just been buried. Just as he passed the mounded grave with the fresh flowers on it, he saw something in the middle of the road. The apparition had driven a knee-knocking fear into him. It was gray in colour and the shape was that of an inverted triangle. It was swaying and making a "thump, thump, thump" sound. His first impulse was to run, but he remembered that the Heron's graveyard had also received a recent corpse, so his other direction was also blocked. He felt trapped and started to panic, but then his father's words came to him "Is nat dead man yuh mus' 'fraid of." Taking courage, he switched on his powerful flashlight and ran full speed at the thing in the road. When he saw what terrorized him, he was overcome with feelings of amusement and relief as the comedy of the situation struck him. What he saw was a donkey standing on three legs and scratching his ears with a fourth. He collapsed on the dew covered road bank laughing hysterically in the soft fragrant grass. That memory lasted forever.

Since then, he never feared the night. He was sure that anything he encountered could be reasonably explained, but he also realized the truth in what his father had said. He altered himself to move carefully and silently. Eventually he came within sight of the goat pen. The animals were all bedded down and resting. Everything seemed to be well. Nevertheless, he would just stay awhile to make sure that all was as it seemed. With tender thoughts of his warm bed and his devoted wife, he sank down on a large stone to wait.

His body jerked upright, eyes opened wide. He must have dozed. But something disturbed him. The night was no longer tranquil. The animals were moving about agitatedly. Some were "may-may-ing" in alarm.

Then he saw the men. Two of them. They were stooped low, trying to blend in with the excited goats. Walford dried his hands on his pants, and picked up the machete. Slowly, he began to crawl towards the pen. Stealthily, he spread apart the strands of barbed wire, and entered the enclosure from the side opposite the bent figures. He watched as one grabbed a protesting ram and dragged it by the legs towards the fence.

When Enid had asked him what he would do if he met a man stealing his goats, he had made no reply. Not only had he lost almost a score of animals, but his Uncle David had been shot to death protecting his animals up at Coleyville a little more than a year ago. He too had lost more than a score of animals. But his vigils had never rewarded him with the sight of any thief. Although at David's funeral he had pledged never to be careless enough to be shot to death by a thief, the truth is that he honestly did not know what he would do.

Now , seeing the thieves, a rage engulfed him. The seething spasm was unlike anything he ever experienced before. Like a wild fire, whipped by hot winds, and blazing uncontrollably through acres of sugar cane fields under a torrid August sun, his anger spread through him until he lost control. He raised his machete above his head and charged like a raging bull towards the thieves.

"A weh de rass yuh a duh? Puddung mi goat before me chop up yuh rass!" he screamed, as he ran in desperate frustration towards the robber who was dragging away his choice ram. In his rush, he lost sight of the other stooping figure who now straightened and stared at the angry farmer with a sad but determined look on his face. With only the briefest hesitation, he pulled his gun, pointed, and fired. The roar of the weapon shattered the quiet of the night.

Walford stumbled. He felt as if his head had struck the biggest rockstone in the world. He slammed hard against the ground. His face had just met the wet cold grass when he heard what sounded like the explosion of a giant fire cracker. Then all went black, and he was enveloped by a warm and dreamless sleep.

"Rass, Bigga, is Mas Walford yuh kill. Is mi uncle yuh kill, man!"

"Come on Boysie, ef 'im dead, 'im dead. Yuh kno' lang time seh sump'n like dis could happen. But we haffi rush now. Sumbaddy mus' hear de shat."

"But, Bigga, yuh t'ink seh 'im dead? Yuh t'ink we kill Mas Walford?"

"Man, Boysie, nuh ax me nuh foolish question! Me seh we haffi hurry now. We haffi leave right now. Come on!!"

"YOU NOT GOING ANYWHERE BUT HELL TONIGHT, YOU KNOW." The soft voice sounded weary and empty of all feeling. "THIS

IS THE END OF THE LINE FOR YOU DIRTY MURDERING THIEVES."

Bigga spun to face the new threat. He screamed in excited response;

"Hell? Hell? Is yuh gwine guh a hell, yuh brute!"

He lifted and pointed his weapon as he spoke. But he had lost valuable time by speaking. Before his finger could close around the trigger, two bullets, like powerful fists slammed into his skull.

By the time he heard the hoarse coughing of the silenced weapon, Bigga had collapsed. A crimson wash of blood surrounded his head and flowed down his neck, and the involuntary muscle spasms which rocked his flailing body, told the story of his unsuccessful struggle to live.

Boysie watched Bigga fall. The now motionless body told him that his partner in crime would never rise to stand again in this world. He felt alone. Nothing seemed to make sense anymore. All he had ever done to make money now seemed so stupid. Maybe he should just have committed suicide like the many others in his village. Criminal acts, like poverty and want, are but opposite faces of the same coin of ignominious tollways to early graves.

But honour, affection, and loyalty informed him that he had a duty to avenge his partner. He dropped the goat he had still been holding and clumsily reached for his gun. He had bought it, but never used it. It was Bigga's idea that he should get something to protect himself. A fleeting thought that his own life was in mortal danger, passed through his mind just before he raised the weapon.

The man before him loomed like a black spectre against the even blacker night. He stood with feet apart and seemed too cool to be a local farmer. Maybe he was a special police officer or some soldier from Up Park Camp. Or maybe even... but no it couldn't be.

Boysie fired. The sound exploded and echoed across the slopes of the surrounding hills. But the bullet went wild. He was afraid, nervous. It had never been his intention to take a human life in this business. Before he could fire again, he was violently lifted and flung by the force of a missile. Just beneath the hole in the centre of his forehead, his eyes filled with tears. Darkness hugged and held him. Boysie died without having time to pray.

Sammy replaced the gun in the sheath beneath his armpit. He walked over to Walford and knelt beside him, placing an experienced hand on the side of his neck. A strong pulse throbbed stubbornly. Next, he looked for the wound that had rendered the man unconscious. A gash exposed the flesh above his hairline. It was bleeding, but not fatal. The crisp night air would soon revive the struggling farmer. His cousin would live. Sammy melted into the night, his darkened form unobtrusively descending the hill. He did not use the well-worn path. Instead, he noiselessly made his way through the high guinea grass and thick intertwining bush. He felt calm. The kill had been justified. Murders were avenged, and an attempted homicide had been prevented. In this Jamaica, where law and order had become impotent, the law of the jungle prevailed, so one had to make justice by the best means at hand. Just as he had effectively done on other battlefields, the seventh son of a seventh son had struck again.

Chapter Two

Mandela Highway, 1995

Sammy smiled mirthlessly. "I wonder if those people know who they are skylarking with when they mess with my family?" He became very serious again. This act tonight held no pleasure for him, even more so now that he knew one of the victims was a member of his own family. He had heard the young boy mention that Walford was his uncle. His battle against the scourge infesting his motherland had now come to include his own kin. The infestation knew no bounds. The starving masses who had been ignored by the privileged few, were now predators without conscience. This disease had to be taken in hand quickly, or there would be nothing left to salvage. The surgery had to be radical enough to excise the spreading cancer.

In the middle of his thoughts, he remembered a literature class he had taken in May Pen decades before. The discussion that evening just fell into place with what he was thinking. The talk had turned to King Arthur and the Round Table. Europe had been laid waste by rough men who, having armed themselves, came to consider might as right. Carnage was everywhere, no one was safe. Not women, not children, not the poor. Teacher Whiteman had challenged those taking private lessons.

"Which do you think is nobler, to believe and act as if might is right, or to use might to defend the right?"

There had been no debate, everyone agreed that force was only noble when used for honorable means. Now, as he took long strides in the dark, he felt a deep sadness at what his country had become. He looked up at the starless sky. He felt at one with the night. Yet, a feeling of purpose came over him. When his family or friends needed him, it was his duty to protect the helpless and the weak. He began to hum softly.

"Sammy nuh dead, Sammy nuh dead, Sammy nuh dead, O!"

Until very recently he had felt destroyed in some fundamental ways. His business destroyed, his family shattered, his character ruined, and his life threatened by cruel men. But Septimus George Gordon the Second, had risen from the dust of depression and ruin. He felt relieved from the constraints of the conservative business class. He could now roam the land and mete out justice to those who schemed to destroy decent people. One day soon, those who had tried to destroy him would be duly punished, but not yet. Before he turned to that last vengeful task, he would do his bit to clean up some of the immoral morass floating atop the cesspool of unlawfulness and violence in his beloved country.

Few Jamaicans dreamed any more of the rewards of hard work. He could not blame them. Life on the rock is tough. Many decent people were just tired of seeing their hard earned goods stolen or destroyed. Many had just packed up and left the terrible place. Many who stayed had become hard, bitter people with little sympathy for anyone. Much of traditional values had been savaged in the turbulence of social upheaval.

He understood, but he could not stand by and watch the downtrodding of those who doggedly tried to keep their dreams alive. These dreams were a legacy left by their parents, who had faith that the tilling of the good soil, of the good land, would eventually reward them. No, he would not tolerate that. He would exercise his skills to expel the rot from the bowels of his beloved hills, then he would settle the score with the elements on the plains that had ruined him.

In mid humming, his mind turned to the sobriety of his situation. He was a realistic man and knew that not even the seventh son of a seventh son was impervious to a well placed bullet.

True, his fortunes had stood him in good stead through many perilous situations, but he knew his day was bound to come. Until that day, though, he would live for the principles that made him a "son of the soil," the loyal patriot he understood himself to be.

Accumulated wealth had never affected his sense of loyalty or genuine love for all things Jamaican. The loss of his family was a dagger in his heart, but the loss of the plush living above Barbican had only been a phase. Then he had been nothing but an adult miming the cruel childhood game of "Puddung an' Galang". All had been phases, necessary steps on the journey to understanding the purpose of his life. His travels across the world, and the experiences and skills he had developed were all stepping stones for what was his emerging destiny.

Yes, living in defence of helpless farmers was a noble thing. Farmers were the backbone of the country, the few generators of real wealth for the nation. These rustic folk, so unappreciated by their city cousins, still understood the goodness and potential of their ravaged land. They were dedicated citizens who expressed hope that in spite of all the anarchy, good would win in the end. It was their due that they should have a champion. He would see to it that he would be there for them for as long as he could, but he knew that time was not always kind. After all, time kept its own counsel.

Sammy had no illusions that anyone would rise to take his place once he was gone. Most people he knew were too cynical and self-centered for that. For many, Jamaica was neither worth living nor worth dying for. Not for a minute did he believe that he could single-handedly eradicate every vestige of the human scum that plagued the nation, but, by God, the farmers of poor small holdings, deserved a chance. If he could drive fear into a few hearts, and thereby slow the wide ranging plunder, then his work would not be in vain. This was his greatest wish.

How he yearned for the return of those days when school, church, and home were united in the task of character building of even the poorest urchin on the street corner. Where had it all gone wrong? Why had the leaders of churches and schools joined others in fleeing the hell hole of an island, leaving the poor and helpless at the mercies of a new breed who had no memory of a noble past, and no vision of a worthwhile future?

It was this abandonment that had caused the sickness of the present generation, who believed in nothing beyond their own survival. Out of the years of hunger and deprivations grew the determination to survive at any cost.

Left to sink or swim, many had little time for niceties like patriotism and community. It was each man for himself and may God take the rest. He understood where their inbred suspicion and cynicism stemmed from. He understood their hostility towards those who returned to Jamaica after the holocaust, with obvious prosperity, to show off to those who had stayed behind and suffered.

But, unlike them, he still believed in the vision and the values imparted to him. He had been fortunate enough to be away during the hell of the revolutionary times. He returned soon enough not to have forgotten all he had been taught by the generation of dreamers, who on the one hand spawned the revolution, but could not foresee the devastation of the mind. That was one consequence of the shock waves of change. A brain drain had broken the link in the chain of a long tradition of excellence. An excellence that had been a mixed blessing, since it had been purchased at a cost of massive social oppression.

His long strides took him at last to the bottom of the hill. He felt a certain contentment. "Let's see," he said to himself, "tomorrow night I'll be up at Royal Flat, or down at Ellen Street where Cousin Raymond's orange trees are being stripped." Too bad he couldn't be everywhere at once.

As he reached the bottom of the hill, he saw the first faint haze of a distant dawn seeping slowly over a far eastern ridge. Much nearer, somewhere below, hidden in a gully near Harmons, was his waiting vehicle. Keeping to little used and overgrown tracks, he took long strides as he walked to his van.

He swung the Isuzu at full speed around the curve, just as the molten ball of a morning sun hurdled a hill and splattered its golden rays across his face. At that very moment, he felt his hands become clammy and so weak, that they could barely remain on the steering, and control the vehicle. He knew the feeling, and willed his muscles to do their work. At the same time, he noticed the return of the powerful lines of a poem that had visited him before in situations such as this.

For all who yield the sweet delight of life

Unasked, unwilling, and with - fear
And voiceless agony
I make my prayer to God and man

"With what, what fear?" Why should that single two-syllable word elude him? He had tried for years to recall it, but the word just would not readmit itself to his mind.

And yet, he was proud of how much he still remembered of the rote instruction from his devoted teachers. Many of his school friends, whom he had met across the years, had admitted that they had forgotten much of what they had been taught as children. On the other hand, many, who like him had migrated overseas, admitted that they too had re-membered much that they had learned in school. He thought he knew why. But why in his case should that one word remain buried? When was the first time had his brooding subconscious dredged up the poem but with that one word missing?

Ah, yes, it was in Viet Nam. He was sharing a foxhole with Sgt. Dent, who was also by coincidence a Jamaican. As they had guarded their perimeter, they had seen nothing at first, as they scanned the ter-rain with bare eyes and field glasses. It was Dent's experienced eye that first saw the bush move. Then the figures dressed in black "pajamas" had rushed towards them.

He and the Sarge both fired sharp bursts from their automatic rifles. One of the attackers fell, but two kept coming. Each had picked a man and delivered bursts of hellish fire. The two enemies never slowed their headlong rush, firing as they advanced. Both Sammy and Dent knew that they had hit the men several times. One of the two stumbled and lowered his weapon, but still came on. The other began a zigzag course without breaking stride. Dent stood up, took careful aim and let go another cruel burst from his gun. Sammy did the same. The black clad figures, as if carrying some urgent message that no force could deter, lunged forward and fell into the foxhole. It was Dent who quickly grabbed and threw away the yet undetonated grenade one man carried. Both bodies convulsed and spurted blood from several bullet holes spread from head to feet.

Sammy had looked in fear and wonder at his fellow Sergeant. This had been his first enemy kill, and although he was not alone when it happened, despite years of training and anticipation, he was still badly shaken. He had also realized how close he had come to losing his own life. As he looked on the babylike faces of the two dead young men, a feeling of remorse had welled up in him and he kept saying "Oh my God! O my God!"

It was as he had looked in the faces of his enemies, now relaxed in death, whose causes he knew to be no less strong than his own regarding his adopted land, that the words of "The Caged Mongoose" had surfaced in his memory. All but the elusive two-syllable word which he could not remember. As the nauseous smell of the spilled blood had swept over them, Sgt. Dent had lit a cigarette and taken deep pulls on the smoke, then handed the anodyne to him saying "Here, take a draw."

And so it had been ever since. At each shedding of human blood, nausea and trembling overcame him. The sense of trembling and helplessness had never lasted long and had never prevented him from doing his duty. He was an excellent soldier, but the feeling never failed to visit him after a kill. He would never take a human life carelessly. He was deeply concerned that the war was now with his own countrymen.

Yet, people for whom he would gladly sacrifice himself in a just cause were now for selfish and destructive reasons, bringing their country to its knees. He was barely able to steer the van off the roadway and into a sugar cane field. He was able to quickly fling a door open and lean outside before the retching began.

The pitiful cry of the desperate young thief rang in his ears. The poor youth had had no idea that he had come up against a fighting machine of the first order. His futile attempt to defend his fallen comrade and a criminal way of life was very wrong. Praedial larceny had existed and thrived for too long in Jamaica. It was a terrible scourge that needed to be eradicated. Yet, the act of taking a life, and that of a blood kin at that, repelled Sammy.

He spilled his guts on the ground, the bile of his agony piping out in forceful spurts. With half closed eyes he watched the colours of his last meal form a rainbow clutter on the grass at his feet. Bits of undigested bammy with green okra and Red Snapper and escallion were floating in a greenish yellow lake of Red Stripe Beer and White Rum. The putrid stench attacked his nostrils and aggravated his nausea.

Tears came to his eyes. His nasal sinuses joined his tear ducts in spilling mucus down his contorted face. Self-pity shook him with fits of sorrow and remorse. He shuddered with the force of his sobbing. He began to blubber snatches of prayers. Deep groans wracked him as he muttered "O Lord! Have mercy! You know somebody has to do something. Things have just gone too far. It's my country I'm fighting for. It's my land I'm weeping for. It's taking the life of a brother man and a fellow Jamaican that I'm weeping for. My God, how did we get to this place? How in Heaven's name are we going to get out of this mess? Will Jamaica ever be the Jamaica it used to be? I confess to Almighty God; to Blessed Mary ever Virgin; to Holy Michael the Archangel; to the holy apostles, Peter and Paul, and to all the saints, and to you, Father, that I have sinned grievously...."

Grievous! That's it! 'Grievous fear'. The connection returned to him a sense of calm. "With grievous fear and voiceless agony." That was the line. He nodded slowly and managed a wan smile. That which had been lost to him for so long, had now fallen into place. His prayer had released the block. He reached behind him and retrieved a towel; he wiped his face, dabbed his eyes, and blew in the towel clearing his nose.

"A how yuh duh, mi bass, yuh sick deh sah?"

Sammy raised his head to see the concerned face of a man staring intently at him. He had come up to the open door of the van, and was searching Sammy's face with his own. Sammy saw the tattered and dirty clothes which hung loosely in shreds about the man. He saw the machete under his arm and the file sticking out of his pocket.

Beyond the man's concerned eyes, Sammy saw the aged skin and the burred uncombed and graying pepperseed hair. This man who was probably only old enough to be his son, seemed aged enough to be his father. How could that be? What bouts with disease, and lifetime of malnourishment had wreaked such havoc? What series of dashed hopes and broken dreams had conspired to cut off from him his chances of enjoying a normal life? This "son of the soil" would never enjoy the benefit of the legacies fought for and won by Bogle and Gordon, Busta and JAG Smith, Manley and Madame Rose Leon and Gladys Longbridge, and so many other patriots, sung and unsung.

It occurred to Sammy, that leaning toward him, dressed in tatters, was the soul of the true and unvarnished Jamaica. Cool waters of care and goodwill still flowed from the "island of springs". Though sullied by brackish pools moving in other directions, subterranean aquifers of compassion and goodness still welled up, and nothing from the outside could destroy them. Yes, he was looking at a Jamaica worth dying for. No, the real Jamaica was not yet dead, it was only covered with the nauseating morass of grasping people with unbridled greed and misplaced dreams. The true Jamaica needed desperately to be recalled to life. His resolve grew. His job was not yet finished. This fledgling, grown old before his time must be permitted to live. There was more vermin to be exterminated. Few would undertake the task, fewer still were prepared to perform the task, and fewer still would understand the reasons why he had to do what he did.

"Grievous fear." What an apt expression. He looked again at the pinched face of the concerned man whose gaze was still fixed on him. He would probably be spending the day in the blazing sun, chopping grass along the intervals of the canefields for a mere pittance.

"Thanks, my friend, I feel better now." he said. "Too much of a good time last night, you know what I mean?" he said with a conspiratorial wink. The inquisitor looked at him without making any response. He was still not sure that the man before him was well. "Anyhow, since you are so kind as to check upon me, take this and buy a little breakfast." The man tucked the cutlass more securely under his armpit and reached for the five hundred-dollar bill.

He stared at it unbelievingly. The small fortune now resting in his palm would not buy breakfast. It would purchase books and pencils for his children. His knees buckled in an involuntary curtsy, and his hands came together as if in prayer.

"T'ank yuh, sah! Gad bless yuh, mi bass. May heav'n smile on yuh, an' keep yuh well, sah!"

As if not trusting that the goodwill of the evidently sick man would last, the labourer turned away and disappeared. Sammy looked around the van. All his equipment was safely stored. Nothing about him could give the casual observer any indication of who he was. He started the engine and reversed out of the side road, raising a cloud of dust. Throwing the vehicle into forward gear, he released the clutch and gunned the engine.

The black Isuzu Rodeo sped east towards May Pen, facing the hot and glorious Jamaica morning. Sammy pulled up to the pump of the filling station. He got out and walked up to the counter. A surly attendant looked at the prospective customer, then looked away.

"I need eleven hundred dollars worth of gas, a Kola Champagne and a spiced bun," he ordered. As the attendant got up to get the items, Sammy saw the glaring headlines of the newspaper. "Vigilante Killer in Clarendon?"

"Let me see that newspaper, please," he said.

"Is ten dolla fi one, sah," said the taciturn seller.

"I mean, please sell me a copy of that newspaper," said Sammy evenly. Without a word, the attendant brought the drink, bun and a folded copy of the newspaper; Sammy took the purchases and handed the man several dollar bills. He dispensed the gasoline into the tank, then started the engine and drove away from the station. He drove a short distance, pulled over and read the story.

The police in Clarendon believe there is a vigilante killer loose in the parish, who has struck for the second time in less than two years. The bodies of Roy Hamilton, alias "Bigga", and Kenneth Nicholson, alias "Boysie", were found near a goat pen in Four Paths, late last night, alongside implements for stealing and robbing, and with revolvers still near their bodies, suggesting a pattern to the police. They believe the dead men are victims two and three of an elusive vigilante.

"So," muttered Sammy, "now I am a vigilante. Three thieves eliminated in less than two years and I am considered a vigilante. I wonder where those newspaper people learn how to write. They keep using words and don't even know what meanings they should convey. Three conscienceless robbers are killed and it makes headlines, while in the same time period five hard-working farmers are murdered including one dead and one wounded in my family alone, and they are not even mentioned. Something is wrong with the way these people think! They know that our country's government is so financially weak that they can't provide police with what they need to even defend themselves. The police have to live in housing conditions little better than a pigsty. They have no transportation and no weapons. But that is not vigilantism. Poor farmers are at their wit's end, and businessmen have to pay all kinds of ways to stay protected. But that is not vigilantism.

People scorn the police and will do nothing to help them. Some of them have to walk miles on empty stomachs to try to perform their sworn duty. Only when trouble strikes people, do they call the cops, and if they don't come running they are criticized on radio and television. This country is in deep trouble and everybody knows it." He swallowed a mouthful of spiced bun and sipped the delicious soft drink. Then his mouth twisted into an angry frown as his self-justification continued. He scowled as he complained "Murdering thieves are not called vigilantes. But if a man takes his life in his hands to pacify a situation, he is a vigilante. Vigilante my backside! I call it defense of the helpless and the weak. This is what Jamaica has come to. And no one raises a hand to help the situation." He popped the rest of the bun in his mouth, drained the bottle of its contents and ignited the engine.

Savagely, he threw the machine into gear and stomped the gas pedal to the floor. The Isuzu roared down Chapelton Road, made a screeching left turn at Guinep Tree, straightened itself from the shimmying, and headed up the hill towards the center of the town. In his fury, he had no idea where he was going. He turned left at the town clock on the road towards Sevens, then he collected himself sufficiently to think that he did not want to go up into the Rock River area. He turned right by the market, circled and came out below the clock and took the road towards Kingston. He slowed his speed, and tried to think. How much did the police know? What signals were they sending with the news article? There had to be a reason why they divulged what they did to the media

He passed through Cross, where he had spent so many wonderful years before he migrated to America. Then he was at the intersection of the Mandela highway. He turned right instead of continuing into Kingston. He sped towards Denbigh. As he drove, he scanned the rest of the article:

> The victims were shot in their heads and abdomen, the Chapelton police told the **Gleaner**. The gun slayings, carried out in similar fashion, are baffling to the lawmen. Nearly two years after the first incident, they still have no clues.

He grabbed the newspaper and threw it to the far floor of the vehicle, then turned on the radio in an attempt to clear his mind of the situation. A talk show was in progress. "Jamaica has been a civilized country for centuries," said a commentator. "This kind of behaviour has been unheard of in our nation before. We just cannot tolerate such activities and hold up our heads around the table of nations. Vigilantism means a breakdown of law and order, and that is a sad commentary on our excellent police force. In fact, it is a matter of disgrace to all of us. Citizens cannot take the law in their own hands, no matter how serious the provocation, and so become as lawless as common criminals. Citizens must allow the police to do their jobs. That's what we pay the police for!"

"Hey!" expostulated Sammy. "I wonder where in the world that person comes from to make a statement like that? I guess they don't read the same newspapers I read, or talk to the same police I talk to, or even listen to their radio and television reports. Vandalism, praedial larceny, thefts, murder, breaking and entering are everywhere, and nobody is able to do anything to protect the defenseless. This country is now a paradise for criminals."

Another voice broke in on the radio programme. "I wonder who that man, or those people are, and I wonder what drove them to take such drastic steps. You know, Jamaica is so messed up nowadays that you can't even tell what anybody will do anymore."

"Sir, you are so right," said the commentator, "I have been wondering the same thing. Just who could the vigilantes be?"

Sammy turned off the radio. He grasped the steering wheel rigidly in both hands as his jaw became tightly clenched, and he stared unseemingly before him. The expression on his face would puzzle a casual observer. It would appear that he was smiling, but a more studied look would reveal eyes that were small glints of steel. This was one angry Jamaican.

Chapter Three

Cocoa Walk, Manchester, Christmas, 1915

The last long rays of golden sun spread their amber trail along the western ridges of Rose Hill. As if on cue, Mal Stennett looked at his mates and asked: "Ready? A One! A Two! A Three! A Four!" Lifting his trumpet to his lips he led the group in a series of rollicking tunes. The sounds caught and held the attention of every one in the pavilion.

The unleashed music echoed across the rolling hills of South Manchester, sending the message that the dance had begun. Mal Stennett was popular. The band was excellent. In the eastern sky, the wide dish of a burnished moon ascended the star filled sky.

The pavilion of the Cocoa Walk Recreation Centre was packed with revelers. This was Boxing Day, December 26, Jamaica's most popular holiday. Many had come home for the holidays from lowland to towns and sugar factories. Others were returning from far away places like Colombia and Cuba, Ecuador and Panama and Venezuela. Some were home from England, France, Germany, and Africa. A relativelty scant few were back from the United States of America. This dance was the social event where they met, renewed acquaintances, and exchanged news before departing again.

All were dressed in the latest finery. The men were spending money freely, and the village girls enjoyed the spree, while family members hovered close to their visiting kin.

Septimus Gordon (Septy) was dressed to kill. He wore a double-breasted cream serge suit, beneath which was a white shirt with pearl studs instead of buttons. There were pearl cuff links to match the studs, and a stiff collar, offset by a dashing maroon coloured necktie. He wore white kid gloves on his hands, and white "oxfords" on his feet. A white "Jippi-Jappa" Panama hat trimmed with a red band was tilted jauntily on one side of his head. To complete the ensemble; he carried a cane on the crook of his left arm, and held a cigarette between his fingers. Descending the red dirt incline to the fair grounds, he walked with a swagger, more reminiscent of a sailor coming ashore, than of a villager used to plodding up and down the steep mountain slopes. His brother David walked beside him.

Turning to Septy, David said with a conspiratorial smile "Bway, I'm going to be sorry for all dem girls at the dance tonight."

"What you mean?" asked Septy, the seventh son among more than a dozen siblings. His affected naivete was betrayed by a twinkle in his eye at the well-deserved compliment.

"Septy, ef yuh only see yuhself, yuh wouldn' ask nuh damn fool question. Ev'y baddy kno' seh yuh boasy, man," said Daniel, a member of the group, with obvious jealousy.

"I still don't understand," protested Septy fearing rejection by his friends. "What's the matter with me?"

"We mean all de girls will fight fi get tuh yuh. Yuh dress well enough to make a lot of them do drastic things tuh hold yuh." said David.

Septy grinned. His parted lips revealed a mouth full of glimmering gold teeth. They matched the lustre of the gold watch, which bounced across his waistcoat, suspended from a golden chain. He raised the lighted cigarette to his mouth. With his pursed lips he pulled in the smoke, as the cigarette tip glowed in the dusk.

"Boy, I don't think so you know," he protested good-naturedly. "I expect to be in Jamaica for only one more week. After that, it's back to Panama for me. I'm going to this dance to have some fun and meet some friends. I don't see any woman even looking at me. I am still the plain country boy that grew up round here,"

"Bway top skylarking. Yuh know yuh change in de five years since you leave here. Even when yuh was roun' here dem seh yuh is de boasyess boy in de whole a Cocoa Walk," remarked Daniel.

They reached the bottom of the grade and started the short incline to the pavilion. The dance drew people from Broughton and Buckup, Cross Keys and Grove Town, Warrick and Stones Hope, and even as far as Plowden. As Septy looked around, it seemed that time had stood still in this place. From the unpaved dirt road and the many broken down stone-walls, to the mongoose that had stopped to look at them before scurry-ing off to continue its hunt. Yet, he could sense the subtle changes. For instance, long gone were the days of school friend camaraderie. Before his eyes, Septy saw a troublesome scene unfold.

"Hey Phonso, how yuh duh?" said an obvious villager who had never left the mountains. He was dressed in an inexpensive blue stripe woolen pants, a thin knit ganzi shirt and brown tennis-crepe shoes. The plea-sure of seeing his friend from school days led him to forget the barriers that the intervening years had made between them. Alphonso, who was being greeted, was one of the lucky ones who had landed a good job. He was also the product of one of the finer homes. He ignored his classmate's greeting. It was his escort who pointed out his discourtesy.

"Did you hear someone talking to you?" She asked.

"Oh, hello!" he said in a weak and formal voice more to accomodate his new love, than to acknowledge the existence of his former class-mate. He kept on walking.

The girl was concerned. "It's people like you who are going to cause problems for all of us in Jamaica," she complained. "As soon as you get a job or a little money, you think you are better off than other people. One of these days we are going to have a riot in this country because of it."

"Uhm, Hmm," Phonso grunted.

They were all at the dance. But the days of shooting marbles and jumping ropes and playing cricket were over. Success or failure now divided old school friends. The humbly dressed fellow shook his head and lost himself in the crowd.

Septy and his cohorts walked with confidence and laughter up the grade to the covered structure where a crowd clustered and the pulsating music beckoned.

Birdie Sinclair's mocking laughter sang out above the chatter of the group that flocked about her. "Heh! Heyy! I tol' you a hundred times that I don' have nutt'n' to do with Denzel. Him is too facety. On top o' dat, him too mean. You know dat he don't even go to church? So, what you think I'm going to do wid a man like that? Cutie, you want him? You can have him, gol' teeth an' all. Me? Denzel Jones can' duh nutt'n fi me." Having made her declaration, Birdie threw back her head and laughed heartily.

"But just de same, Birdie, everybody aroun' here know that you and Denzel are bosom friends. Even from infant school, you and him used to walk home together. You can't just throw him 'way now. What happen that all of a sudden we cyan even call him name to you? Denzel is at dis dance, and you should watch how you dance with everybody here. We know him is goin' to want to dance wid yuh."

"Cutie, Denzel is a big man. Him can go to any dance him want, an' dance wid who him want. Him didn' come here wid me. Mi gwine dance wid anybody mi please. The only one man ah won' dance wid tonite is Denzel. You hear me? Ah say ah don't want to have anything to do wid a man dat is stingy. Is not dat mi want anything from him, but de way mi see him treat him pickney dem, an' de baby madda dem, mi seh him nuh mean nobaddy no good unless is himself? Mi cyan bother wid him. Me at dis dance fe have fun tonite. Please don' mention dat bwoy name again."

She was the loveliest girl at the dance, and both men and women alike admired her beauty. She was accustomed to all the attention, yet she was unaffected by it. She was friendly with everyone, and equally gracious to all the male admirers who competed with each other to get a dance with her. She stood with the intention of returning to the dance floor, when the group around her parted, as Septimus and his friends came up the steps. Septy flipped away the luminant butt of his cool Zephyr cigarette as he climbed the remaining step. He came to an abrupt halt as soon as he spotted Birdie. They stared at each other, seemingly lost in time and space.

Septy recovered first. Still wrapped by the magic that enveloped them, he glided across the remaining distance to Birdie, and in awed tones said:

"Good evening Ma'am, may I have the pleasure of the next dance?"

Birdie was entranced. "With pleasure, Sir," she replied, forgetting who was next in line to dance with her.

Admission to the dance was "A bow for gentlemen, and a curtsy for ladies." Septy paid the fare with a low and courtly movement. He removed his hat, handing it along with his cane to a member of his group. Then, taking Birdie by the hand, he led her through the crowded room to the dance floor. The music lifted and whirled them with a power of its own. For a long time they moved dreamily and silently, not trusting words to convey the power of what they were feeling. It was Septimus who finally broke the silence.

"And what's your name?" he asked.

"Birdie. Birdie Sinclair." she said.

"I'm Septy. Septimus Gordon. And where have you been all my life?" he asked. He felt daring and dizzy.

Birdie giggled. "Is de same question ah been askin'. Where yuh been all my life?"

Again, they melted into each other's arms, content to simply enjoy the moment. They kept swaying together long after the music had ceased, and were brought out of their reverie by the teasing laughter of those nearby. They stopped dancing in shy embarrassment, but they did not leave the dance floor. Etiquette required that Septy escort Birdie to the sideline where her friends were waiting. Instead, with a restraining hand, he insisted that they remain on the floor until the next number began. It was a sizzling rumba. The sensuous cadences drew them together and the rapid pace gave them an excuse to vent the emotions that had been restricted by the previous sedate waltz. Their supple bodies wheeled and turned feverishly, shoulders shimmying and fingers snapping. Their hips gyrated as their feet traced elusive patterns on the floor. The thrill of their attraction to each other intoxicated them. They spun away from each other as if to test how well they could do without the physical contact of each other, but soon the pain of their separation overcame them and they reached out eager hands above their heads catching hold of each other. Coming close again, they clasped each other as they danced.

"You having a good time?" asked Septy

"Yes, man! Lawd de music sweet, yuh see!" Birdie answered

"That's Mal Stennett and his Lively Five. Seems like they got even better since I went away."

"Oh, where yuh did guh?" inquired Birdie

"Panama," Septy said

"Panama? Which part? Mi have friends ova deh yuh kno'."

"Canal Zone where everybody from Jamaica go."

"It pretty ovah deh?"

"Some parts look just like Jamaica. But there are a lot of swamps. And a lot more mosquitoes than here in Jamaica."

The village green was sprinkled with a hundred varicoloured bulbs. Their soft glow eased the darkness, and gently illuminated objects. A 'Delco' generator which powered the lights hummed steadily beneath the din of the dance. Against this backdrop, the first attraction of Birdie and Septy blossomed into mutual affection. The young couple spent the rest of the night dancing with each other, politely, but firmly rejecting all attempts to disturb the growing intensity of their twosomeness.

"I wish dis night would never en'!" Birdie whispered at one point during the evening.

"I know what you mean," responded Septy, tenderly stroking her head, which now rested on his shoulder.

When the dance was over Septy asked Birdie: "May I walk you home?"

"Yes please!" gushed Birdie. They held hands as they joined their friends.

"We're going to walk Birdie home," Septy announced.

The two groups of friends now divided into couples and singles. The couples huddled closely, talking in whispered intimacies. The singles congregated together conversing loudly with their laughter filling the early morning air.

Septy and Birdie walked ahead of the group. He told her of his school days at New Broughton. She told him of her days at Woodlands School. He told her of his travel to Panama to visit his older brother. She told him of her life at home helping her mother and the rest of the family. She even told him of Denzel whom she had expected to make trouble at the dance, but who had left her alone all evening.

"Suh, wha' happen to you in Panama?" Birdie queried.

"Well, my brother Thomas was there to meet me at the port and take me home to stay with him and his wife, Esme. They looked after me very well. I guess because I am the baby in my family, they felt the need to care for me. I didn't have to pay rent or anything. Even after I found a job they charged me much less than what other people had to pay. They encouraged me to save my money and prepare to return home to make a good life.

"Panama is no place for a Jamaican to live forever," my brother said. Even though he married a nice Panamanian himself. That's why tomorrow I have to go to Mandeville and buy presents to take back for them next week."

He told her that workers risked their lives every day to fulfil the dreams of engineers who wanted to link the Atlantic Ocean with the Pacific. Many died from accidents. Many gave in to the vices of alcohol and gambling. But his older brother had coped with the situation. He had married a good wife who helped him keep his balance. His brother gave him good advice and provided a family for him. He would return to Panama and would spend about two more years there. Then he would come back home and set up shop as a merchant tailor, with his brother, David who was a shoemaker. He would join him as a partner. He was sure he would prosper in life, with the help of God.

Birdie had been listening intently as Septy talked. Now she said three words that would change their lives forever. "Don't go back."

"What do you mean, don't go back?" he asked incredulously.

Birdie looked at Septy's slim five feet eight inches frame with smooth and fine skin, the colour of rich coffee with a liberal dash of coconut milk. His high forehead held jet-black hair that was parted and brushed slick and wavy with Yardley's Brilliantine. His high cheeks accented a large nose with a broad bridge and flaring nostrils. His mouth was wide with lips of medium thickness and his chin pointed and hairless. He was good looking, she thought, and she felt that he was kind as well. He was definitely industrious. And he was spiritual. She felt her body shiver with emotion.

"Jus dat," she insisted imperiously, "don't yuh go back, I wan' yuh tuh stay here wid me."

They were holding hands. They had come to the gate that barred the way to her house which now loomed dark and silent beyond the shrub lined path. Septy stopped, and looked searchingly into the face of the impulsive woman whom he had known for only a few hours. Her expression, illuminated by the lunar glow, gave convincing evidence of her sincerity. Returning to Panama was his plan. All his belongings were there. His future as he had outlined it. He didn't have enough money saved up yet to fully establish the business he had in mind, he thought. Yet, Birdie's impetuous demand was infectious and he felt himself caving in to her request. What could be more perfect than spending the rest of his life with this wonderful woman standing before him?

"Well," he said gently. "Since you ask me like that, I will stay." He felt a wave of tenderness wash over him as he said it.

Birdie slipped into his arms and their lips met. Any lingering doubts Septy may have had, dissolved. He enveloped her within the folds of his jacket to shield her against the morning chill. At that moment, Birdie knew that with Septy she had found a safe haven. He was kind, gentle, and God-fearing. That was enough. They clung to each other, sealing their pact with kisses. Reluctantly, they released each other.

"Well, I can't keep my friends waiting all night." Septy said.

"All right," Birdie said softly. "Walk good and come see me tomorra."

Septy stood and watched until she was safely inside her house, then walked slowly to rejoin his waiting friends. He remained silent as they headed home. After a while his cousin Daniel could not pass up the opportunity to tease him about this latest turn of events.

"Um Hm! Wha' me did tell yuh? All a yuh nuh hear me seh it was gwine happen? Jus' look pon de man! De bway look like wet fowl inna de rain. Me seh, de man can't even talk!"

Wham! A sudden swing of Septy's strong right fist landed on Dan's jaw sending him sprawling to the ground.

"Septy!" roared David. "I keep telling you 'bout your temper. Now what did Dan say for you to lick him down like that. All of us thinking the same thing."

Incensed, Daniel struggled to his feet and rushed towards Septy, wielding a piece of wood he had managed to pick up during his fall.

"Unna betta hol' me," he screamed. "A gwine kill dis facety, dutty bway. Me neva duh nutt'n fe him cum thump me. I gwine kill him!"

"Come on! Come, nuh!" shouted Septy in nervous malevolence.

So much had gone differently than he had expected tonight. Everything seemed to be out of his control. A fight would provide an avenue to release his frustrations and embarrassment that his friends had been proven right, despite his assurances earlier in the evening that he could guard against the charms of any woman.

"Dan," said David protectively. "Watch what you say. Is only decent people 'round here, you know."

Daniel dropped the club, and spoke with intensity.

"David, me nuh care weh yuh seh, all me kno' seh is me cousin life mash up. Jus' look pon' 'im. Me still seh im look like wet chicken. One likkle dance wid one likkle dry foot gal an' de man t'un fool-fool. Yuh evah see nutt'n like dat, ehn Stanley? Yuh evah see nutt'n crazy suh?"

"Suh, Dan," Stanley countered devilishly, "tell me man, is how much time yuh try fe cut in pon Septy tonite, and de same likkle dry foot gal wudden even look pon yuh?"

"Cho man, Stanley, yuh kno' what I mean," protested Daniel, "Jus' look pon Septy. Yuh evah see a grown man look like dat, like a shame dog. It mus' be lightenin' strike him. Me seh, him is me cousin and we grow up togedda like breddas, and me love him to deat', but me nevah see 'im like dis before in me whole life."

"Dan, me seh shut your mouth and leave the man alone." said David again. As the oldest in the group, he commanded respect.

"Alright," said Dan with a note of resignation, "me naw guh seh a word to none a yuh. But Septy, me haffi ask yuh one question."

"What?" asked Septy cautiously.

"Man, wha' happen to yuh tonite?"

"Nutt'n much," said Septy quietly, thoughtfully. "I just met the woman I'm going to marry. That's all."

"Yuh what?" expostulated Dan. "But man, yuh don' even kno' de 'oman!"

"I know enough," said Septy, "She is jus' the sweetes', pretties', and bes' woman have ever met in my whole life, I can't let this chance pass me. I told her I'm not going back to Panama."

"Lawd, me nuh tell yuh, me nuh tell all a yuh seh de man tun fool-fool!" Dan exclaimed.

"Bway, I saw the look on yuh face when yuh buck up pon her on the steps this evening," said David. "I just had the feeling that you had met your match. But married? Don' you think that's a little bit sudden?"

"Master, I've been to Mandeville, Clarendon, Spanish Town, Kingston, and all over Panama. I've never met a girl as sweet as this. I know this is the woman for me," declared Septy.

"Well Septy, you are a lucky man, But who is she, anyway?"

"She is a Sinclair. Her people come from Resource and Victoria Town, and Pushy Hill."

"Well," sighed David "the Sinclairs are solid people. They are well respected and hardworking. Boy, I hope she makes you happy. But are you sure you are not moving too fast? Why don't you go back to Panama, correspond with her, then see if you two really love each other or not?"

"Man, David, I know I found what I've been looking for. I don't need to go nowhere or think about it. As people used to say, 'If you think long, you think wrong'. I know I want this woman for my wife."

"Well, just make sure you can take good care of her, yuh hear. Us Gordon people always take good care of our family. You have the Gordon name to live up to, you know that?"

"David, I love this girl, Birdie. She won't have to worry about a thing when we get married." pledged Septy soberly.

"Then God bless you, my brother. I hope she makes you very happy," said David fervently.

The Birdie Sinclair who entered the dimly lit living room, was a different person from the flighty carefree girl that had left the house a few hours earlier. Her mother could tell immediately that something had happened to her oldest daughter. Her best friend and confidante.

"Suh," she greeted her child conspiratorially, "Wha' happen tenite fe mek yuh come home a look like de puss wheh fin' ripe pear unda de pear tree?"

"Mamma, I meet the man I'm going marry. Him just come back from Panama. Lawd, Mamma, de man sweet yuh see! 'im seh 'im was planning fe guh back ovah deh next week. But I tol' 'im tuh stay here wid me. Mamma, yuh kno' seh de foolish bway agree fe stay?"

"Suh, ef 'im stay ya, wha' 'im a guh duh fe mek a livin'? Yuh know seh life tough fe true inna Sout' Manchesta?" asked the practical mother.

"Mamma, Septy have money. 'im work a Panama fe five years, an' im save all a 'im money. An' 'im is a taila tuh; 'im seh 'im plan to make a big success outta him life. Lawd, Mamma, im sweet yuh see! I cyan even begin fe tell yuh how a feel. I wan' fe sing. I wan' fe cry, I even feel like I wan' fe vammit! Lawd, Mamma, is suh love guh? Tell me, is suh love guh?"

Mrs. Sinclair's eyes widened as her concern for her daughter increased. Questions were being posed to her that she could not answer. Her own marriage had held none of the excitement she now saw in her child. She had married a good man whom she had known since infant school days They admired and respected each other and she thoroughly enjoyed life with him, but she had never felt any of the wild kind of nonsense she heard her daughter talking about. She shook her head in an effort to find some words of motherly wisdom, but nothing came to her mind except an old saying of her mother's, "An idle mind is the Devil's workshop." She decided that the best course was to get her daughter's mind off the madness by filling it with something practical like work.

"Anyway," she said, breaking the delirium of the moment, "yuh betta gwan tuh sleep. Tomorra mawnin' is a big Morning Sport. We haffi get up early fe start de food an' t'ings. De man dem gwine start wuk by six a'clack. By eight a'clack, dem gwine be starvin'. Suh, yuh betta get tuh bed right away."

"Yes, Mamma." said a subdued Birdie.

"An' by de way, when yuh tell yuh fatha 'bout dis t'ing tenite, yuh betta change up yuh story a likkle bit. Yuh fatha won' kno' nutt'n 'bout yuh tellin' a grown man nuh fi guh back a sea. Jus' tell 'im dat yuh meet dis nice man who is gwine come an' ask ef yuh can marry wid 'im. Tell 'im how nice de man was tuh yuh, an' don' feget de part 'bout how much money de man bring back from farrin. Now, gwan tuh bed."

"Yes, ma'am," said Birdie, "Goodnite, Mamma."

"Good nite," said Mrs. Sinclair.

Chapter Four

Cocoa Walk, Manchester, 1916

Nine months after they met, the wedding day came for Septy and Birdie. The rains that had been falling for days stopped to permit a golden sun and clear blue sky, even though the road was pockmarked with pools and puddles. The lovely Anglican Church at Smithfield stood in grandeur with its freshly painted walls gleaming white, and the wood work tastefully trimmed in red. A mild breeze blew through the open windows stirring the air and refreshing the expectant crowd.

He and his brother David, his Best Man, waited nervously by a window near the altar rail. The restless clergyman stood near them. Birdie was two hours late.

"See them here!" announced a spectator.

Everyone craned to see. Down the lane came a horse drawn buggy; the horse decorated in flowers from mane to tail. In the driver's seat sat Birdie's father, and beside him sat her mother, dressed as if she herself were the bride. Behind them sat Birdie and her sister, the Maid of Honour. Following the slowly moving conveyance was a troupe of young ladies and men. Some were bridesmaids and groomsmen. Others were close family and friends.

The party turned into the churchyard and the crowd took available seats. The groomsmen joined Septy, as Birdie, her father, and the brides-maids waited at the door.

Birdie's shoes, a size too small, began to hurt her feet. She bore the anguish heroically. Her heart pounded as the huge pipe organ swelled the sanctuary with the opening notes of "Here Comes The Bride." She felt faint. Then she felt the tug of her father's arm as he guided her forward.

Septy looked at her move towards him. Their eyes met and she smiled. He smiled in reply. Then his eyes moved to look at her father's face. He seemed as sternly unsmiling as the day when he had gone to ask for her hand. He remembered the day well.

"Yes, I hear that yuh meet my dawta at one dance, and yuh come tuh ask to marry har. I only want tuh know one thing: what is yuh inten-tion for my dawta? Where you plan to live? How will you care for har? I didn't raise my chile from a baby for a poppyshow to come and sweetmouth har, and mash up har life?"

He had looked in surprise at David who had accompanied him. Neither of them had expected the barrage of questions. He had replied that he was hardworking and had saved his money. He had bought some land and would build a house. He fully expected to care for his wife and family and expected no help from anyone. "Mr. Sinclair," he had said, "if I did not think I could afford to care for a family, I would never decide to get married." There was a silence. Then Mr. Sinclair was heard grumbling, talking more to himself than to them.

"I tol' Birdie she is welcome to stay wid har Madda all of har life. She don't want for nutt'n here. She don' have tuh run off wid de firs' strange man dat come aroun' wid gol' teet' and tu'n har head. But, she is a big 'oman now. Parents can't duh nutten wid pickneys nowadays. Yes, she say she wan't to married tuh yuh, suh I guess is allright, yuh can marry mi dawta."

"Thank you, Mr. Sinclair." He had said quickly, wanting to con-clude the uncomfortable interview.

"But!" insisted the father, refusing to be hurried, "let me tell yuh something, young man. I know your people and they are respectable and hardworking, but I know nothing about you except you went tuh farrin. If yuh ever mistreat or hit my child because you are angry wid har, yuh will regret de day yuh bawn. Yuh hear me?"

"Yes sir, Mr. Sinclair," Septy replied humbly as the full weight of accountibility impressed itself on him. With that memory came a feeling of panic. Had he been too rash? Was he really ready for the responsibilities of marriage? Was he strong enough to head up a family as was Mr. Sinclair? A swath of perspiration bathed his face. He looked left and gazed at the door leading to the outside and freedom.

"RUN!" ordered a voice within him. "RUN BOY, THIS IS YOUR LAST CHANCE!! AFTER THIS YOU'RE DEAD!" He turned towards the door and freedom. As if reading his mind, his brother David took hold of his arm and without looking at him, held on tightly. The moment of doubt left and Sammy looked again at his still advancing true love, who was now but a few feet away. He stepped forward, took her arm and together they stood before the minister.

The ceremony was brief yet memorable. Septy went through it all as if in a dream... Later he could not recall the wise counsel given by the Parson. He did remember repeating the vows mechanically, and did remember coming alive when instructed to salute the bride. He had made the kiss chaste and brief under the watchful eye of Mr. Sinclair who had smiled for the first time since they had met. The minister blessed them and they led the procession from the church.

Meanwhile, at the house, while the wedding service was in progress, a crew of busy people was getting all ready for the reception. "About how many people are we expectin?" asked a dark, thin woman who was sweeping the last bits of trash and debris from the yard.

"At least a hundred," replied another woman who was putting the finishing touches to some floral arrangements on several table.

"So, where all these people coming from?" asked the first woman.

"Missis, they are coming from everywhere- Panama, Cuba, and Englan', then in Jamaica from Four Paths, Vere, Kingston, Spanish Town, St. Elizabeth, and all over Manchester. Birdie Sinclair didn' stop til she found a man that came back from farrin' wid a lot of money and a big family and lots of friends."

"Well, I believe you, because I never see that many animals kill for a wedding before."

"Well, they should be comm' any minute now, so we must have everything ready."

"You think we have enough food for all those people?"

"Oh yes! We killed three goats including a big ol' ram that weighed fifty pounds alone. Then we killed a lot of fowls too. That along with rice and yams and bananas should be enough."

With a last look at the beautifully arranged tables and the seething and steaming pots, the woman in charge nodded her head in satisfaction and walked out into the cleared pathway to look down the graded unpaved roadway. She was greeted with sounds of shouting and singing as the wedding party came up the pathway and entered the yard.

The jubilant crowd thronged into the booth and the reception got underway. The Parson offered prayers and blessed the wedding cake, after which toasts to the groom and bride were offered. After the well wishing of the couple, a meal was served. Then they were given knives and asked to cut their wedding cake. It was supposed to be a "race" to see who would reach the bottom first. But the Master of Ceremonies declared a tie and used that as a lesson in cooperation in all the further activities they would perform as a family.

The top layer of the cake was removed and carefully wrapped in muslin. This would be stored to be served on the first anniversary of the marriage. The remaining layers were sliced thinly and served with wine.

The couple then stood and thanked all for helping make their special day a memorable one Then they moved among the guests greeting and thanking as many as they could. As the day yielded to evening, the couple bade farewell and retired.

Inside the dimly lit room, Septy turned to Birdie. "So, why were you so late today?"

"Were yuh worried?" asked Birdie mischievously

"No, man!" boasted Septy, "where would you find a better man than me?"

Birdie threw back her head and laughed in merriment. "Bway, yuh 'shurance, yuh see!"

"Come here, Birdie." he said huskily. She moved into his arms. Septy kissed her with a passion and a desire he had chosen not to show at the church when he had saluted her under the watchful eyes of her father.

Chapter Five

Cocoa Walk, Manchester, 1942

Like a pair of ripened mangoes floating on a steadily flowing river, Birdie and Septy were carried by their fervent love across the passing years. Septy invested his savings in buying twelve acres of land, and in building a house. The living area was a modest structure of two rooms called a "room and half", but it provided warmth and security for the young family. It was painted a cheerful sky blue, and the wood trim was painted a bright red. A separate building also of two rooms housed the kitchen and a storage called the "buttery".

The twelve acres were planted with mixed crops of oranges, grapefruits. tangerines, bananas, coffee, sugar canes, pimentoes, ginger roots, red apples, sweet potatoes, cocoas, peppers, avocados, and cassavas, plums and guavas. A few heads of cows, goats, pigs, chickens, and donkeys, rounded out the stocks of the small farm. The virgin soil yielded abundantly in the early years.

Even as the soil produced, so did the love of the couple; as an increasingly larger flock of children crowded the modest home. First came a boy, Thomas, named for Septy's caring uncle in Panama. Then came David, named after his best friend and favourite brother. Then there were George, and Timothy, nicknamed "Tarzan"; then the only daughter Joyce, affectionately called "Girlie", then the twins, Henry and Lester, and finally, Septimus George Gordon, the Second: the seventh son of a seventh son. Of whom, much more later.

Septy senior was born in the mountains, but he was not a mountain man. He was born in the country, but his experiences were town experiences. After leaving school, he had been apprenticed as a tailor. He knew nothing about farming and cultivating the land. He made costly mistakes due to his lack of judgment where human character was concerned. One was when his father-in-law promised to get him some volunteer workers to give a "morning sport". This community help provided valuable free labour in performing the most gruelling tasks of small farming such as land clearing and soil preparation. A dozen men, providing their own tools and singing encouraging work songs, could in two or three hours provide a tremendous boost to the labour needs of a small planter. When called upon, each labourer reciprocates, and so life in the community is made easier.

The day came. The men arrived promptly. To show his good faith, Septy had steaming pots of food waiting, and bottles of rum ready for the pouring.

"Come on gentlemen!" he hailed them. "There's plenty of food and drink. Enjoy yourselves." Without further words, the men enjoyed themselves, eating well and partaking liberally of the rum. It was well past eight o'clock when Septy asked if the men planned to spend the whole day with him, or just a half-day. He wanted to know if he needed to prepare more food for them since what he had provided was running low.

"No, sah!" one man declared, "We did tell Mass Johnny dat we haffi leave by nine a'clock."

"But you men didn't do any work!" complained Septy. Mass Johnny said, "You would come by six o'clock and help me clean some land and dig some hills. Now you eat all the food and tell me that you have to leave. What kind of business is that?"

Some of the men guiltily picked up their tools to clear a small space of brush. Others dug a few hills for yams or potatoes. Others explained that they were sorry but that the sun was getting high and they had to leave. Septy's father-in-law saw his crestfallen features and tried to console him.

"Septy, man, I fegat tuh tell yuh, yuh poor thing. Yuh mus' nevah feed de man dem nor gi' dem any likker until dem duh some work. Where yuh wrang is yuh feed dem firs'. If yuh feed dem firs' dem wi' always get lazy and sleepy. I don' kno' when I can get dem tuh cum again, but nex' time, let dem wuk firs', den while dem working, let dem see de pot boiling and smell de food. Den dem will wok even harda. But, if yuh feed dem first... Well yuh see what happen today."

Having given his explanation, the father-in-law also left, taking his sons with him.

"Son-Son, Manley come on!" he called. "We have a whole heap of litter fi chop befo' de sun get too hat."

It was a despondent but wiser Septy who picked up a hoe to dig the hills he had hoped would be dug for him by a happy group of men. He drove the blade vigorously into the red soil with a desperation forced by the urge to provide for his family, and from the embarrassment that he had so easily been misled. He had put all his money into land purchase, house building and family support. Each year the task seemed harder to wrest a livelihood from the increasingly stubborn soil.

After many days of deep brooding, Septy awoke one hot and dry August morning to the realization that the hardy land had reached its limits. It would never produce the quantity of food and supplies needed to maintain his family in the manner he desired. He knew he had to supplement his income from some other source. His eyes burned with tears as be looked at his growing family and realized that his reserve of cash was gone and he was sinking into debt. The fear he had felt on his wedding day returned in full force. He looked at Birdie pregnant again, and wearing a threadbare thin cotton dress, and said:

"You know, Birdie, I've been thinking. I have to do something to get some extra money. I talked to our Member of the House of Representatives and he said he could get me a contract to go to America."

"Is dat what been botherin' yuh? Yuh been puffin' dat cigarette all mawnin."

"Yes, I'm worried. Just look at the poor children. They are growing up. Their world is changing, right now we can't do a thing to help them. Birdie, I think I have to go away and make some money. I can make some good money in six months and come back here and pay off our debts, and have some money to invest in the place."

"I don' t'ink suh yuh kno', Septy. None of my family evah haffi lef' home fe mek money. De furdes' any of den evah guh is Mandeville or Vere. When yuh talk 'bout six mont's, no one of my family evah stay away dat lang.. we jus' not use tuh dat kin' of life."

"Vere. I didn't think about that, maybe I could go down and work my tailor trade for a little while. What you think? At least I am a tailor, even if tailor money come in slow."

"Septy, is hard tuh watch yuh guh away, but Vere nuh too far. I guess is allright for a likkle while. At leas' yuh can come up pon de market truck on Saturday night and go back down Monday. Me an' the children dem will try to manage while yuh gawn, but please, Massa, don' be gawn too lang. De work 'round yah hard and I not as strang as I use to be."

Septy promised not to stay away long.

"Taking care of my family is my responsibility. But I did mention it to Son-Son to keep an eye on you while I am gone and he understands that I'm not a mountain man. There are some things I just can't do to make a living up here."

Septy left. The several months he had promised to be away turned into three years on the plains of Vere working in shops at Alley and Lionel Town and Water Lane. By the time he had paid rent and bought materials, the low paying trade allowed only small amounts left over to be sent home to Birdie. That did help for a while. It provided for the older children to attend school in St. Elizabeth and Mandeville and Kingston. Still, on his monthly trips home he would return to the subject of going abroad and earning good money.

"Birdie, just look at our situation. We can't keep on like this. We are already deep in debt that we can't pay. Is mash up our lives going to mash up if I don't make a move. I can't stand around and let that happen."

"Septy, we see hard times up here all de time. We don' always get rain on dis side of the mountain, and when drought come we expec' t'ings fi get bad and money fe get scarce. But de rainy wedda always come again, an' de plant dem spring back, and de animals get fat, an' we ketch anodder good crop. Is suh it guh all de time. I know dat since de twins dem did bawn me did feel weak all de time, an' me not been helpin' like me use tuh duh, but I will du betta. I can get a man fe bush out de half acre we didn't clear dis year. We can plant some cawffee an' gungo peas. I can start sewin' again. We can cut some corners, an' we can save a likkle here an' dere. We will mek out, Septy. Yuh wi' see."

Tears welled up in Birdie's eyes in support of her impassioned plea. Septy was touched, but his mind was made up.

"Birdie, I still say that I am a Gordon. Men in my family are raised to take care of their wives and children. You know that since our twins came you are not as strong as you used to be. I can't have you out there in the hot sun wrecking yourself and getting sick, I know you hate to see me leave, and I hate to go with all my heart, but I have to do something. I can't stay around here and get worthless like some men I see."

Birdie wept quietly in her helplessness. She understood Septy's sincerity and his concern. She knew deep within that he was right. She too had watched their growing inability to provide for the needs of the family. She knew also that Septy had travelled and had seen the world. He was a man of pride. He knew much more than she what was needed to prepare the children to face the future. She pleaded because she had to. But she understood the dilemma.

Septy was mollified by her pleading for a few weeks. His love for his wife kept him close to her. He was tender and attentive to her every wish. But the reality of unmet needs finally deafened his ears to her strong objections and tearful pleadings.

"I seh don' guh, Septy. I beg yuh not tuh leave we. I don' kno' wha' I'll duh ef I haffi raise dese chil'ren by mahself."

"Birdie, I really sympathize with you, but try and see things my way. We can't go on like this. I can't stand by and watch our lives mash up. I have to do something. And I'm not going anywhere to chop bush nor turn into a yard boy. I have to scuffle and get some good money to pick us up again. I have to go away, Birdie!"

She became quiet. She had exhausted all her arguments. She knew he was right, but she hated to see him go. She felt some guilt that her way of life had reduced him from the dashing and flashy young man she had met and married, to the concerned and aging man before her. Like a colt that could not adjust to the tension of a rope, Septy was trying but finding it difficult to adjust to the deprivations of country life.

On his part, Septy was sad but unbent in his determination to break away. When he could no longer resist the strong pull to provide for his family, he visited his brother-in-law again.

"Son-Son, man, I can't stay here and watch my family mash up. It's my job to support them and I'm letting them down. We can't even afford school clothes and books or something decent to eat. It is not their fault that things are tough, but a man must do what a man must do. I promised God to care for my family. I realize that God bless me with more children than the land can support, Son-Son. Man, I've got to go away and make some money."

"Septy, bway, I hear wha' yuh seh," Son-Son commiserated. "Yes, dis country life is rough, yuh kno'. Is nat eve'ybaddy build fe tek it. Yes, man, I see wha' yuh mean."

"Anyway, Son-Son, I won't stay away any longer than I have to. Help me talk to Birdie. And I beg you to keep an eye on them while I am gone. You know that my brother David would help, but he is gone to Vere with his tailoring. I promise to write often. You understand, don't you, Son-Son?"

"Yes, man. A man mus' duh wha' 'im haffi duh. Ah wi' look afta me sistah an' de pickney dem."

Some days later, Septy left the house before dawn and walked to Cross Keys. There he boarded a blood red van with the gold painted imperial lion and crown on both sides. Large gold letters declared the van to be the carrier of the ROYAL MAIL.

He made his way to Williamsfield where he took the train to Kingston. In Kingston he boarded a ship bound for the United States of America.

In America, he picked apples, and reaped asparagus and tomatoes. He enjoyed the work and he enjoyed life with his fellow contract labour colleagues. He gathered valuable information about farming. He was pleased with the money he earned. Dutifully, he mailed Birdie as much as he could each month. His letters were tender as he assured her of his constant love.

Each week the children would visit the Post Office at Cross Keys. They would be delighted when that special envelope was handed to them. The paper texture was light blue and very strong, with red and blue stripes etching the borders, and the words "Par Avion" printed at the top. There would be rejoicing as they ran into the yard shouting.

"Mamma! Dadda write again! We get a nodda letta!"

And every month, Birdie took the Mail Coach to Mandeville. She would cash Septy's check and deposit most of it in the bank, taking out only enough to buy necessities. The bulk of the money would await Septy's return.

When Septy had been gone about six months, he wrote saying that he had been invited to stay for another contract period. Instead of nine months, he would be gone close to two years. But the time would pass quickly. He was sorry that he would not be there for the birth of their baby, but he was sure that with her mother and sister nearby, things would work out all right. He would be sending more money each month as the salary would be increased. As always, he closed assuring her of his love.

Septy's seventh son was born on a starless night. Mrs. Jane Douglas the village midwife was sent for to assist Birdie. She fussed and worried as she encountered an unanticipated complication, a breech birth. The baby boy lay athwart the mother's womb and gave no sign of voluntary turning to make his way out. With a dexterity that came from years of experience, Mrs. Douglas coaxed the young life into the world, stripping the caul that covered his face.

"You know, Miss Birdie, this veil over your baby's face is a sign. This boy of yours will never be ordinary. He may be an angel or he may be a devil, but he will never be ordinary. All of you will have to pray for him and ask God to help you raise him right. So, what you going to name this baby?"

"Well, Miss Jane, I have been laying here thinking. This baby almost killed me, and his father just keep on traveling. I don't intend to have any more children, and he is my seventh son, so I will name him Septimus George after his father, and I think we will call him Sammy."

"O Miss Birdie, that' a good name. I just know that his father will be proud of that name and of his seventh son."

"Yes, Miss Jane, I think he will. I really think he will."

Chapter Six

Cocoa Walk, Manchester, Mid 1940's

The wind blew in gusts, its billowing waves flapping the clothes on the line. The afternoon sun hung high in the sky, draped by beige coloured clouds. The children jostled each other as they lined up to get a drink of water. They had been running and playing among the fruit trees and were now thirsty.

Sammy shivered. His blue and white sailor suit with its short pants scarcely protected him from the cold day. This was his first week at the new kindergarten. He knew no one. He had not played much. He felt alone. But he did not feel sad. Soon, he would be joining his cousins and friends for the run home. But he was thirsty. He moved with the line towards the tank where each child was given water, dipped from the full tank by an older boy of about five or six.

It was his turn and as he reached up to take the water, he saw the boy's shirt billow like a sail as his body was lifted and thrown into the tank. Sammy closed his eyes and opened his mouth to scream. Then he opened his eyes and looked again. There was the boy, still stooping on the rim of the tank, extending the tin cup to him. His eyes showed impatience at Sammy for slowing the line.

Sammy squinted at the boy in confusion as he took the water and lifted the vessel to his lips. The water was cool. He began to drink deeply.

"Miss Powell! Wilfred Fagisson fall inna de tank! Miss Powell Wilfred Faggison fall inna de tank!"

Sammy lowered his cup. All around him, children were screaming while the announcer of the mishap was trying to explain to the teacher what had happened. Instructions were given to find a diver. A crowd seemed to gather out of nowhere as people came running up the hill and assembled around the tank. One after the other, men probed the tank with bamboo poles and yam sticks to no avail. The boy could not be found.

Then a man was seen hurrying through the crowd. He was stripping off his clothes as he ran. At the tank, he kicked off his shoes, climbed the two steps up a ladder and dived. He disappeared under the cover of the tank. A splash of cold water catching the nearest members of the crowd.

Sammy stood stock still grasping the cup in his hand. He felt responsible for what had happened to Wilfred Faggison. He kept his eyes fixed on the tank with a mixture of dread and bewilderment. People around him spoke in hushed voices.

"What happen?" Asked a late arrival, "Some pickney drop inna de tank."

"Lawd have mercy! Den a which pickney? Yuh kno'?"

"Dem seh him name Faggison."

"Lawd have mercy! Den nuh mus' be Mass Bertie Faggison likkle bway?"

"Me nuh kno', me jus' come ya, meself. Wait likkle bit something a happen."

"Him a cum. See him ya."

The diver surfaced. He swam to the opening of the tank pulling a limp form. A man, stooping, lifted the small body from the diver. Water poured from the drenched clothing as the little boy was lifted out. The body heaved, and Sammy saw large pink bubbles ballooning from the nostrils as they managed to get Wilfred breathing again. Strange wheezing sounds accompanied each ragged breath.

Sammy dropped the cup and ran through the rose garden, down the hill and across the street to the big school where he usually met his Cousin Walford and his brothers for the journey home. Sammy never mentioned the accident to anyone. He never told anyone that he was the last one to receive water before the lad fell in the tank. He felt stunned and couldn't understand how he could see the boy fall into the tank before it actually happened. Did he somehow make it happen?

Sammy never heard anyone mention the name of Wilfred Faggison again. But the image of the limp figure with the pink mass of foam coming from his nostrils would remain with him for the rest of his life. That was his first introduction to the fact of death, and his mysterious ability to glimpse into the future. He was almost four years old.

* * * * * * * * *

"Sammy! Getup! Is time fi yuh go tie out de goat dem, an' bring back sum fiah wood." It was not quite dawn. The chill in the air made him unwilling to leave the warmth of the covers. The boy pulled them over his head and continued to doze.

"Bway, me seh get up. Yuh have work fe duh an' yuh gwine be late fe school. Yuh kno' seh Teacha Williams sen' message seh yuh late yestiday. Me seh get up! Yuh wan' me t'row col' water 'pon yuh?"

His mother roughly shook Sammy as she pulled the bed clothes off him.

He got out of bed and dressed quickly. He poured water from a goblet into an enamel basin and washed his face and hands. Vigorously, he toweled his skin to dry it and to get some warmth in his body. He stepped down from the house and faced the mist shivering on the tracks as he tried unsuccessfully to avoid the branches heavy with the condensed dew.

He went to where the goats were lying in a pen under a breadfruit tree. Bypassing the kids and the ram, he went to the ewes whose distended udders were full of milk. He washed the nipples, then began to extract the milk with gentle squeezing tugs, enjoying the musical sound the milk created as it hit the bottom of the bucket. He worked steadily until the bucket was frothing at the brim. Carefully, he put the bucket aside and released the kids who ran eagerly to get what was left of their milk. While the kids fed, Sammy took the milk to the kitchen.

He returned to the pen and released the goats, driving them on a track to the field where they would feed that day. There the guinea grass was thick and interspersed with other grasses and shrubs enjoyed by the animals. He tied the goats to trees while leaving the kids to run free. Then he began to gather firewood. When he had gathered as much as he could carry, he walked briskly back to the kitchen. He placed the wood by the fireplace and picked up a bucket. He went a few steps from the kitchen to the water tank. The tank had seen better days. His mother's father had built it many decades before with walls and floor lined with a foot or more of concrete. But it had fallen into disrepair. Large holes and cracks could be seen on the sides and bottom. After a heavy rain only a few inches of water was held at the very bottom. These would last for a mere week or so. The tank would then be dry again.

He climbed to the rim of the tank and carefully placed his feet on the top rung of a ladder that descended about twelve feet inside. Using a "butter pan", Sammy scooped the precious liquid into his bucket. When he scooped as much as he could carry safely, he climbed up the ladder rungs making his way to a wooden barrel by the kitchen door. He emptied the bucket into the barrel and made a number of trips between the barrel and the tank. A muddy trail marked his progress.

"Bway, yuh nuh done yet?" urged his mother from the kitchen. "It a get late yuh kno'. Yuh betta hurry. Me nuh wan' no more message from yuh teacha come to me yard. Me seh hurry!"

"Yes, ma'am." said Sammy.

He quickened his pace. As he started down the ladder, he held the bucket above his head, while looking toward the sun and noticing that it was rising high above the tree line. Hurrying down, his feet slipped. The bucket fell from his grasp and rolling past him, struck him a vicious blow on the side of his head. He felt fear and closed his eyes to concentrate, while he probed with his feet for foothold. He found one and drove his foot into it. Regaining his balance, he placed both feet on the ladder and let his body relax. Trembling in every limb, he made his way to the bottom, retrieved the bucket and gathered the water. He ascended slowly and walked gingerly to the barrel. As he emptied the bucket, he was satisfied that there was enough water to meet the needs of the day. He stored the bucket and walked into the kitchen.

"Jesam Crime, Massa, wha' happen to yuh?" demanded his mother.

"Me fall dung inna de tank, Ma'am," he said calmly.

"But bway, how much time me haffi tell yuh fe be careful when yuh guh dung inna de tank. Wha' happen?"

"Me foot slip , ma'am, and de bucket lick me pon me head."

"Lawd, den mek me see it, nuh?"

"Is alright, Mamma, which part me breakfast deh, ma'am?" Sammy shied away from Birdie's maternal hands.

"Den come ya, nuh pickney, mek me look pon de cut."

"Me seh is all right, Mamma, me jus' hungry." he protested.

"An' I seh come here chile, and mek me look pon de cut!" commanded Birdie.

"Yuh see it still a bleed!"

Sammy gave in. Birdie poured hot water in a basin and shook a generous amount of salt in it. She used a soft towel to tenderly sponge the wound. When she was through, she sat Sammy down at a wooden bench in the kitchen, and served him breakfast. The morning's events had sharpened his appetite. On the blue enamel plate set with knife, fork, and spoon, were several boiled green bananas, a slice of boiled white yam, a few spoonfuls of salted mackerel cooked up with scotch bonnet pepper, escallion, tomatoes, and chochoes; and two slices of buttered hard dough bread. He attacked the food, eating quickly and saving the chocolate drink for last. It was deliciously sweetened with sugar cane juice and coconut milk. Draining the cup, he left the kitchen table.

The sun was now high and it was almost eight o'clock when Sammy set out for school. Most of his classmates were already far ahead with only a few stragglers in sight. These children did not care about being late. Teacher Williams, the Headmaster, was unforgiving of lateness, and would make latecomers recite the story of Solomon Slow, the indolent boy who missed the bus. If the young scholars were not in their seats by the time the school bell rang, they would be disciplined by four judicious licks from the dreaded leather strap.

Sammy began to run. He caught up with the slow ones and passed them. Perhaps they had no fear of the strap, but he had no desire to be beaten. It was not so much the pain as the humiliation. What made him furious was that the teachers had no mercy on children who had many things to do before getting to school. Many had to get up early before dawn to help their parents before going to school. His anger made him run the faster. The indolent children, seeing him run, began to run themselves.

Many of them were barefooted. All picked their way over the rough stones of the macadam that was being upgraded. They ran past fields where workers were already busy. It was weeding time, coco planting time, and the season for cutting litters for mulch. Some of the workers were shouting across fields to each other. Others sang to cheer themselves. An occasional bread van chugged by leaving the tantalizing aroma of "bulla" cakes, fresh baked bread, and spiced buns in the air.

Sammy turned into the school yard trotting between the ancient graves, and hastened up the hill, to the school building. Breathlessly, he collapsed into his seat just as the bell rang.

Every child stood at the sound of the next bell, which signaled morning devotions.

"God the Father, God the Son, God the Holy Spirit

Bless, direct, and keep us, and give us thankful hearts. Amen."

The task of learning now got underway. The busy hum of the various classes in the one-room school spoke of the activities as teachers led students through their lessons.

"Crack!" went the leather strap making hostile connection across the starched khaki shirt of an unfortunate student. In a class adjoining Sammy's, the headmaster was reviewing a poetry lesson.

"Crack!" and "Crack!" came two more sounds in quick succession, followed by the wheedling voice of the pedagogue, still flexing the strap.

"Say it again. Start at the very beginning and this time don't form the fool or make any mistakes! It's two weeks you have this poem and it's time you learned it. Say it again! Start at the beginning!"

With brave yet trembling voice, the boy began to recite. A tiny tear formed in the corner of his eye, but his head was held high and his voice grew in confidence with each memorized and repeated syllable.

Tis good to see the school we knew, the land of youth and dream,
To greet again the rule we knew, before we took the

stream.

Though long we've lost the sight of her, our hearts shall ne'er forget.

We've lost the old delight of her, we'll keep her honour yet,

We'll honour yet the school we knew, the best school of all

We'll honour yet the rule we knew, till the last bell call.

For working days or holidays, for glad and melancholy days.

They were great days and jolly days at the best school of all.

The boy's voice grew stronger with conviction and confidence as he quoted the school poem. His eyes were fixed on the teacher knowing exactly what would happen next. He saw the sadistic glow spread from the intent eyes to the rounded cheeks and down the now relaxed lips as the next lines were said:

The men that tanned the hide of us, our daily foes and friends,

They shall not lose their pride in us, e'er the journey ends.

"Well done!" exclaimed Teacher Williams, "why did you not do it like that the first time? Heh? Its like I always say, it takes Dr. Discipline to get the best out of you boys."

The reference to the thick leather strap sent a chill of fear through the boy as he took his seat. The day droned on and Sammy, unable to keep his mind on the lessons, started to daydream. He saw himself running through fields with his dog, Hector. He thought of playing a game of marbles with "nickols", those gray and yellow round seeds that were as hard as porcelain and would last for a lifetime. Or even a game of hopscotch.

Sammy was jarred out of his daydreams by a question from his teacher "What do you think, Septimus, what do you think is wrong with the statement?"

"Please teacher, please ask de question again."

"Of course, The statement is this 'The bird flew over the wall, which was six feet tall. If the wall had been seven feet tall, we would have trapped the bird."

"Well, teacha, I don't kno' what is wrang wid de statement, but ah kno' about birds. If de wall was even seventeen feet tall de bird would still fly ovah it, ma'am."

"Very good, Septimus! This was a statement that called for you to think. Your answer is right."

Sammy smiled in relief and pleasure. Then his growling stomach informed him that it must be near lunchtime. The bell rang and children from all classes rose in anticipation and made a dash for the door. Those who had brought lunches went to find comfortable seats under the trees and among the tombs. There were ham sandwiches and bully beef sandwiches, mashed boiled green bananas, fried fritters, fried plantains, and a variety of fruits- ripe bananas, oranges, tangerines, and even a few soursops. All this was washed down with bottles of milk or lemonade.

The lunch hour was a happy time for Sammy. After eating, he would move about joining in one activity after another. There were games of "cashews", marbles, hopscotch, cricket. He also loved the "ring games", but above all he enjoyed joining in the singing of the work song "Sammy Dead, Oh!" There were also tricky games that tested the wits of those who dared to join in them. As Sammy ran merrily across the playground, he heard his name called. "Sammy! Pudding an' Galang." The unfortunate lad had been "PG'd". In rueful good humour, he placed the colourful and delicious grated coconut confection on the ground, and watched as it was quickly scooped up and gobbled by his wily adversary. As the boy ran off in triumph, Sammy called after him: "That's alright Fonso, today for you, tomorrow for me. I'll catch you next time! Just wait!"

The day became warmer. Sammy began to feel a gnawing fear for the next class which was Arithmetic and was taught by the headmaster. His favourite teacher, with whom he had been deeply in love, had left the school in the middle of the term. The boy became heartbroken. No one ever explained why she had to leave, and the pain her departure caused was almost physical. He used to impress her with his work. He was always first with an assignment, and every problem was always correct. Now, the very thought of arithmetic caused him to be ill.

And the insensitive headmaster was the cause of it. For the rest of his life, he would never forget or forgive that teacher for not realizing his grief, and for adding to his suffering. For weeks now he would sit shivering with his exercise book turned to the page. He would dutifully write NAME, DATE, SUBJECT, then put the book aside, his mind filled with thoughts of his missing teacher. And every day for the many weeks, the head teacher would line up all the children who had not finished their work and deliver four licks across the back without ever giving a single thought to why this otherwise productive and healthy child was not performing in this particular subject. The headmaster came to the class. The names of the children with incomplete or incorrect work were called. The line before him grew shorter as the children each took their licks. Then it was his turn.

"And what is your name?" he asked as impersonally as if the thing before him was not human. The boy remembered the day his father had come home saying that he had met his old school classmate who was now a headmaster, and so he was transferring his children to his school. Sammy thought that the change from Woodlands to New Broughton was for the better. When he was in Junior A Class, he used to see how the headteacher, Miss Benlos used to mistreat the big boys. She had no mercy! And no boy had better hold onto the strap when she was giving a whipping. Then the sounds of her strokes could be heard all the way across the schoolroom. She was especially tough on the big boys from the orphanage across the street. Sammy was afraid of Miss Benlos and was glad to leave.

This Teacher Williams was apparently an exact copy of Miss Benlos. It seemed that they really enjoyed beating the boys. So, this was the reward he got for smiling at the teacher that first day and saying "My father said you and he were friends in school so that is why he sent me to this school." He should have known then from the unsmiling way the man had recorded his name while saying "uh hmm". Things had gone from bad to worse. Now, he was before this man who had beaten him every day for weeks without even noticing. Tears of self-pity and grief for his lost love poured down his face.

"I said, what is your name?" So, he thought, after beating me every day for weeks, and asking me the same question every day, the man still does not even know my name.

"Septimus, sah. Septimus George Gordon, but everybody call me Sammy."

"Aha! A good and proper Latin and English combination is your name. You have a lot to live up to young man, a lot! So, where is your good and proper English industry, my boy? Here, these licks ought to wake you up and help you do better."

And he was dismissed. He never cried aloud, but the tears streamed down his face; not so much from the pain of the strap which he never truly felt, but from the despair and hopelessness that no one understood his grief at the loss of his dear Miss Hewitt whom he would never see again. As far as he knew, she was the only one who ever really loved him, and now she was gone. He was truly heartbroken, and no one cared.

The day was brighter and warmer after that ordeal and Sammy breathed easier as his internal clock informed him that it was almost time for school to let out. There was a certain rose apple tree that would be loaded with sweet, aromatic, and golden fruit. He wanted to be the first to raid clusters of their trove and to collect the purple tasseled buds as bullets for his bamboo "pop gun". But before the day was over there was the music class. His favourite was the national song:

> Hail to Jamaica sweet island of springs,
> Peace on her meadows her radiant springs,
> Beauty and gladness make thee dear land,
> The happiest spot on earth's wide watered sand.
> She lies mid white foam and blue waters at rest
> Like a maiden clasped close to her true lover's breast.
> Not for the realms of earth's mightiest kings
> Would we change thee Jamaica, sweet island of springs.

The words of the song moved Sammy's mind to think of the white caps to be seen on the sea looking down at Calabash Bay from a shop piazza at Cross Keys. He thought also of the lovely pastures with fat cattle grazing in the tall grass at the Experiment Station at Grove Place. He thought of crimson ripe tangerines bobbing in the breeze, and of lovely birds perching on high tree branches. He thrilled at the beauty of his country. The pathos of love for their native land that was struck by these songs would be so indelibly hammered home that regardless of where her children were dispersed, their hearts would only find full rest in Jamaica.

The bell rang. It was time to gather pens and pencils and books. A final clang of the bell officially dismissed the school. He dashed from the building, and was soon galloping ahead of the pack to the place where the rose apples bobbed in the breeze. He found a branch with several apples blushing pink and yellow. He filled his pockets quickly, and harvested a few buds for his popgun.

As Sammy made his way back to the main road, he heard his name called. He turned to see a fleet footed girl hurrying towards him.

"Sammy! Sammy! yuh have a rose apple fi me?"

It all came rushing back. He became embarrassed because the day before, Daphne had brought her Catechism Book to school. They along with several others were studying for confirmation, and preparing for taking their first Communion. All looked with anticipation to travelling to Mandeville for the sacrament at the Catholic Church.

The day before, he and Daphne had huddled studying the manual.

Question: Who is God?

Answer: God is Spirit.

Question: What is Man?

Answer: Man is a creature composed of body and soul and made in the image and likeness of God.

Question: Who made you?

Answer: God made me to know Him, to love him, and to serve Him in this world, and to be happy with Him forever in the next.

As they studied further, the booklet led them to an understanding of the meaning and purpose of the human family. It explained that the love of adults for each other was God's way of providing loving and supportive homes in which children would grow and become happy people. It was then that Daphne had taken hold of his hand and said in a voice suffused with passion that belied her twelve years of age:

"Yuh see how dem a teach we fe bad a'ready?"

Sammy was confused. As an altar boy who could pronounce very well the Latin words whose meaning he vaguely understood, he knew nothing of the libidinal excursions Daphne was now suggesting. The boy was speechless. But he felt that there was a challenge being hurled to which he had to make a response, or lose his place in the girl's affections. So he had said with as little conviction as possible that maybe they could marry while they were in Mandeville. The girl had agreed with enthusiasm. Having demonstrated his bravado, Sammy had found an excuse to leave that seat and join some of his male friends.

He had forgotten his brash proposal until now, but the eager girl before him was claiming rightful support and sustenance. He would not ever again be able to eat an apple or a guava in peace. He felt fear and anger as he looked at the beautiful and precocious girl now extending her hand for his food. Reluctantly, he gave her two of the apples as she looked searchingly in his face.

"Yuh 'memba wha' we seh, yestiday?" she queried. "We still ah go get married we'n we go ah Mandeville?" Fear dilated Sammy's eyes. His tongue froze in his mouth, he mumbled...

"No, ah change me min'. Maybe later, but we too young fi' get mash up a'ready." There it was out. He had said his mind.

He expected some defiant reply. But, without changing expression or showing any emotion, the girl turned, bit into the apple and moved towards her friends.

"Thanks fe de apple." she said over her shoulder.

Sammy turned from the girl and ran towards home, and towards the safety of a group of boys. He ran to escape a situation that threatened him with a life for which he was not yet ready. He looked back once and saw Daphne gazing at his retreating back with a look of puzzlement on her face. He could not believe what he had said to her the day before. He could not believe what he had just said to her in a fit of panic. He could not believe that he was now running away from a mere girl. But something inside impelled him.

He ran until he turned a bend in the road, which erased her from his sight. The curve was sharp and he held his head down while thoughts of Daphne filled his mind. The breeze whipped by his ears, and then, too late he saw the big lumbering car weaving and skidding towards him. It was out of control and seemed determined to attack him. He zigzagged taking as much evasive action as he could to escape the intrepid monster who followed his every twist or turn. He cried out in alarm as he stared in horror at the pursuing car, his mind flashed to the bucket pan hitting him that morning, his licks at school for not doing his work; his lost Grater Cake to 'Fonso; and his flight to escape Daphne. What was happening to him? Would he survive this unlucky day? He cried out in alarm. A fender struck him. He felt himself flung beyond the muddy ditch and into the bushes. A soft, warm dark hugged him. He knew no more.

He heard a woman's excited voice.

"Me seh, is ongle Gad save de likkle pickney. Me see de whole t'ing. Me certain seh 'im a guh dead."

"But thank God, he seem to be alright," said a man's assuring voice.

His father's voice. But he never heard his father's voice. Had he died? Was he in heaven? Yet, that would be how his father's voice would sound. Was he dreaming? His father was somewhere in America. He felt a warm gently caring hand touch his cheek. Like when his mother was feeling for a temperature. But this hand felt masculine, yet it was pleasantly perfumed. He wanted to hold onto the hand. But if he was dreaming, he did not want to awaken.

"Mr Gahden, me sorry yuh see, sah. Is yestiday me put de car inna de shap fe de whole day yuh know, sah. De man dem tell me seh dem fix de steering. An' now see me crosses ya. If yuh likkle bway get hurt, sah, nuh matta what it cost, jus' mek me know sah, me we carry de expenses."

Sammy did not see the worried taxi operator twist his hands and lean over to look at his bandaged head.

"That's alright Mr. Delgado, yuh know I was sitting beside you and saw the whole thing. I just didn't know it was my own son. It seems like he hit his head but there seem to be no broken bones. I will take him to a doctor in Mandeville and let you know if there is anything you can do."

"Well, Mr. Gahden, me glad fe see yuh sah. Welcome back. But what a home comin' eenh? Yuh almost come home fe bury yuh own likkle pickney. Me seh me see de whole t'ing. Is a mirrickle de pickney nuh dead. Which part Miss Birdie deh?"

"Me right here. Tank yuh suh much fe tell us wha' happen. But yuh see seh, me own husban' was in the de taxi weh lick me son. Is alright, Mr. Delgado, Me husban' wi' take care of every thing now."

"Mr. Gordon? Husband? Everything is going to be alright?" Sammy smiled. If he was dreaming he did not wish to be awakened. If he was in heaven, he wished he would see his father's face. It seemed that his father was indeed home, and if that was true, then all was well.

Chapter Seven

Vere, Clarendon, early 1950s

Two years after his return from America, Septy decided that he was not a mountain man. Wrestling a living from the rocky mountain sides held no charm for him. He needed to be with a crowd where action steadily occurred. Birdie reluctantly agreed. She was not prepared to be separated from her husband any more.

They moved to Vere, the sugar belt of the parish of Clarendon. The move put a special stamp on Sammy's character. He became closer to his father. Septy took a deep interest in his namesake and attempted to make up for the absent years. He encouraged Sammy to spend time with him in the tailor shop he opened. He imparted the wisdom of his years through pithy proverbs such as "If you watch the skies, you will neither sow nor reap;" and, "the fruits of the labouring man is sweet," Sammy relished being in the presence of his father. He especially enjoyed the warmth of his personality and his easy friendliness. Septy made friends easily. But Sammy was more deliberate and cautious in his dealing with people. A serious demeanour and thriftiness with words were his nature. Sammy's outlook on life became a mixture of the hills with the inclination to make one taciturn, individualistic and self-reliant; and that of the plains with its tendency to egalitarian camaraderie that typified those who are forced to rely on others for survival. It was as though all the sorrows and pain of Birdie, converged with all the extroverted adventures of Septy, to make for a balanced youth who mixed well, but never trifled time nor emotions. In the mountains, space between people was natural and expected. On the plains people lived very close together and interacted to survive. Sammy carried both senses in his character.

He never forgot Manchester. The red dirt. The undulating hills. The cool mornings bathed with dew. His love for Daphne Haffenden.

But he adapted to the plains. He made new friends. He learned to ride a bicycle. To swim. To fish for shrimps under stones, and mud fish under the sand. He came to enjoy guineps, "jimbilins", tamarinds, which were plentiful, instead of mountain guavas, plums, and rose apples, which were not. He also learned to compete.

He learned to steal rides on the back of cane carts where he had to match wits with the dray drivers. As the loaded mule drawn carts passed by, boys would pretend disinterest. Then they would rush to dive beneath the loads where the lashing whips of the drivers would not reach them. Sometimes the boys wished to steal a ride. Other times they desired to filch a length of sweet, juicy sugar cane. Stealing the cane from the carts was wrong because a dislodged piece of cane could undo the entire load. Stealing the cane from the cart had three steps. Move in; select, grab a likely piece of cane; and move out before the driver could see what was happening and snap the wicked whip.

On occasion, an unlucky youth would pay a terrible price for being slow. He would feel the sting of the lash and retreat with howls of displeasure and without a trophy. Often, the unfortunate lad would be mollified by a piece of Shiners or Red Cane, thrown by a compassionate driver or sideman. After all, they too had but recently been cunning youngsters.

School for Sammy became focused on the studies for the Jamaica Local Examinations. Passing the "Third Year" was the passport to apprenticeship to professions, admission to schools and colleges, or to employment in the better clerical jobs. Fear of failure to pass, spurred boys and girls to study hard and memorize the contents of aged notes. These had been copied by hand from textbooks that few alive had ever seen. Books that many students had never seen. Definitions of the Amoebae and the Spirogyra. The botanical orders of the Lily and the

Morning Glory. Studies of the works of William Shakespeare as reflected in Portia's Speech, or Mark Antony's Speech. All these were handed down from one generation of students to the next. Each group of students selflessly sharing what had been received with classmates who were in fact an extended family. When a "scholar" heard, or read in the Jamaica Gazette that he or she had passed an examination, the rejoicing would be widespread across several districts, for those children "sat" together.

These years were busy ones for Sammy and his friends. Many were involved with the Boy Scouts, Girl Guides, Boys and Girls Brigade. They memorized Laws and Promises. Even those who did not join the organizations could still repeat the first Scout Law: "A Scouts Honour is to be Trusted," and parrot the summary of the Ten Scout Laws:

"*Trusty, Loyal helpful, brotherly,*
    courteous, kind
Obedient, smiling, thrifty,
    pure in body and mind."

The hymn with which Boy Scouts ended meetings was also widely known and loved:
"*Softly now the light of day,*
    from each campfire fades away,
Solemnly each scout should ask,
    have I done my daily task,
Have I kept mine honour bright?
    Can I guiltless sleep tonight?
Have I done and have I dared,
    in everything to be prepared?"

Sammy grew in height and weight and strength. He lifted weight with his friends. These were the years of courtship for many. Sammy compared all the girls he met to Daphne. He found them all lacking something, so he read books. Without openly stating the matter, the boys and girls in Sammy's inner circle held on to dreams that required the delaying of family life until other goals were achieved. All held high ideals of what they wanted to become.

"What are you going to be when you grow up?" One would ask.

"A lawyer, like my father." Would come the spontaneous reply.

Or doctors, teachers, engineers, secretaries, telephone operators, chemists, and accountants. Others planned to enter civil service, or work in the offices of the sugar factory where their fathers had connections. One by one members of the group separated. Stated dreams and ambitions bowed to the realities of special circumstances. Some became apprentices at the various trades to become electricians, mechanics, truck and tractor operators, builders, and smiths. Others became office helpers who would become clerks, book-keepers.

A small core of students remained at their studies. These held out for opportunities they could not name. But the values of their religious communities guided and identified them as Anglicans, Baptists, Catholics, Church of God, Methodists, Salvation Army, Seventh Day Adventists, or Jehovah Witnesses. The East Indians in the groups who were not Christians, followed the teachings of Hinduism or Islam. Whatever the base, the values they shared influenced even those classified as "No Whereans."

Times were tough for many, following the end of World War II. When the sugar crop was over, jobs were few. Severe drought made matters worse. Many people lived at a mere subsistence level. Those in the towns and cities suffered more than those in the rural areas where ground provisions and fruits were available. In the towns, those who had, had to share. There was laughter, and songs even in the toughest of times. Even when many had to weep. All looked to the future with hope.

Sammy and his group studied their books to the lilting beats of the popular songs, "Too Young", "Mona Lisa", "Begin the Beguine", "Young at Heart" and the challenging lyrics that may have energized the scattering of young Jamaicans across the globe:

Faraway places with strange sounding names,
Faraway over the sea,
Those faraway places with their strange sounding names
Are calling, calling me.

And so mates going to England, to Canada, to the USA, further decimated the group. It seems that every week there was a "send off" function for someone going away. And every week Sammy received letters from friends in distant places. Sammy solidly determined that his lot was in Jamaica. He would not join the exodus. He would remain at home and enjoy the company of his mother.

A secret society developed. It was no mystery why the captain of the cricket team who was also a Leader in the Boy Scouts became Frank Hardy. Or why the leader of the Girl Scouts became Nancy Drew. In the excitement they made the mistake of wearing badges. Sammy had been named Yaqui after a sagacious and fleet footed Indian whom the Hardy Boys and friends encountered on one of their adventures.

The Headmaster was against secret societies as a matter of school policy. Life at school was supposed to be egalitarian and predictable. No form of elitism was to be permitted in the parochial school experience.

Every member of the Hardy Boys/Nancy Drew gang had been sworn to secrecy with terrible threats of unimaginable punishment promised to any who betrayed its secrets. The Headmaster called in Sammy. Sammy, the trustworthy and admired youth; the scout patrol leader and apparent paragon of youthful virtue. He the loved and trusted friend of teachers and students alike, was summoned before the solicitous and non-threatening presence of his surrogate father, the Headmaster.

"Tell me son," he coaxed, "what is this new group I have been hearing about, this secret society?"

Sammy's expression was that of near mournful candour. He looked the teacher in the eye and said "I don' kno', Teacha. Seems to me the club is only for the big boys, and the important students."

The headmaster stared at Sammy as if to search his very soul. "So," he insisted, "you don't know anything about this group?"

Sammy looked back at the teacher who had never beaten him. That had been unnecessary, because he was a model student. The closest he came to getting a whipping was when he had given the teacher some money to buy a textbook, and the teacher had failed to deliver the book. He told his father that he still had no book and his father went to the school to talk to the Headmaster.

"My son said he gave you the money to buy his book. I've come to ask you about it." Said his father.

"The boy lies!" Shouted the teacher. Sammy's father had taken the teacher by the collar in a moment.

"My boy never lies!" Septy had shouted at the man. Sammy received the book. The teacher had looked at him with coldness for weeks, but he was not spanked. Perhaps it was the strong attestation to Sammy's character, which impressed the teacher. Their relationship became one of mutual respect. So he knew that his words were believed and he was being taken seriously.

So, he lied.

"No Teacher, I don't know anything about it."

"Alright, Sammy, you may go." Said the headmaster.

As he left the presence of the teacher who loved him and believed in him, the youth thought of the first Scout Law "A Scout's Honour is to be trusted", and was wrenched by remorse. He also felt a sense of pride that he had prevailed against the authority of the teacher in loyalty to his pledge. He had not betrayed his friends. He remembered how the group had discussed the matter.

"Suppose teacher calls and asks us about this society, what must we do?" One had asked.

"I don't care if he beats me, I won't tell anything," Sammy had said fervently. So, he had been prepared. Sammy knew that many others had been summoned before the teacher. All would respond to the ponderous authority according to decision. Later he learned that none had told what they knew.

It came as a shock to Sammy some days later when every member of the Hardy Boys Mystery Club was lined upon the stage by the desk of the headmaster. None was flogged. The teacher showed no signs of anger. In a quiet and authoritative voice he stated clearly to the whole school that since it was against government policy, the secret society was disbanded. There would be no more meetings of the group on school premises.

The burning question when the boys met was "who betrayed us?" It was later revealed that the culprit was an adopted grandson of the headmaster. He had been initiated into the society. Under pressure he told all he knew. He was loved, he was forgiven. When Sammy heard, he thought to himself. If it had been me, they would have to kill me first. Once I have given my word, I will not go back on it. I would never betray my friends."

Sammy and his best friend Fitz were riding into Water Lane from Race Course. Sammy pedaled while Fitz sat on the crossbar.

A voice from one of the shops shouted:

"So, Fitzie! You wouldn't pass your exam until your best friend came, huh? Boy, you two are just like David and Jonathan. Anyway, congratulations. You past First Year. Both of you. We read it in the Gazette!"

That's how Sammy heard that he had passed the First Jamaica Local Examination. The boys then decided to skip the Second Year and study for the Third Year examinations. But Sammy had other plans. He decided to pursue a career in Agriculture. The best preparation was to be trained at a technical school. To get there, he needed a scholarship. To get scholarship, he had to be recommended. Recommendations were made by a special committee headed by the Custos of the Parish. He had been invited to meet with the committee.

The day came. Sammy and a group mounted bicycles to ride to May Pen. The meeting would be held in a room at the Courthouse. The road from Water Lane crossed the Rio Minho River at Alley.

When floods washed down from the mountains, the river would be impassable. The water would then be a rich chocolate brown, carrying logs and soil to be disgorged in the sea at the historic but now discarded Carlisle Bay. Today, the waters ran low, cold, and crystal clear. The lads removed shoes and socks, rolled up their cuffed pants above their knees, and pushed their bicycles across the stream with their shoes suspended by the laces from the handlebars. On the other side of the stream, they used handkerchiefs to dry their feet and dust off the sand. They then replaced socks and shoes, retied the laces, rolled down the pant cuffs, and reclipped them to prevent their being caught in the oiled drive chain of the bicycles.

Remounting, they rode through the busy market village of Alley. To their right, they could see the smoke lazily swirling from smouldering fires of the "dungle" or garbage dump. The trash accumulated from the weekend market was still burning. They passed the barracks of the Indian settlement on one side, and that of the Afro-Jamaicans on the other. Then they passed the shops of the grocers, and tradesmen.

They came to Amity Mall. Fitz looked at Sammy and said:

"So, what happened that day that made you run away from school?"

"What day? Which school?" asked Sammy.

"Infant School. You remember when you came to spend some time with your father at Alley and you ran away from Infant School?"

"Oh! you remember that. It seemed so long ago."

"Yes, but I never did know what happened."

"You know, now that you mention it, that was a terrible day for me. Here is what happened. The children were playing leap frog on the school grounds. While I was leaping, I fell and cut my knee on some broken glass."

"Yes, I remember that I was right behind you. I saw you fall, and I remember the blood." Said Fitz.

"Well, I went to the teacher, and she sent me to the Dispensary, next door. While I was standing in line, before me was a big man with the biggest sore on his foot you ever saw. The Dispenser had two assistants to hold the man while he cut out the dead flesh that was preventing the ulcer from healing. The removed dead flesh caused the sore to bleed. The wound was then bandaged. The man was groaning and moaning all the time. After the Dispenser had finished dressing the wound, he turned to me with the bloody scissors still in his hand and said "Next!"

"Boy, I just decided that I didn't want that man cutting out any of my flesh. I bolted out of that room and did not even go back to school for my books. I even forgot that my body was bleeding and in pain. I ran straight home, and hid under my uncle's bed. The covers touched the floor so I felt very safe under there. I stayed there until I was sure that school was over. It was at suppertime when everybody was seated for the meal that I heard my uncle say "But stop, where is Sammy?" I didn't wait for anyone to call me twice. I rushed out from under the bed and said "See me here." I took my place at the table and started eating that red peas and rice. I don't even believe I went back to that school. I believe I went home to the country to be with my mother."

"Ha ha! Now I see. Boy, I would do the same thing. I guess the Dispenser was too busy to run and catch you."

"I don't know about that," grinned Sammy, "all I know is that he would have to be as desperate as I was to catch me. I was one frightened little boy."

The boys parked their bicycles, removed the riding clips from the cuff of their pants, combed their hair, and wished each other good luck. They climbed the stairs and braced themselves for the meeting with the committee.

Sammy sat before the fair skinned and white skinned men. They seemed to view him as some specimen that had just been placed under their microscope. He remembered the instruction of his teacher to look at the men directly. In addition to the Custos, there was an estate manager, a parish education board official, a member of the clergy outfitted with his wide stiff white collar, and an engineer. None gave the youngster a reason to believe that even one iota of compassion resided in the room. The committee meant business. Theirs was the obligation of selecting the most promising youth for the tasks of leadership. The merely average and below were to be relegated to the labour pool that powered the farms and factories.

The youth was not intimidated. He had been conditioned to marshal his mental powers to good thinking, quick recall, and skilled wit, as careful lines of questions were followed. To his surprise, he was asked no question about his success at passing the First Jamaica Local Examination. He was asked no question about his present studies. He was asked why he wished to attend technical school.

"What are your plans for the next five years?" asked the clergyman, with a bulge in his windpipe jiggling while he spoke.

"Sir, by then I should be working as a Busha, after completing my studies."

Other such questions followed, then came one that shook his composure. The engineer fixed on him a wicked glint and asked:

"Tell me, what is the difference between a dynamo and a generator?"

Sammy was baffled. He did not know the answer. He remembered the advice of his teacher: "You are not supposed to know the answer to every question. Be frank. Don't stall. Think carefully and if you don't know the answer, don't guess." So Sammy was frank.

"I don't know sir," he said.

The man smiled. He was the only one who smiled during the entire interview.

"They are the same thing, young man. The same thing. You must read, read!"

On that note he was dismissed. He was quiet when he rejoined his group. All the boys were subdued. Some more than others. On the way home they stopped for lunch. Over buns, cheese, hot beef patties and cold ginger ales, they compared notes. All felt they had done badly. Only one, Fitz, had correctly answered the question about the generator and the dynamo. All returned to their studies while awaiting the results of the interview. At the most only two would be selected from that school that year. When the letters came, two were selected. Sammy and Fitz. All the classmates celebrated with them.

Chapter Eight

Dentwood, 1953

The first week at Dentwood was hell. Not in the literal sense. The Christiana-Spalding area was colder than Sammy had remembered being, when as a little boy he ran around in south Manchester. Maybe his years on the plains had softened him. But he had never seen thick sheets of ice on boxes of ice cream before he went to the North Manchester school. The cold of the place terrified him. But worse than the cold was the hell of adjusting to the new world of technical school.

He had not even unpacked his grip before the teasing started. It began with the dismantling of a self he had cherished. It began with his admiration of the second year student who was assigned to guide him to his dormitory room. It began with his attempt at friendliness. The young man seemed an unusual creature. He impressed Sammy with his impeccably neat uniform, his exquisitely shined shoes. His immaculately clean skin and very clean and neatly shaped fingernails. Sammy wanted to be like him. But his cautious attempt at friendliness was met with a coldness he did not expect.

"So, how long you been here?" He had asked his guide.

"You will get answers to all your questions later," was the reply from barely moved lips.

"As soon as you put up your things, come down the hall to the meeting room, we will have some information for you."

Within a half hour, all the new students who had come in that day were gathered in a room. A troop of sober faced second year students faced them. These viewed the newcomers as if they were so many mosquitoes to be swatted. One who appeared to be the shortest and scrawniest of the group served as the spokesman.

"Now, listen," he said in a surprisingly authoritative voice. "We are going to tell you this just once. You must learn it just as we say it. You hear? Now, all of you are Grubs! I said, you are grubs. That will be your name for the rest of this year. Whenever you hear the word "Grub", you must stop immediately, right where you are, and find out if you are the one being addressed. If you are being addressed, you must respond to the orders or needs of the upperclassmen immediately and without question. You hear? Without question."

"Now, what is a Grub? Say after me. 'A Grub is an infinitesimal specimen, accidentally dropped on a wall by flies, and miraculously hatched by the rays of the sun'. Repeat!"

The terrified newcomers now found themselves in a world and a situation for which nothing in their previous experience had prepared them. They repeated the definition. Then they repeated it again.

Sammy felt a mounting disquiet. He had serious reservations about what was being drilled into him. He remembered when he was being trained for Confirmation as a Catholic. Then he had been defined in ways that gave him dignity. That definition had never left him and had been very important to him, as he grew older.

"What is man?" The Catechism had asked. "Man is a creature composed of body and soul and made in the image and likeness of God," was the answer. He had believed that definition and staked his life on it. If that was so, how could he now accept being defined as a "Grub"? How could he affirm being insignificant, and being hatched by flies, of all things? Was this stripping of his being really necessary to make him adjust to this place? He felt he was not going to fit in well at all. But, he would go along for now and see where things would lead. The next words of the scrawny guide intensified his uneasiness. "Now, there are some Grub laws that you must learn. Say after me: 'A Grub must see, but never be seen'." The assembled novices repeated the words in bewilderment.

"A Grub must hear, but never be heard. Repeat."

"A Grub must be here, there, everywhere, and at the same time be nowhere. Repeat."

Feelings of deep foreboding filled Sammy. Every instinct told him that this place was not what he had expected. Some things here were very wrong. He had thought he was going to be educated. But the place was turning out to be more like a prison camp. He wondered if the Principal knew what these boys were doing. He would have to go and report this out of order activity as soon as he could.

"Grub! Grub! I'm talking to you!"

Sammy was jarred from his thoughts by what seemed to be a rock colliding with the side of his head. He had been severely boxed. Rage gave impetus to his reflexes as his ears rang from the blow. His usually quick temper exploded. He had been no slouch in the few fisticuffs in which he had been engaged in school. He had viciously blackened Boasy Harry's eye. He had taken Papa Son by surprise and savagely slugged him driving fear into the muscular youth. He had been lifting weight and his muscles were as hard as iron. Above all, he was accustomed to acting with lightening speed, that often took his opponent by surprise. His clenched fist swung at the ruffian who had dared offend his dignity. To his surprise the blow landed nowhere.

Steel-like hands held and secured him as other upperclassmen came to the aid of their mate. Sammy was pinioned. Even as he wondered what was happening, several powerful punches landed on his midriff in quick succession. The apparently skinny little fellow who bad been doing most of the talking was not so puny after all. The blows that now engulfed him in misery were from his fists. He had been rendered a panting and praying bundle of raw nerves.

Then as if indicating they had nothing to fear from the tall lean young beginner, those holding him released Sammy. He was breathless and sore, and he doubled over in agony. As if nothing had happened, and that no perturbance had taken place, the little lecturer patiently continued his pedagogy.

"As I was saying, Grub, when I speak to you, you must pay full attention. We have no time to waste, and you don't either. And by the way, in case any of you are thinking about it, you may freely report this orientation to the Principal or any of the teachers here. If you do, though, make sure your grips are packed. We will gladly carry you to the transportation to take you back home. That's all for now. We will see you later."

Sammy watched the retreating figures of the second year students. Their confident and secure manner fuelled his fury. He had never felt so humiliated in his life. He broke into a run after the group, and tackled the little leader, grasping his neck and choking him. Two of his classmates, also collared upperclassmen. With apparently minimal effort their attack was countered by the quiet strength of the second year students who silently freed their colleagues and held the newcomers apart until they were quieted. The skinny fellow carefully brushed himself free of wrinkles and looked at Sammy with a smile that was almost a sneer. "Yes, Grub, as I said, we will see you all later." They walked away without looking back. Sammy clenched and unclenched his fists. His breath heaved in gasps. He controlled himself.

He lay in bed struggling to sleep. The night was bitter cold. His stomach ached. He tried to make some sense of the events of the day. What had he done to deserve such inhuman treatment? Did people really know of the cruelty going on here? How could well-groomed and apparently well trained young men act in such brutish fashion?

His thoughts were interrupted by a sudden and unusual quiet in the dormitory. It was as if someone had flicked a switch and ordered an unnatural stillness. He was sure he had heard noises and movement only moments before. In his room there were about twelve beds, all occupied. His roommates were either asleep or pretending to be. The building had become as quiet as a cemetery. He began to hear a hissing sound that grew in volume. At first it was like a low rumble of escaping steam. As it grew louder, it became intelligible as the sounds came nearer. It was as if scores of voices were whispering the word "WASP?" But without the "p".

"WASS! WASS! WASS!"

"WASS! WASS! WASS!"

The chanted whisper swelled to scream as the door of Sammy's room was flung open. Several juvenile throats screamed the battle cry as the room was invaded and each bed viciously attacked in the dark by shadowy figures with flailing belts, sticks, leather straps, and other instruments for inflicting pain. The voices of screaming attackers were joined by those of terrified and surprised victims against whose vulnerable bodies the malicious blows were connecting.

One resourceful sufferer sprinted out of bed and hurried towards a light switch. Someone guarding that instrument from illumination hurled him back to the centre of the melee where moans and curses mixed.

As quickly as it began, the scourge stopped. The attackers vanished. None could explain with certainty what had happened. Someone turned on the lights. The batch of new students looked at each other in stunned questioning. Most had received blows which left smouldering welts on all parts of their bodies. They were a group of victims weeping without shame.

Sammy was a cowering, whimpering, shivering mass of hurt and anger. The tears came profusely. He had been on the receiving end of several blows that left their mark as reddening welts on his arms, legs, back, chest, and shoulders. He felt anxiety. He felt that he was the cause of the terror.

Three of the boys stood in the centre of the room nursing their hurts. They cursed and promised physical harm to the cowards who had surprised them and victimized them in the dark. They thought they knew who the attackers were. Just wait. They would have their due. They would get their sweet revenge on the morrow. "Just wait 'till tomorrow!" they shouted in defiance.

In the middle of their shouts of rage and recrimination, a tall senior student entered the room. His name was Ben. He was a cool, unruffled, and dignified gentleman who did not lift his voice as he looked at the motley assembly of excited boys.

"What's going on here?" he asked. His voice conveyed the sense of an irritated father whose well deserved rest has been carelessly disturbed by errant children. A brown robe covered his pajamas. His feet were clad in shined brown house slippers. His hands were in the pockets of his robe.

Several voices tried at the same time to explain that an outrage had occurred. They had been cowardly attacked. They had not even been given a chance to defend themselves. Ben stared at the loudest of the talker and braggart and queried him levelly. "So, you wish to fight back at those you believe cowardly attacked you?"

"Yes! let them come back right now! Let us see them. We can fight too!" Ben's eyes drilled into the ringleader.

"So, you really want to fight?"

The braggart suddenly wilted under the steady gaze of the senior man.. There seemed to be more to his look than a mere question.

"Well, we didn't do them anything for them to come and beat us up in the dark. That's not fair!"

"Uh huh! So you want to fight then?" insisted Ben

The room became quiet. There seemed to be a challenge to combat for which none felt quite ready. The quiet became eloquent and signaled that all were in assent that things had better be left alone for the time being. They had welts enough for one night. Ben's eyes surveyed the group with condescending charity.

"All right since you boys can't sleep, come to my room. You, you, you and you," he said pointing to Sammy and three others of the more avid talkers. "I have a job for you to do. The rest of you had better get some sleep. I believe tomorrow will be here soon and YOU have a hard day ahead of you. You four come with me."

The boys exchanged cautious glances as they followed the senior man down the polished hallway to his room. Ben reached beneath his bed and pulled out several pairs of boots and shoes. He showed them to the youth who gathered around him.

"Do you know how to shine shoes?" he asked apologetically. The ones he showed glistened from recent burnishing.

"I tried to shine these," he said, "but I was in a hurry. Just look, I can't even see my face in them. You lads will have to do them for me." He handed the footwear to the dumbfounded fellows.

"When you bring them back, I must be able to see my face in every one of them. Get them done as quickly as you can. They had better be outside my door before breakfast. And by the way, you had better be quiet. If you wake up any of the upperclassmen, I won't be able to help you. Go."

"Yes, sir!" chorused the boys quietly. They felt they were in the presence of an authority that could not be questioned. Only obeyed. As they trudged silently to their room, they whispered several questions among themselves. Who knew how to really shine shoes? Did they really have to shine the shoes? Did they really want to find out what would happen if they didn't shine them? Who had shoe polish and polishing cloths? Had any of them ever seen shoes as shine as the ones they were now holding in their hands?

Sammy had spent time in his uncle's shoemaking shop. He shared his knowledge and shoe shining materials with his new chums. The experience of the first night at technical school forged friendships. As Sammy and the boy who had talked so forcefully sat on adjoining beds, they had introduced themselves.

"What's your name again?"

"Ralph. Ralph Myers, from down near Newport, right here in Manchester."

"Well, my name is Sammy Gordon. I come from Vere, but I know Newport. I was born at Cocoa Walk, near Cross Keys, and during the War, I had to go to Newport to buy kerosene oil."

"I know Cocoa Walk. I've been there to picnics. My father comes from Resource."

"What a small world, heh? I have a lot of relatives at Resource. We could be family, you know."

"Yes, is possible. At least we both have quick tempers. Anyway, let's shine these shoes. That Ben looks like a pugilist to me. These boys are rough, henh?"

"Boy, it looks like they are too rough for my blood. I don't like it here at all."

The shoes and boots were shined and placed before Ben's door. He was either charitable or they had done a fair job. The boys never heard a word from him about his shoes.

The school routine at Dentwood was challenging. Early morning exercise was followed by breakfast, then daily chores, then class work. Sammy enjoyed tending the cows, farming the land, and maintaining the machinery. But he never grew to like the place. And the harassment never stopped. He enjoyed the class work and he loved the teachers.

His batch mates were transformed by their uniforms, the discipline of the Cadet Corps, and the regimen of school life. They aped the style of the upperclassmen in shining shoes, scrubbing face and hands, and seeing that their clothes were cleaned and neatly pressed. They were not yet as polished as the seniors, but there was a noticeable improvement.

Sammy's life as a Grub humiliated him. Try as he might, he could not avoid further thumps and beatings. His spirit rebelled and was almost broken. He saw other boys respond and become the minions of second year students, but his sense of personal dignity would not permit him to bow. He refused to be broken and rebuilt into the likeness of the Jamaican technical school version of a leader of men. He did well in class work, but he was always sad. In a letter home to his father he said that he would rather be a dray driver than return to the wretched place.

Septy jubilantly replied that he need not stoop that low. There was a place for him in the tailor shop to learn the trade and take over when he retired. Sammy put the letter aside. He enjoyed the Cadet Corps. As a former Boy Scout Patrol Leader, he took well to the regimentation. But he resented being brutalized. The life of discipline should not make a person brutal, he thought. Above all, he enjoyed church parades. He sang the hymns with enthusiasm, and he listened to the sermons with keen interest. He enjoyed the company of Ralph Myers and a small circle of friends. These fellow sufferers supported each other during the first year of technical school. They pledged to remain friends whether or not they returned for the second year. They visited the local shops together. They danced with the same group of girls at socials. They were the only ones to see Sammy smile.

In the life of the technical schools, not all could conform. At the end of every term there would be those who washed out. Sammy was among those who did not return at the end of the first year. He remained at home doing token tasks in his father's tailor shop. But the longer he worked with his father, the more convinced he became that the life of a tailor was not for him. The customers were too slow in paying for their ordered clothes. Many creditors disappeared owing balances that could not be collected. He heard enough of his father's complaints to discourage him. Often as he looked out at the world passing by the door of the little shop, he wondered what was his next step up his personal ladder to manhood and independence.

Chapter Nine

Vere, Water Lane, 1953-54

He was leaning against a corner post that held up the blacksmith's shed. The mid-morning sun struck his face and highlighted the perspiration on his forehead. He looked intently at the man who was studying the piece of red hot metal he held between the jaws of a pair of tongs.

Sammy was despondent. He had given up trying to please his father as a tailor, but he was finding it difficult to find any work that would earn him some money. He had walked from place to place for much of the morning, visiting two factories and a number of farms. All his efforts had proven fruitless. Ever since he had come home from school, it seemed nothing else would work for him.

His mind returned to his month as a pupil teacher at Race Course. He had about eighty children under a tree and was reviewing a lesson with them on the blackboard. It was about one twenty in the afternoon, and he had had very little to eat for lunch. He had also left home without eating any breakfast.

"Please teacha, I want to go to the toilet!" "Please, teacha, Junior, tek away my pencil." "Please, teacha, tell Mary not tuh pull my hair."

It seemed to Sammy that all around him were gaping mouths and writhing bodies. He felt like screaming. When he came to himself, he was holding a little boy by the neck and his feet were dangling off the ground. Carefully, Sammy had put the little boy down. He had taken the leather strap, the duster, the chalk, and the easel back inside. He had given them to the teacher without a word and left the school yard. That was over a month ago.

"Sammy, why don't you just stop rambling and settle down with me. This tailor trade has put food in your mouth for years. I don't see what you find wrong with it. You don't have to do it forever, but it can be a good thing to fall back on hard times." He had listened, but he had not been won over.

"Dada, all I can tell you is that I remember how people would not pick up their clothes from your shop in the hard times when you wanted money so badly. I promised myself then that I would not ever get into a trade where I have to wait until people have eaten and are satisfied before they think of my services. I don't know what I am going to do for a living, but I know that tailoring is not among my choices. I love and respect you, and I thank you for raising all your children right; but no sir, tailoring is not for me."

So, he had walked all day trying to find a job and on his way home, in final desperation, he had stopped at the Blacksmith's shop. He had just been told that there was no employment there but he felt too tired to go any further. The combination of fatigue and disappointment had drained him completely. As he leaned against the post, he remembered how children would stop to listen to the music made by the smith and his assistants. The larger children would nod their heads, and the smaller ones would uninhibitedly dance. All that seemed so long ago.

"Bway, yuh nuh 'ear me talking tuh yuh, yuh deaf?"

"Sir, were you talking to me, sir?"

"Den 'oo helse I tuh talk tuh? Yuh see hany one 'ere but hus? I ask yuh is whose pickney again?"

"I am Tailor Gordon's son, sir."

"Which Tailah Gahden? De one at Halley, hor de one 'ere at Watah Lane?"

"They are brothers, sir. The one at Water Lane is my father, sir. Mr. Septy Gordon."

"Bway, I know all de Gahden dem. Suh, yuh his Septy's bway. Han' yuh seh vuh wan' tuh be a blacksmith? Yuh really serious?"

"Well, ever since I was a little boy and used to stop by this shop after school, I said that when I grew up I would like to make tools like you sir, and make music on the anvil like you, sir."

"Suh yuh t'ink blacksmith work is fun, huh? Yuh t'ink his music I ham makin' when yuh see me workin? His 'ard work this yuh kno' bway. Yuh know 'ow tuh work 'ard? Yuh evah 'ave a job in yuh whole life, huh?"

"No sir, I have never had a real job. But I am strong and I am not afraid of hard work, I will prove it to you if you only give me a break sir."

"A break! Dat's hall I ear hevery day from yuh fellas. Den when I gi' dem a chance, dem soak me. I don' 'ave no time tuh waste, yuh kno'. I 'affi mek a livin' for my family, hevery day. I can't form de fool han' skip work ron Monday han' Friday, jus' because Hi 'ave a likkle change in my pocket. I haffi work hevery day. Las' week work can't buy nex' week salt thing. Yuh handastan wha' mi a tell yuh? Mi don' 'ave henny time to was'e han' I won' make yuh come 'roun 'ere han' was'e my time. Yuh handastan me, bway?"

"Yes sir. I understand you, sir." The misplaced aitches of the black-smith were familiar to Sammy. He still found them interesting to hear.

"Hall right. Since yuh gwine 'ang 'roun' 'ere all day, yuh may has well make yourself useful. Hi will pay yuh hate shillings a week tuh start. When yuh know something tuh hearn some money, hi will gi' yuh ha raise. Yud wi' get yuh money hevery Monday heevenin' hat four ha'clack. Now come 'ere, han mek me show yuh somethin'."

"Yes, Mass Eustace," Sammy whispered. He could hardly believe his good fortune. He had a job! And at the least likely place at that. What had won a change of heart in the workman? Was it his interest in not rushing off? Would he have been employed somewhere else if he had stayed around longer? Was rushing and running and trying to do so much in so little time a hindrance to creating a good impression? He would never know, but he was glad to be doing something at last.

"A seh come hova 'ere, bway. Wha' mek yuh suh slow, henh?"

"Yes, sir, here I am sir," said Sammy with renewed eagerness. He moved quickly to the side of the sinewy blacksmith whose features had suddenly changed from being relaxed and sociable, to being a dark and stormy cloud with blazing eyes.

"Wha' yuh seh dem call yuh?"

"Sammy, sir. Everybody calls me Sammy."

"Hall right den, Sammy. Yuh see dat t'ing what look like a fiah side wid the black fiah coal on it? Dat's de furniss. De black t'ing dat look like a fiah coal his coke. Hit stranga dan wood coal, han hit carry mo' 'eat. Now dat ledda t'ing dat look like a bullfrog is de bellas. Yuh see dat lang pole dat hook to de chain at de back hof de bellas han come hout tuh de front hof de furniss? Pull dung 'pon de pole."

Sammy took hold of the long pole, the end of which was just before his face, and pulled down on it. A strong swooshing sound of escaping air came from the mouth of the bellows which was half buried beneath a heap of coke. A soft red glow of fire came to life from the middle of the coke pile.

"Keep pullin' on de pole. Nice and smood, huntil de hair keep blowin' hin a steady flow. Dat's hit. Jus' like dat. Yuh don' 'affi kill yuhself, yug gwine 'affi duh dat all day lang."

Sammy dutifully pulled and released the pole, and watched in awe as the steady stream of air fanned the coke into a lively flame.

"Good, Sammy. Good! Now, de 'ole t'ing, furnis, an' bellas, put together mek up de f'oge. Yuh handastan? Well, yuh betta, beca'se me nah waise me breat' an tell yuh nutt'n moh dan one time. Nobaddy heva 'affi tell me nutt'n mo' dan one time, han me nuh repeat nutt'n. Yuh handastan me?"

"Yes, Mass Eustace."

He didn't tell the man that he had learned painfully that it was important to get the message correctly the first time.

Mass Eustace picked up a hammer and showed it to Sammy. The head weighed about eight ounces and it seemed quite ordinary except that it had no claws for removing nails like a carpenter's hammer. "Dis is a workin' "'ammer", he said, "an' dis", he continued, pointing to a large hammer with a head that weighed several pounds, "dis is de sledge. When we wuk, hi will use de workin' 'ammer tuh show yuh where tuh strike the hian. Has lang has hi don' show yuh anodder place, keep 'itting de hian on de same spat. Mek sure yuh strike de metal square pon hexact spat hi show yuh. Hif yuh 'it it wrang, yuh will pinch de hian han' spoil it. Dat will cost money han hi will charge yuh for hit hout of yuh pay. Yuh handastan me?"

"Yes, Mass Eustace."

"Uh hm. W'en hi wan' yuh tuh change han 'it anodder place, hi will 'it dat spat wid my 'amma. Den yuh mus' change right haway and strike de new place hi show yuh. Handastan?"

"Yes, Mass Eustace."

"Hall right, gimme some hair."

Dutifully, Sammy pulled down on the pole and began a smooth up and down movement which caused air to be pumped through the bellows to the smouldering coals in the furnace. A bright flame leaped upward. Mass Eustace selected a piece of iron from a pile beside the forge and placed one end of it in the middle of the burning fireplace. He used a pair of tongs to stoke the coals and spread them evenly. As Sammy pumped, he watched the iron on the fire gradually change colour from black, to brown, to pink, to red, to yellow, to almost white With a deft movement, Mass Eustace lifted the glowing metal with the tongs and placed it on the anvil. Sammy picked up the big sledge hammer.

He kept his eyes on the blacksmith who raised the working hammer and struck the soft metal a sharp blow. Immediately, Sammy responded by hitting the heated iron on the same spot.

"Tickey-tickey; Tickey-tickey!" sounded the small iron as the artisan light tapped it on the horn of the anvil. That informed Sammy to keep striking the same spot on the iron with all his strength, flattening it with the force of his blows.

"Boom! Boom! Boom! Boom!" sounded the impact of the sledge hammer.

"Tickey! Tickey! Tickey! Tickey!" countered the working hammer, pacing and guiding the work of the big sledge.

The day moved on. The workman and his new apprentice laboured steadily. The sun passed its zenith and by the forge, a growing pile of new made tools and implements was heaped. They stopped for lunch. Sammy was sent to a nearby shop to buy bread and sardines and drinks. They ate silently, each busy with his own thoughts. Sammy looked with pride at the work they had accomplished. As they had been pounding their hot iron, he had been repeating softly the lines of a poem he had learned in school:

"Drive the nail to the right boy, hit it on the head,

Strike with all your might boy, while the iron is red."

Then they returned to work. Now the long shadows of an evening sun hurrying to keep tryst with the western sea beyond the promontory at Round Hill, released the children from school and sent them scurrying to the blacksmith's shop. Some were youngsters Sammy had taught recently as a Pupil Teacher. He became excited. Mass Eustace had taken a piece of white hot iron from the furnace and placed it on the anvil, indicating with his hammer where the blows were to fall.

"Tick!" pointed the working hammer.

"Boom!" struck the sledge hammer.

"Tickey-Tickey" countered the working hammer.

"Boom! Boom!"

"Tickey-Tickey!"

"Boom- Boom!"

So went the teasing rhythm of the hammers at work. The children began to move in time to the music. Some danced. Others popped their fingers and nodded their heads. Sammy became a percussionist on special command performance. He was playing to a home crowd. He was their hero. He became caught up in the euphoria of the moment and forgot that he was at work.

"Tickey-Tickey!"

"Boom-Boom!"

The perspiration glistened on his face. His clothes became soaked with the moisture from his body. His tongue protruded from the corner of his mouth as he salivated in excitement. Then, without warning, the sledge hammer forcefully struck not the soft metal on which they were working, but the highly tempered anvil. It rebounded and hit his forehead, the impact knocking him to the ground.

Children cried out in alarm. Many scattered in different directions. Hot crimson blood spurted from Sammy's forehead and soaked the ground beside him. He shook his head to clear it. A searing pain shot through him. For a moment he did not know where he was or what he was doing. The older children surrounded him in deep concern.

"Move back! Move back!" roared Mass Eustace. "Gi' 'im hair!... let 'im breeve." The children backed away and gave him some space. Slowly, Sammy moved, then looked up. The blacksmith was staring at him with an expression that was so compounded with meaning as to defy easy description. It seemed to convey equally proportioned parts of anger, vindictiveness, pedagogical tact, and deep, stern, Jamaican parental concern.

"Pick up de sledge." He said.

Sammy lifted his hand to nurse the wound and ascertain the severity of his injury.

"Hi seh pick up de sledge!" Mass Eustace insisted sternly as the children looked on in alarm. "Yuh can tek care hof yuh cut hafta five ha'clack. We 'ave wuk fe duh."

Obediently, Sammy picked up the big hammer. Despite his throbbing head, and oblivious to the blood still trickling down his face and on to his shirt, he looked at the blacksmith.

"Gimme some hair." said Mass Eustace.

Sammy pulled down on the pole and pumped. Apparently concluding that all was back to normal, but that the place was no longer a source of entertainment, the children disappeared. Sammy was quiet for the rest of the afternoon. His eyes never left the working hammer, nor the metal on the anvil.

The day came to a close and the workman showed his new apprentice how to clean and close down the forge. Dead coke was disposed of. The newly made tools and equipments were stored, and so were the tools they had been using. The artisan showed the apprentice how his inattentiveness had "pinched" the metal and had ruined it for any further use. That piece of iron was now placed with other bits of discarded metal beside the forge, its faulty spot looking up to remind Sammy of his carelessness. Sammy was contrite as he indicated that despite his aching and swollen head, he held no grudge against his boss.

"Mass Eustace," he said, "I notice that you never use any iron from this heap over here. Why is that, sir?"

"Hi can't use dem because dem rotten. Dem can't tek de 'eat. Hevery time me try tuh 'eat dem and strike dem wit' de 'ammer, dem jus mash up an' won't form hinto de t'ing hi ham trying to mek. Dem jus' rotten han' can't stand de 'eat. Yuh handastan?"

"I see." Said Sammy. "Well, thanks Mass Eustace. See you tomorrow, sir."

The blacksmith stood tall, wiry, and serious holding on to the pole of the bellows with one hand, his other hand on his hips, akimbo. His expression was thoughtful as he watched his new apprentice walk away.

That Monday came quickly. Payday. Sammy was elated. Finally, after months of taking small handouts from his father, he would be holding in his hands some real money he had earned. He and Mass Eustace worked steadily all morning under an overcast day. The thick rain clouds gathered low in dark formations that stirred a wind, making their hard work much more comfortable.

It was about two o'clock in the afternoon when Mass Eustace called a halt. He cleaned up the work area and stored the tools, then said to Sammy:

"Bway, hi 'ave to mek some rounds. Hi will get back by four ha'clack. Don' leave hantil I come back. Hif ennybaddy hask fe me, jus' tell dem dat a soon come." He straddled his bicycle and rode away. It was a stripped down version of a bicycle with no fenders in front or rear, no brakes nor lights nor reflectors, and no licence tags. It wobbled as he tried to get control of it, the front wheel turning now to the left, then to the right; in time, he achieved a balance and pedalled out of sight. Sammy found a box, sat on it and made himself comfortable for the wait.

The slow evening hours passed. Before he realized it, night came on. He became concerned that Mass Eustace had not returned. He had promised to pay him at four o'clock. The time was now after seven. Could something be wrong? Had his boss met with an accident? Maybe the man had fallen down with no one to help. He decided to go to his house and see if his wife had heard anything. He walked to where the man lived and stepped up to the door and knocked. After a short wait, he heard slow footsteps coming. The door opened. There was Mass Euctace. Sammy was relieved and expressed it.

"Mass Eustace! I thought something had happened when you did not come back!"

The blacksmith glared at him with hostile and bloodshot eyes. "What yuh want?" he demanded.

"Well, today is payday, sir, and you told me to wait until you got back so..."

"Clear hout hof me yard right now!" ordered the man, leaning drunkenly on the door. "Clear hout, han' don' you heva come to my 'ouse widdout permission again. Yuh hear? Meh seh leave now, befo' a tek a stick han' break yuh head!"

"But Mass Eustace, is not the money sir, I just came to see if you are allright, since you never came back."

"Bway, a seh leave me yard now! A nat gwine tell yuh again! Has a matta of fac', yuh fiahed. Don' come back tomarra. Yuh 'ear me? Yuh fiahed! Don' come back tomarra!" He slammed the door in Sammy's face, leaving the stunned young man standing in the dark and feeling gloomier than the gloomy night. Tears of injury and disbelief flowed down his checks as he walked away.

Chapter Ten

Vere, Clarendon, 1953-54

As he walked down the pathway from the house, he looked back to see the light in the living room turned off. Mass Eustace did not expect him to return. At that moment, the skies that had been darkening with rain clouds all afternoon, gave vent to their feelings with loud rolling explosions of thunder and sharp cuffing flashes of lightening. Sammy began to run towards some shops he saw in the distance. The rains came down in drenching sheets. He was soon soaked.

He ran into the nearest shop. In the adjoining rum bar, he saw a group of men passing the time by drinking and regaling each other with stories. At least one face was familiar, a classmate he had not seen for more than a year. He walked to the entry of the bar.

"Sammy Gordon!" he was hailed, "Bway, wha' a gwan? What yuh doin' here, I thought you was up at Dentwood."

"Hey, Henry! How you do? Yes man, I did go up there, but I didn't like it at all, so I came back. I've been around here for a few months now. So, how are you, Master?"

"Man, me can't complain, me a gwan. I still study electrician down at Paradise Farm. Suh, mek me buy yuh a drink, nuh. Yuh soakin' wet. Mr. Bartender, serve my frien' here a gin and wine. Him look like him gwine catch him deat' of col'."

Sammy joined the men. Although he never frequented bars, he saw the wisdom of the offer and took the drink gratefully. He sipped from the glass that was placed before him. The concoction forced a radiated warmth through him from his head to his toes. By the time he had imbibed a good portion of the mixture he was no longer aware of being either cold or damp.

He entered their conversations and listened attentively. One member of the group was a fisherman from Rocky Point. He was talking about barracudas and sharks:

"We spen' de night on a sand bank out by Pedro Key's an was comin' back in. All of a sudden we see dis t'ing come up out of de watta and circle 'roun de cunnu (canoe). Eh! Eh! Next t'ing we kno' de fish grab one of de skull oar an' start tuh twist it out of the man han'. Him haffi wrastle the oar from de fish and lick him 'pan him nose wid it, before de fish would swim off. Yes, man. Is a lot of big fish out dere. Den one time, we did ketch one big barracuda. When we did cut him open, guess wha' we fin' inna him stomach? Nuh one gol' ring! Me seh, when yuh guh a sea, yuh see all kinda t'ings. Sometime at night when yuh ketch a nap, yuh hear some t'ing a splash inna de watta dat mek yuh 'fraid fe even open yuh yeye. Yuh t'ink seh fishaman life, a plaything? Cho! Every time dem guh a sea, is dem life dem tek in dem han'!"

As the fisherman paused to catch his breath, Henry turned to Sammy.

"So, what yuh doin' these days, Massa?"

"Boy, I'm struggling, you know I just had a rough time awhile ago. I was working for Mass Eustace. You know, the blacksmith around at Broken Bank. I worked and he said he would pay me today at four o'clock. Well, about two o'clock he left and told me that he would soon come back and I must wait for him. I waited until it got dark but he didn't come back. I wondered if something had happened to him, so I went to his house to tell his wife."

"When I knocked on the door, who opened it but Mass Eustace. I was so glad to see him, and I said "Mass Eustace! I was worried about you!" The man came down the steps staggering and stinking of rum. He was rotten drunk. He told me to clear out of his yard and that I was fired.

He used a 'whole heap of bad words that I am not accustomed to. I was shocked. Henry, I never did the man anything for him to treat me like that. Nobody ever talked to me like that in my whole life. Now I don't know what to do. I won't work for him any more, but I've tried so hard to find a job, and now I don't even have any money and my father is getting impatient with me."

Henry nodded his head in understanding. "Sammy, let me tell yuh something. Almos' everybody around here know 'bout Eustace. If you did ask anybody, they would tell you that he is the last man on earth you want to work for. Even if you are starving. The man is evil."

"I believe that. He was cruel to me," Sammy agreed. "Look here. This scar on my forehead comes from a sledgehammer that he let bounce off the anvil and hit me."

"Bway, yuh lucky," replied Henry. "When I lef' school, guess where I got my first job? Yes, wid Eustace. Me seh, de man mek me believe him was gwine make me into the bes' blacksmith in the worl'. And you haffi agree seh him is an expert blacksmith. De man is great! Him can tek an ordinary piece of iron and turn out tools that are as good as any you can get from England or Germany. Him can make ames, augurs, chisel, bridle bits, collars, horseshoes, plough board, you name it. One day a man bring a shotgun to the shop with the trigger broken off. I was thinking that the whole gun was now spoiled. But Eustace take the gun and look 'pon it, then him unscrew the broken part. Next thing I know, him put a piece of iron in de fire and heat it red hot den start to shape it wid him likkle hammer. Den him punch a hole in it an' file it down. Him screw de new t'ing in place an' call de man tuh guh outside wid him.. Him put two shat in de gun, point it in the air, and pull de trigga. Badam! Badam! De gun shat like it jus' come fram de facktry. Eustace charge de man five shilling. De man was suh happy him give him a whole pound note an' shook him han' suh hard, him nearly break it off."

"Yuh see dis mark on me forehead?" continued Henry, pointing to a star shaped scar. "Is Eustace lick me dere wid a axe hangle. An' wha' mek him dweet?"

"T'ank God, t'ings fine wid me now. Suh, wha' yuh a guh duh now, man?"

"Henry, I don't know. It seems like everything I try I fail. I know I don't want to be a tailor like my father, but I need money and I can't ask him for any more when I refuse to enter his shop. I seem to be up against a stonewall. But this thing with Mass Eustace still hurts me a lot."

"I see what yuh mean. I tell yuh what. Even though yuh don't want tuh ask yuh Father for anything, maybe his name can still help yuh."

"What you mean?"

"Yuh 'memba Headman Lorasingh that used to work down at Ol' Monymusk?"

"Yes, he's my father's good friend."

"Dat's what I mean. He is a big man down at Paradise now. I see him all de time. He is my father's good friend tuh. I will see him tomorra an' tell him that I saw yuh an' yuh lookin' for a job. I will tell him dat yuh pass Firs' Year an' dat yuh spen' time up at Dentwood. Den I will tell him dat yuh are Tailah Septy Grant son. Den I will tell him dat I tol' yuh tuh come see him because if anything open down deh him will kno' 'bout it. Give me tomorro tuh talk tuh him, den yuh can come down on Wednesday. If anybody can help yuh 'roun here, I kno' is Mass Lora. Once he kno' seh yuh Tailah Gordon son, he will do every-thing tuh help yuh, I kno' dat."

"Boy, Henry, thank God for the rain that forced me to come in here. I feel better already."

"Yes, man. Something good, bound to happen now." They turned back to the group where the man from Rocky was still talking.

"Me seh, nex' to Ol' Harbour, dere is no fishing beach betta dan Racky Pint on do whole south side of Jamaica. And when yuh include the white san' up at Jackson Bay, we even betta dan Ol' Harbour. But de dundas watta fram de facktry is wha' mash we up. When de stinkin' watta run aff fram all ovah de fiel' dem an' get inna de sea, all de way fram Carlisle to Jackson Bay, no baddy want fe come tuh Rocky fe nutt'n."

"What de dundas duh?"

"It stink up de place. Is refuse dirty watta yuh, kno'. An' it smell sour, and it dirty up de sea suh yuh can't swim or even fish out in de Bay. Is not poison, is jus' insanitary an' ugly. It mash up Rocky, man."

"Well, if de dundas is a problem, why can't you all complain to the factory people and see if they can do something to help the situation?"

asked Sammy.

The man laughed showing toothless gums with one giant tooth incongruously jutting out of the top mouth like a lone mast against a black horizon. "A seh scoo here!" he giggled tipsily. "Massa, yuh kno' is who yuh talkin' 'bout? Is Tate an' Lyle we talkin' 'bout yuh kno'. Tate an' Lyle can buy an' sell Jamaica over an' over, an get back change. Nobaddy at Rocky fool-fool enough tuh guh mess wid Tate an' Lyle. All of we can duh rum talk here at Watah Lane, an we can wurry if we pickney will tek sick from de stinkin' brown watta, but we kno' seh we nah get nutten if we raise a row. We may even lose de likkle bit of bread we have now. Is a pity tho', I still seh we could get some tourist bisniss at Rocky if we could clean up de place."

Another round of drinks was ordered. When it came, another member of the group named Likkle Man proposed to recite a poem. It was entitled "Jamaica" by H.S. Bunbury.

Here through leaf fertile valleys flows the cool caressing breeze
Luring sunshine. Forth it sallies from its ambush in the trees.
Rich savannahs, plumed and spacious, sweep and fade in
    golden haze
Till they melt into the gracious curve of seas and sapphire bays.
Out of these rise up the crested mountain masses. Many hued
Sunset crowned, and dawn invested with a sovereignty renewed.
Now the glimmering expanses of the rainbow tinted Main
Hide the treasure ship romances and the splendour that was
    Spain,
Still shall Drake and Raleigh's story to Jamaica's youth be told
For they held all England's glory, higher far, than Spanish gold.

On and on recited Likkle Man, in spirited inebriation, waxing more and more loquacious as he crescendoed to the forceful finish. Then, lifting his glass as proudly as Little Jack Horner, he drained its contents, while the others drank in salute to the orator.

Sammy took a sip of his drink, but he was deep in thought. He wondered how this motley group of tattered and unlearned black Jamaicans could be grouped with Drake and Raleigh. Was the poet thinking of people like them as he wrote those patriotic lines? Somehow, he did not feel included in the "Jamaica's youth" of the poem, although when it was taught to him in school he had felt that it was intended to send him a message. England's youth was considered interchangeable with Jamaica's youth by the writer, but his experiences as an Afro-Jamaican had informed him that there were differences that could not be ignored. England's children had enslaved Africa's children. The consequences of that history was still evident in Jamaica. England's grandchildren, even the brown ones, tended to hold proudly to their "skin colour" as a badge of difference which set them apart from the "blacks" whose social place was below them in every respect.

Poor blacks seemed destined to be hewers of wood and drawers of water for ever. Even in a world where such kind of labour was no longer needed, the class lingered. Africa's pure blooded children in Jamaica were till considered inferior to their kinfolk of fairer hue. He remembered when he worked for a few weeks on a farm. He along with some others had helped to drag a horse with a broken leg to a spot where it was to be put to sleep. The owner of the property, a Jamaica white man, unpacked the biggest handgun Sammy had ever seen. The man expertly despatched the horse from its misery with a single well-placed bullet. At the sound of the explosion, the boys with Sammy jumped.

"Lawd, Mass Jim," said one of the lads, "is where yuh get a gun suh big? Is wha' yuh gwine duh wid a gun dat big, sah?"

Ignoring the first question, the man grinned broadly revealing gold teeth darkened by years of accumulated Craven A cigarette smoke. He looked at the still smoking weapon, then looked at the boy and said "Run, and I'll show you."

The lad shrank several sizes smaller than his frame as he said "Who me, sah? Me not gwine run anywhere, sah?" The man returned the gun to its case with a self-satisfied chuckle. The workers laughed hilariously at their discomfited mate.

All except Sammy. He had not found the situation humorous. He remembered that he had gone with some friends to fetch firewood on the man's property. Trees felled by tractors were in heaps to be burned. They were busily tying bundles of dried sticks and roots when a boy dropped his bundle in fear and fled shouting "Run! Missa Jim coming!" Sammy joined the retreating youth in a deep excavation in the bank of a gully. They watched as the man picked up the bundles and threw them back on the pile to be burned.

Sammy remembered going to church and seeing the man singing the hymns, praying the prayers, and kneeling reverently to receive the Holy Communion. Then why did he act so uncharitably? As the children had walked home, Sammy had heard them recite past acts of cruelty the man had done. He had felt anger. So, as he heard the man say "Run, and I'll show you," he felt there was a deeper meaning than mere humour. He was not amused.

Yes, he had observed and experienced the differences between England's youth and Africa's youth in Jamaica. The former were landed and privileged. The latter were landless and poverty stricken. The former were haughty and self-aware. The latter were humble and self-deprecating. And Sammy had reserved to himself the right to feel as equal in value as any person of any colour. That had been the power of the Confirmation and self-definition he had internalized at the altar of the church. That no one could take from him. He knew he was different, and he knew why. But he still wondered why as the darkest of his parents' children he was reminded of his skin colour constantly by fairer family and even friends. Why did he pick up on things that were considered trivia by others, and ponder their deeper meaning?

So, now he wondered about the poem so glibly spoken by Likkle Man. The words held implications for him that made him feel very uneasy. He felt excluded from the closing lines and the exclusion reminded him of a place in his society that limited his access to comforts and opportunities and power. He felt sad that the reciter did not catch the exclusion, and could so easily repeat words not written with him, and is ilk in mind.

He took another quick sip of the potent tonic and put down the glass. Thanking Henry for the drink and the advice, he assured him that he would follow up on his counsel on Wednesday. He said goodnight to everyone and gave a special handshake to the man from Rocky Point, who was so near and so far from seeing his dream become a reality. As he stepped out into the street, he noticed that the rains had ceased and there were stars in the sky.

As he walked away, he heard Henry say to the others.

"Is one different and ambitious bway that, yuh kno'. But something is wrong wid him. He get a scholarship to Dentwood that only a few people get, but he wouldn't stay up there because he wouldn't let dem beat him. Everybady know seh is suh it guh up at those schools. Dat's how dem make men out of boys. They can take the littlest fraidy boy, and when they get t'rough wid him, if he finish de program, even duppy fraid of him. But Sammy seh he is not a slave and nobody has to beat him for him to learn anything. The boy is smart, but something wrong with him, for him to throw away a good opportunity like that."

He paused in the dark to listen with sadness to the comments about him. Was Henry right? Was something really wrong with him? True, he felt that he was different from others. He felt he was born to achieve some high purpose. He felt that he had to control his quick temper, and he had to manage the flashes of images that from to time blurred his mind and forewarned of things he could not always understand. He felt unsettled and rudderless in navigating the voyage of his life. He felt he needed help or special advice. He had no idea where to turn. He unlocked the door to his room and dressed for bed. He lay awake a long time then drifted off to a heavy sleep.

That Wednesday he had gone down to Paradise. Mr. Lolasingh was impressed with him and found him a job as a scale clerk. For several weeks, Sammy impressed everyone with his punctuality and dependability. Then things began to go wrong. He became detached and absent minded. While he made up the payroll for the cane-cutters and dray drivers, he suddenly found he would miscalculate weights and numbers of loads; and he would have to compensate the people out of his cheque and makeup the deficit on the next payroll. He would daydream and ignore details of his job such as keeping good records of store house inventories. The straw that broke the camel's back was when he was given strict instructions by the section manager to see that a truck of sand was emptied at a spot where a building was being erected. Sammy was at the scale when the truck arrived. Instead of telling someone where to tell the driver to dump the sand, he allowed the sand to be dumped at a spot far from where it was needed.

"Mr. Gordon, it is clear that your mind is not on your job. Why don't you be a man and resign?" suggested the manager. He did.

Chapter Eleven

May Pen, 1954-1958

After resigning from Paradise Farm, Sammy had returned to his father's tailor shop, deciding that since all else had failed he would settle down and learn the tailor trade. One day, after he had been with his father for a few months a car pulled up by the shop and a man got out and called for his father. He was a supervisor of the Motor Repairs Division of the Monymusk Sugar Factory. Unknown to Sammy, his father, knowing of his dissatisfaction with tailoring, had been trying to find him a more satisfying position elsewhere. His father now told Sammy that the man wanted him to report to work on the next Monday morning. Sammy was deeply touched by his father's concern for him.

Two years had passed since Sammy had been employed as a mechanic's apprentice. Now, he stood beside a master mechanic preparing to start the engine of the tractor on which they had been working for the past several months. They had stripped the machine of all its moving parts, examined each, and ordered replacements for the worn ones. In the months while they waited for the new parts to arrive, they cleaned and painted the chassis, overhauled the electrical and cooling systems, and made sure everything was made ready for the rebuilding of the machine. Now, all was installed and the freshly painted tractor was ready for the test of the mechanic's skill.

This was Sammy's first experience of overhauling a tractor. His teacher was standing beside him. Sammy was anxious to see how well they had done their work. He was told to press the starter switch. The tractor groaned into life, belching white smoke. The mechanic made some adjustments and the smoke spewed blue as the engine settled to a smooth humming. The pride of accomplishment was clear on the mechanic's face. Sammy shared in his pleasure. Sammy had become settled in the position of becoming a mechanic, when one day his father asked to talk to him.

"Son, I hear that there is land for sale near May Pen at a place called Cross. I never did enjoy life up at Manchester, but I believe we can open a tailor shop and grocery store near where the new settlement is going to be, and we can grow with the area. What do you think?"

"Well, Dadda, what do you know about the area? Have you seen it?"

"No, I was thinking we could ride up there one day and take a look."

"I don't see anything wrong with that. What does Mamma say?"

"She says she will do whatever I decide, but since it's only you and me at home now, I will do what you think is best. I just think paying this rent and not getting anything back is not sensible."

"I will ride up with you Dadda. Let's go look over the place."

They had seen and liked the place, and in a matter of months had moved to Cross. Septy opened up a tailor shop, and Sammy gave up his job at Monymusk and found a job at the Storks DeRoux Store in May Pen. He settled down to the routine of being a sales clerk. He began to make new friends.

He had not been to Mass in years. He had grown out of the habit. Yet, he was still a very religious young man. One evening he went with some friends to attend a revival at a neighborhood church. They had stood outside an open window of the packed church. The saints on the inside were joyful. They seemed filled with something that was strange to him. He felt a hunger for their confidence about life. They stirred within him a yearning for direction for the life that he had given up. The lost sense of being born for a special purpose returned as a feeling of nostalgia. He listened intently to what was being said and done inside the church.

As the saints clapped their bands while playing cymbals and timbrels, and beating drums, their repeated chorus caught and held his attention:

I am feeling sweet with new wine.

I am feeling sweet with new wine.

The Holy Ghost came to me, Makes me feel like rejoicing,

I am feeling sweet with new wine.

He felt drawn to the song. He seemed to be waiting for some force to take all the frayed edges of his checkered life and knit them into a whole. The singers seemed to be telling of something that had moved them to say "Yes, that's it!" He wanted that. The waiting for a break-through carried its own deep anguish.

The tempo shifted as the people onstage began to stomp with such show of energy that it seemed the wooden floor would crash at any moment. The frenzy was hypnotic. Their songs and movement enveloped Sammy. He felt infused with a special appeal. The words and music confronted him, flowed through him, and washed over him. He felt as warmed through just as the Gin and wine had done on that rainy night. But this warmth was more profound than any he had ever experienced. The songs began to stir him. He began to feel that he knew what the people knew, and could join them in celebrating what they celebrated. He felt a Presence within him guiding him. He no longer felt alone or afraid.

The tempo shifted again. A young man came to centre stage and spoke convincingly about the change God had caused in his life. The words were low keyed but impressive. Sammy listened attentively. Then the man sang a solo. The words echoed Sammy's feelings at that moment: "Search Thou even me. Search Thou even me. Take my heart and know my thoughts. Search Thou even me." He joined the singer in asking God to examine him and make him worthy. To make his life count for something.

When an invitation was extended for people to give their lives to God, Sammy ignored the fact that he was already a baptized Christian and a confirmed Roman Catholic. The appeal was too soul-searching, and his hunger for spiritual focus was too sharp. He ignored the fact that for years he already had a personal praying relationship with God. He ignored that his parents would never understand how he could leave an established religious faith, and join one that was a mere step away from being "pocomania". What he did recognize was that this worshipping community was witnessing to something that promised fulfillment. His needs for meaning were being met. He knew that he wanted what these people had.

He walked down the narrow aisle through the thick crowd. He looked at no one as he made his way to the crude wooden rail and knelt. For a moment he was struck by the contrast between the dirt floor beneath him and rustic appointments around him, and the attractive and well appointed altar and furniture he had been accustomed to all his life.

The feeling of being out of place did not last. He closed his eyes and turned his thoughts to God. He became aware of a steadily increasing noise around him. Hands were placed on his head. Many voices were praying, apparently praying for him. He thought that curious since he could very well pray for himself. He let that thought pass. Let them shout and holler if they want to, if that is their way. Then he felt a peace enveloping him. He felt alone with God in that moment. At long last he had arrived in a safe harbour after a long and perilous journey. There, at that crude altar, he felt secure with God.

Oblivious to the din, he poured out his soul to God. He spoke of his longings and his puzzle that his deepest prayers had gone unanswered. He told God that he was still willing to go where he was sent and do as he was told. "Only, please Lord, give me a clear and firm purpose. Only give the constant peace that comes from knowing that I am truly home at last."

Sammy rose from his knees. The voices around him had become silent. He felt refreshed and unburdened and steady. He was announced as a convert. He did not correct them. He accepted their love and friendship. This was different from the formality he had known when he had attended other churches. The sense of being in a large family nourished him. He no longer felt alone.

One Sunday morning he was taken to the river and baptized. He felt foolish that all the sacramental things that had been done in his life before were so carelessly set aside, yet he said nothing. He was also puzzled that he was baptized without instructions. He felt that he was much more solidly trained as a Christian than his fellow converts, but he did feel that this new experience had deepened his personal relationship with God.

Again he was plagued with his old malady of daydreaming. Again he became incompetent at his job. He spent many hours at the church taking music lessons and practising on the organ and the piano. He spent many hours in fasting and prayer, pleading to discover God's will for his life.

One evening, the Pastor entered the church and came to where he was sitting. They greeted each other, then he listened to Sammy practise for awhile. Then he came to the point:

"Brother Gordon, what do you really want to do with your life?"

The question took Sammy off guard. His mind reeled under the images of dashed hopes and shattered dreams and disappointments. He thought of his ventures at Dentwood technical school, at trying to be a Pupil Teacher, at trying to be a blacksmith and also tailoring. The thought of his embarrassment at Paradise Farm, and his leaving the work he enjoyed at Monymusk. He even thought of the present concerns his boss had expressed about his slowness in doing his work at Storks DeRoux. He even remembered how he had gone to Kingston to take an entrance examination for a college. When the letter came announcing that he had been awarded a half scholarship, he had shared it with his father who had advised him:

"Sammy, never hang your hat where your hand cannot reach it. Look at me. I never went beyond six class in school. But I have travelled abroad. I have saved my money, and I have cared for my family. Son, if you join me in this tailor trade, you will never want for anything. I will buy you a sewing machine, a pair of scissors, a table, and all the tools you will need. But this college business you are talking about is nonsense. Later, when you earn your own money, you can do as you please just as your older brothers have done. I don't see what in the world you have against tailoring."

Yes, at every turn in his life he had lacked true sponsorship. That had been his handicap. And yet, there was something special about the way the minister asked the question. The thought pushed to a memory long hidden deep in his being. It flashed to the days when he was an Altar Boy and just knew he would be a priest when he grew up. It drove onto that day when he had gone searching for firewood. He had found a lovely dried branch that when brought home and cut in pieces would feed the fireplace for many days. On the journey home, the burden of the branch became very heavy and very painful to the shoulder on which he carried it. He looked at the steep ascent of the hill ahead, and the thought of how far he had to go made him begin to cry. Just when he was about to give up and throw the wood away, he had a picture in his mind of Jesus carrying the cross up the hill of Calvary. His confirmation class had taught him that it was love for him that made Jesus carry the cross. He had stopped crying. His love for his family made carrying the wood home tolerable. The experience was so impressive to him that he had told his mother about it when he arrived home. She had looked at him in a funny way, and this had conjured a Bible verse in his minds "Mary pondered all these things in her heart." He didn't tell his mother of the new flash of insight. He had wanted to be a priest, but no one had taken an interest in him nor showed him the way. At every turn, there had been walls and fences keeping him from finding a way forward. The minister's question indicated an interest in him. He decided to tell the Pastor the truth. It could do no harm, even though his true desire seemed an impossibility.

"Well, Parson," he heard himself saying, "I have always wanted to be a minister, but it never seemed possible. I have never had anything in life I really wanted. My Dad says I always hang my hat too high."

The minister seemed to come alive. It was as though some suspicion he had was verified.

"Oh" he said, "If you want to be a minister, that is very possible. I can help you."

"Well, sir," said Sammy cautiously, "if you could do that for me I would be very happy." He held his breath. He did not know what would be said next. He was now quite accustomed to excuses and second thoughts. Could his prayers be finally answered? Could this man be an agent of God to rescue him from the doldrums of his present situation?

"Very well, Brother Gordon, meet me in my office at eleven o'clock tomorrow morning. We will talk at length about your interest," said the Minister.

"Yes, Parson, I will be there."

Sammy had kept the appointment. It was explained to him how the process for becoming an ordained minister would work. He was advised to return to private studies towards sitting for the Third Year Jamaica Local Examination. He had sought out Teacher Whiteman at the May Pen School. The Pastor had recommended Teacher Whiteman highly.

In time he had been licensed to preach. He continued to work at Storks, DeRoux with increasing disinterest. He devoted his time to Bible study and prayer and music practice. And he read English Literature and Science for his planned taking of the Third Jamaica Local Examination.

Chapter Twelve

Mississippi, USA, 1958-60

The big, red bus rocked and shimmied as it negotiated the sharp curves of the foothills of the Mocho Mountains. Its engine whined in loud protest as the driver, hunched over the steering wheel, held it at speeds that would have shocked the manufacturers, and had the heads of expectant mechanics nodding in glee. Sammy sat on the back seat of the crowded vehicle. He held his big black - covered and redlined Bible possessively close to his chest. His eyes were closed, but he was not asleep. He was meditating. He was returning from his preaching mission in the mountains of upper Clarendon.

He stirred and opened his eyes. He looked at the scene around him, and began to wonder what he was doing there, and where would he be going next. In the two years since he had started preaching, the romance of the work had dulled. Not only that, he had given up his job at De Roux to spend all his time on his studies and preaching. The net result was that his nice clothes were now wearing out and there was never enough money to replace them. The people with whom he laboured were loving and kind, but they were poor and never had enough cash to share.

There was still joy in proclaiming the Gospel, but there was no indication that he would ever be able to make a living or support a family at it. Again he felt boxed in.

He turned to look behind him and gazed at the obfuscating dust. Then he turned to look before him and stared speculatively at the unwinding road. Clutching the Bible, he wondered what awaited him around the next bend. The dusty unpaved road of the mountain became a paved way, and the dust cleared as the hills gave way to level ground. The slopes became meadows. Orchards of citrus and bananas dominated the scene.

The letter from the college in America was awaiting him when he arrived home. It came when he had given up hope of ever hearing from them again. It announced that he had been awarded a full scholarship for two years. They expected him to arrive at the first possible semester. He was overjoyed. He immediately began making plans for an early departure.

The send-off was an unforgettable experience. The speeches were touching. The gifts were tokens of affection and care. All were deeply appreciated. The church, which had been his extended family for four glorious years, was gathered to express its profound affection for him. He looked across at the packed audience from the gas lantern illuminated daze. When the moments came for him to express his love and gratitude, the words could scarcely be spoken. But he spoke of his abiding affection for them, and he assured them that the years of study would pass quickly, and he would return.

His church family had accompanied him to the airport in Kingston. Now he sat over the wing and watched as the giant propellers of the DC8 roared as they spun at breathtaking speed. It seemed from the vibration that the airplane would fall apart at any minute. He looked out at the waving people who crowded the departure stand at the Palisadoes Airport. He could not recognize any faces from the distance, but he knew that many were his friends. So he waved in reply.

The airplane pivoted around to face the open sea. It paused to increase the revolutions of the propellers to maximum speed, then it lunged. The wings lifted and the plane was airborne. Sammy looked down to see foam specked seas directly below him. Sea birds skimmed the waves. The wide expanse of the Caribbean spread to the distant horizon. He whispered a prayer of thanks to God, and a commitment of his life to the future God had opened up for him. The airplane lifted and he mused that he was "mounting up with wings like an eagle." He thought of the mysterious ways in which God had guided him to that moment. For years, since the end of the Second World War, Jamaicans had been migrating to Canada, England, and the United States. He had seen many of his family and friends leave, but it had never occurred to him to go away. He had felt that his destiny lay with that of his beloved island. But here he was, on a plane heading north.

It seemed as though a powerful spirit of the age was siphoning many of his generation and relocating them where they would prosper, instead of exhausting the limited resources of their homeland to sustain them. It occurred to him that the restlessness he had been feeling was not unique to him. It was probably an instinctive hiving of age groups with an impelling drive to establish new colonies where more commodious space existed.

Those, like him who were leaving, would never forget the land of their birth. Wherever their travels took them. And regardless of the destiny encountered, that piece of "rock" now receding would always be home, and would always claim their first loyalty. It was easy to sing with new meaning the song drilled into him as the anthem of his country:

"Jamaica, fair Queen of the blue Carib Sea
We hail thee, we crown thee, we shower on thee
The praises which sons to their native land give,
The love which in fond hearts forever doth live."

The Pan American Clipper touched down in Camaguey, Cuba, but was soon aloft again. The very attractive stewardesses in their sky blue uniforms were an exquisite touch to the attractive decor of the inside of the airplane. As soon as they were airborne again, the stewardesses came around to serve a meal. The small portions of food shocked the country boy, but the colourful arrangements caught his attention. He was surprisingly well satisfied when he had eaten. He enjoyed the meal. When the plates were cleared, he wrote in his diary which he had begun some weeks before.

The airplane shuddered. Turbulence. Sammy remembered his father's stories, that his plane flight was like a market truck travelling over rough roads. Thus prepared, he was not unduly alarmed as the plane shook. Once, it seemed to him that the propellers had stopped turning. He was just about to notify the stewardess of his observation when he realized that his eyes were deceiving him. He was glad he had not spoken too quickly.

The flight north seemed to have only just become enjoyable when the airplane turned sharply and began to descend. He looked out the window as the clouds parted, and saw buildings reaching up to the sky. They were the tallest he had ever seen. He had indeed crossed the ocean and was now circling the airport in Miami, Florida. As the plane glided lower and lower, he glued his face to the window so as not to miss a single detail of the sights before him.

He deplaned, claimed his baggage, and called the clergyman whose name he was given by his Pastor in Jamaica. He was told to take a taxi. The journey would take about twenty minutes. As the taxi travelled through Miami, he was impressed with the giant size of everything he saw when compared to what he had known before. As he saw the buildings up close, he remembered his father's description of a trip to the Empire State Building in New York.

"I had to take off my jacket, lay down flat on my back, and look straight up to where the top of the building was hiding among the clouds."

He had thought his Dad was exaggerating. Not only were these buildings huge, the cars and trucks were bigger than any he had seen before. For many minutes he was lost in the awe of the wide streets, big people, and the magic of everything around him. Then he began to feel uneasy. He had to have been traveling for more than twenty minutes.

"Say, mister, where are we going?" he asked the driver.

"Oh, I thought you wanted to see the city. I'm giving you the tour," was the reply.

"Man", said Sammy, lapsing into patois, both for effect and to show his agitation, "Tek me tuh de address me gi yuh, right now! If me did wan' fe see de city, me wudda tell yuh. An' I'm not gwine pay yuh fe de extra time neitha. I'm paying yuh only fe de regular time!" His agitation had the expected effect.

"All right, keep your shirt on. I'll get you to your address in a minute."

True to his word, the driver made a sharp turn and in brief minutes pulled up beside a lovely white frame two storey house with green trim and awnings. Sammy got out. The minister came out to meet him.

"Good afternoon, Rev. Carter, Rev. Knight, my Pastor in Jamaica sends his regards. But I seem to have a problem with this taxi driver. He tried to take me on a tour of Miami which I did not request. Could you tell me the average fare from the airport to this address?"

"Let me handle this," said the minister.

"Now, what's the problem with the passenger, sir?" he asked the taxi man. Sammy was struck by the obsequious demeanour of the minister.

"No problem, Rev., I just thought he wanted to see the city. I charged him fourteen dollars and ninety-five cents. That's what is on the meter."

"Well, that may be what's on the meter, but the fare from the airport to this address is eight dollars and fifty cents. Will you take that or do I have to report you to your supervisor?"

"Okay, Rev. I'll take the fare, but these people must learn to stop me before I go too far out of my way."

"Sir," said the minister, "it is people like you who give taxi drivers and this country a bad name. It is your job to take people to their destination by the shortest and safest route possible. Good day to you, sir."

The minister took one of Sammy's bags and led the way up the walk to the house. He met the Pastor's family. One son was about Sammy's age who looked at him and asked:

"What do you know about the state of Mississippi?"

"Nothing," Sammy replied.

"God deliver me from Mississippi" said the young man fervently. "If am coming from California and the train has to stop in Mississippi for water, I will take the plane and fly over that state."

"Why?" asked Sammy. "What's wrong with that state?"

"Mister," said the young man ominously, "you are going to the right place to find out. All I can say is God deliver me from that place."

His words made a deep impression on Sammy. He wondered what he was about to encounter in that mysterious place so far from his home. And yet, he knew that God was leading him and he could trust God to protect and deliver him from every adversity. The family was still trying to gather information from him about Jamaica when he heard music and noises coming from another part of the room. He turned to see a highly polished box resting on a stand. It had a square panel in the side facing him, and glossy black pictures were moving across a screen. The pictures were of cowboys and cattle. He recognized the contraption from pictures he had seen in magazines. But he was not sure.

"Is that a television?" he asked.

"Yes," someone replied.

"May I look at it?"

"Of course."

Sammy became engrossed in the "Rawhide" story. He became oblivious to his hosts and to their continued attempts to engage him in conversation, until dinner was announced. He knew that he had exhibited bad manners, but the television was such a wonder to him that he had not been able to pull himself away.

"Please excuse my bad manners," he apologized. "I have never seen a television before and I became so fascinated I could not pull myself away."

The pastor chuckled. "Don't worry about it. We get used to people from the Caribbean as visitors in our home. It is always the same situation. They get trapped by the magic of the television, and we can't get them to talk to us."

Dinner was broiled steak. Sammy stared at the enormous piece of meat on his plate. He reflected that back in his home in Jamaica, they would not cut meat in the same way, and the portion he was served, more than a pound in raw weight, would easily feed a family of four. "Even a country boy like me can't eat this much meat," he said to himself, as the Pastor said grace.

* * * * * * * * * *

It was a Chapel assembly; and he was seated in the front row of the auditorium. The Chaplain of the college was giving his usual inspirational message. The Choir had just given a rendition of the Negro Spiritual, "Soon Ah Will Be Done Wid De Troubles O' De Worl'." Sammy's eyes became fixed on the back wall of the stage where the curtains were drawn back to reveal a mural that covered the entire space. The scene was of a forest that stretched to the far horizon. In the foreground stood a powerfully built black man. He was naked to the waist and wore a tattered pair of shorts cut off above the knees. The man was looking at the forest as his muscles seemed to ripple off the canvas. In his hands he held a double bit axe at the ready. Beyond the trees was the glow of a rising sun. A legend at the bottom of the painting read: THE TIMBER LIES BEFORE US-WE WILL BUILD. That painting had fired Sammy's imagination from the day he first arrived. He felt a sense of refuge on the hallowed grounds of the college. In the auditorium with the painting exposed, he felt he was at the centre of his new universe.

The speaker was warming to his subject of the day. He spoke of obstructions that stood in the paths of those who were trying to realize the goals of life. He encouraged his listeners to make sure that nothing stood in the way of their reaching their objectives. Sammy loved the speech because it fell in line with his determination to find and fulfil his destiny in the world, and his self-imposed discipline to be excellent. He was proud that he was doing well in his classes. Except for the courses in the Bible where his teachers began to foster doubts in his mind. Their ways of interpreting the Bible left him reeling with questions that were deeply troubling. Most of his fundamental beliefs were being called into question. On a single day, one teacher had questioned the validity of the Virgin Birth, the Resurrection of Christ, and the fact of miracles. All concepts that were central to his faith and preaching. He could hold his peace no longer.

"Professor Johnson, if you really don't believe in the truths of the Bible, why are you teaching students who are being prepared to preach those truths?" he had asked bluntly.

"Well, Bro. Gordon, like you, I was educated to be a preacher and that's all I was prepared to do all my life. A guy has gotta eat." He said with a rueful smile. Sammy was shocked at the answer. His unease got in the way of his better judgment. Before he could restrain himself he blurted out:

"Personally, if I did not believe the things I am preaching, I would rather dig ditches to gain an honest living rather than collect a paycheck under false pretenses." The teacher winced but did not reply, Sammy felt that he had spoken out of line but he did not apologize.

But the seeds of doubt had been sown. Despite the flippant defence of the teacher, he had put forward rational arguments that started serious questioning in the mind of the young scholar. The moral relativism of many churchgoers further eroded his confidence in his faith.

Then too deep loneliness invaded him as he felt compelled to hold on to long subscribed values without the support of a Christian community far away from home.

He had many opportunities to preach and he declared his beliefs, as he understood them. He tried to compare the practice of religion in Jamaica with what he now observed. He concluded that in Jamaica many refused or postponed becoming active Christians because they fully understood and were not yet ready to embrace the lifestyle. That was understandable. Their sermons were geared to inviting these to decide to become converted. In America on the other hand, Christians held values and lifestyles that he found strange; Racism for instance, was rampant. Many church leaders exhibited hatred and jealousy and malice against their fellows. He had not encountered these in Jamaica, even if they existed there. After three semesters in America he was troubled about whether he could still preach without the foundations of beliefs he had held sacred.

Chapter Thirteen

Texas and the World, 1960-65

It was a disturbed young man who strode out of the chapel service and walked the short distance to another nearby college campus. He was keeping an appointment with a West Indian college professor. When he entered the office of the man who had invited him, he was impressed by the spacious office and the distinguished bearing of the man from his home country. In his study, books were stacked on shelves from floor to ceiling, unlike the dozen or so possessed by the teachers at his college.

"Come in! Come in!" invited the professor in response to his knock.

"Thank you sir," said Sammy.

"Please, have a seat. Tell me how are you getting along at your college?"

"I'm doing well. I'm earning A's and B's in my courses and I now have a B-plus academic average. I enjoy the people and the place but I am still not accustomed to the food."

"Good, good. Yes, I understand about the food. It does take awhile to become accustomed to change in food types and their preparation. What I really want to talk to you about though, is this. You know that you are attending an unaccredited school. I can imagine that at the present time your mind is set on returning home. But whether you remain or return, the name of the game in academia is "credentials". A degree from an unaccredited college will not get you very far these days. I have already made some inquiries and I can get you a scholarship to this college if you would like a better education."

Sammy thought of all the foreign students who had been admitted to the college he was attending. After arrival, being sponsored by his college they were siphoned off by other institutions. He felt a keen sense of loyalty and gratitude to the college that for more than two years had expended so much effort to finally get him to America.

"I thank you, sir," he said. "But as you know, I am a ministerial student. My college has been preparing clergy for our church for many years. I thank you for your kind offer, but I will remain where I am until I graduate."

The professor wished him well, and said "If I can help you in any way, be sure to call on me." After a few words of pleasantries, the interview was over. Sammy felt good about his sense of loyalty as he left the man's presence.

He returned to his campus to find several letters for him in his mailbox. Several were from family and friends. One in an official looking envelope was from the United States government. Another was from his best friend at his church in Jamaica. He read and replied to the letters from his family and friends. Then he opened the letter from his best friend. The contents disturbed him:

Dear Sammy:

Boy, I am sorry it took me so long to write to you, but a lot has been happening here in these past few months. First of all I am sure you have heard that Rev. Knight died. We had his funeral three months ago. It was a big funeral. There were people from St. Elizabeth, St. Ann, Upper Clarendon, and from all over Cross and May Pen. Everyone was crying. He was such a good man who loved and cared for everybody. Anyway, what happens is that the man they sent to take his place comes from some-

where in St. Catherine. He is a different kind of person and don't understand the way we do things here. As you know, Parson Knight used to leave a lot up to us to carry on. Well, this man says there will be a lot of changes because there is too much slackness in how things operate. He wants to change officers around and keep the books himself. The people are in an uproar. They say you were to be gone for only two years, and they want you to leave off your studies and come back right now and take over the church. But you know it's not that easy.

Since Parson died, a new man is now Superintendent. It is he who sent the new Pastor, and it will be he who would have to appoint you. I don't think he will send you to this church because he will feel that you will be on the side of Parson Knight. Even though he is dead, he still has a strong group of people who are loyal to his memory, and the superintendent was part of another group that never did get along with his group. He will probably send you to a church somewhere in the country. You can do what you want, but that is how I read the situation and I would not like to see you hurt. I believe you should stay where you are until things cool down a bit out here. I will tell you when I think it is alright for you to comeback. All here send their love. Then send me a few dollars, no man. Boy, dutty tough out here, you see. Write soon. Always your Brother in Christ.

Glenville Sampson.

Sammy reread, then folded the letter and replaced it in the envelope. What should he make of what his friend was trying to tell him? Yes, he had been told of the death of his beloved Pastor. That had been a source of sadness and anxiety for him. But he had wondered why his best friend had not written to give him the details. He had come to expect letters with informing contents from his friend. Then, he could not ignore the jealousy of his friend who felt that since he had been a member of the church longer than Sammy, he should have been the one picked to go overseas to study. Could it be that his friend had designs on the pastorate he now described as being in turmoil? Could he be a cause of some of the trouble? He would never stand in the way of his friend's ambitions.

More troubling was the demon of church politics. The capacity of church people, both lay and clergy; both in America and Jamaica, to lapse into acts of cruelty, had become a source of shock and dismay to him. At least his friend was right regarding the point that animosity from the faction which opposed his sponsoring pastor, could be a source of hurt to him for years to come. He needed time to think. He was a bit sorry that he had rejected outright the offer of the college professor mere minutes ago. Had that been divine intervention?

The news from home coupled with the conflicts he was facing in his religious studies caused a turmoil in Sammy's soul. On the one hand, although he had promised to return home and serve his people, he felt certain that he would be mistreated by the ministers in control of appointments. Without sponsorship, even with the best of training, he would suffer. On the other hand, he would not be a hypocrite and try to preach, if he had grave religious doubts.

His mind was reeling as he opened the next letter. It was from the Selective Service of the United States. It began with a greeting, then invited him to visit the nearest office to be registered for the draft into the military forces of the country. Although he was a non-resident student, apparently they had got his name from an indiscriminate scanning of the male enrolment of the college. He could visit the nearest centre and appeal for a deferral on the basis of being a foreigner or being a ministerial student. On the other hand, he could join the military, and if he survived hostilities in wars, he would become eligible for citizenship based on service to the nation.

Was it the Lord moving in his life again? Was this a way out of his dilemma? He had always considered himself a pacifist on what he considered sound Christian Biblical grounds. Now, it seemed all his assumptions were open to questions. He patted the letter in his hands and thought about the many twists and turns his checkered life continued to take. Why did the letters come at the same time? Why immediately after he had turned down an invitation to study at another college, and even pursue some other vocation besides the ministry? Was this another omen, another pointer in the direction he should go? With a sense of sadness, and even feelings of betrayal of his people and his country, Sammy decided to leave the college and join the armed services of the United

States of America. He felt that he was doing an opportune thing, not necessarily the right thing. He did not seek Divine guidance in making the decision.

Too many conflicting emotions depressed him. He only hoped for the best.

"Well," he said to himself, "If I die, I die. But if I live, I will become a citizen of the United States and escape all the wicked bickering of those religious hypocrites back home, and even over here." He enlisted in the military and was sent to Fort Knox in Kentucky for training. After that he was stationed at Fort Hood in central Texas.

* * * * * * * * *

With some reluctance, he had decided to accept the invitation to attend the Christmas party. The affair had been sponsored by a local group of the United Services Organization, and was held in the spacious and gaily decorated living room of a matron who lived in the town nearby. Cheerfully covered tables were loaded with meats, nuts, pastries, sweets, fruits, and drinks. Music from a record player enlivened the air with strains and lyrics of popular songs. A festive aura did much to break down the barriers among the strangers, left over soldiers from many places too far away to go home for the holidays.

The soldiers were resplendent in their dress uniforms. Some, like Sammy, were fresh from basic training. Others were veterans who had seen action overseas. A flock of young ladies dressed in assorted evening apparel of every imaginable colour and style, mixed gaily among the strutting military men who boasted ribbons and bars. The women wore corsages.

The silver haired matron with dimpled cheeks, smooth ebony skin, and an infectious smile, made the rounds of the milling young people. She played her role of hostess perfectly as with encouraging words she guided stragglers into groups to play games and engage in conversation. Bashful girls were coaxed from corners and walls to entertain shy young men who lingered alone or in groups of two, scattered in places around the room.

It was Sammy's third Christmas away from Jamaica and his first in the military. He enjoyed his posting at Fort Hood because the climate was much closer to that of Vere or May Pen. The occasional cold snap in November or January was far less severe than the winter he had experienced in Kentucky. He was happy to be stationed there. He nursed his cup of punch as he surveyed the room of more than twenty GIs who were there.

Some of them he knew, but many were from other units, three of the group were West Indians, the others were Negroes from all over the United States, hailing from such distances as New York, and Virginia and California. Under the gaiety, there was a soberness of thoughts mixed with missing home and an anxiety about their next assignment, which was expected any day now. An assignment to Korea and the dangerous 38th parallel, where hostilities were still very real, was not far from the front of any of their minds.

Sammy's eyes shifted in turn from the hostess working the crowd, to the young people milling around the room. At twenty-five, he was older than many who had joined the military fresh out of high school. He was even older than some of the veterans. His experiences as a Boy Scout and in the Cadet Corps at Dentwood had stood him in good stead. His three semesters of college also helped. He wore his two stripes as a Corporal with pride. He looked at the two others from his platoon who had come to the party. After graduation from rigorous training, the original platoons and companies had broken up, with their members reassigned to units across the world. These two along with himself were now part of a new outfit. The rumour was that they were headed for Korea. But it could be Germany.

He walked to a table, picked up a napkin, and filled it with cookies, then stepped out to the porch. He really preferred to stand apart and watch people. Although he had done his share of dancing and socializing during school days, his recent life as a clergyman, had disciplined him to be reserved. But he was glad now that he had decided to leave the lonely barracks.

The porch faced south with towering branches of pecan trees still showering dried nuts as a lively breeze shook them. Through the leafless branches, a golden moon was seen to fill the sky. The large disk was accompanied by a necklace of stars. A sadness overcame him. What was he doing here? What was he doing in this strange city, with these strange people at Christmas time? The thoughts played hopscotch across the landscape of his mind. He looked south following the trail of stars and tried to imagine whether his family and friends back home would be looking up, and seeing the same constellations as he did: He wondered what activities would be going on in Jamaica at that moment.

A deep sigh heaved his breast as he exhaled and gazed in the distance. He thought of his mother and knew she would be thinking of him this night, even as she thought of all her children. But he knew that she had enjoyed him the most when they were able to spend much time together, without the crowd of other brothers and sister. They had fun. Especially after Girlie and the Twins had left home, and before his Dada had returned from America. Some lines from a song referring to the Prodigal Son came to him, and he wondered if his mother was even then humming the lines, despite the fact that some of his siblings were doubtless with his parents for the holidays. He would bet anything that they were talking about him, and wondering what he was doing. Was his mother humming the lines?

> "O where is my boy tonight?
> My heart overflows for I love him he knows,
> O where is my boy tonight?"

A painful lump gathered and enlarged in his throat. His eyes misted. He had left home following what he thought was the bidding of God. Far from home, he had met the impersonality of Christians who meant well, but assumed that each individual must make friends and develop support systems by themselves. He had never been left without family or church support before. He had no inclination to associate with those who did not know and love the Lord as he did: He found those people scarce here. He missed the families he had left. The haunting ache for home was worse than usual this Christmas.

Sammy knew for himself how his longing for home and family was like a physical pain. True, as the youngest child, born after his older siblings had left home, and enjoying the younger ones for but brief years before they too went away to school or work, or establishing their own families, he had come to look to his parents and cousins for love and support. Then they had moved to Vere, then to May Pen. The moves had disrupted his ability to cultivate deep friendships and confirmed him as a loner. He bit into a cookie to ease the lump in his throat. His mind turned from his mother to his father who loved him and whom he loved. He wondered what would have happened if he had stilled the calling voices and rejoined his father in the tailor trade. He probably would have become industrious, made a decent living and started a family. He would have been home with his parents during their declining years. Although he was the youngest, he was closest in intimacy to his parents. A part of him knew that they needed him.

Now here he was, after years of chasing elusive stars and shifting his commitment from one movement to another. Always, he was putting his blood kin second. It was not that he felt regrets about following the call of God, or the guidance of the Scriptures. Nor was it that the new God-given families he had found in the church had grown stale. It was more that these secondary families for whom be had sacrificed his true parents, now seemed conditional and impermanent.

He had discovered in recent years that there was a difference between the promises of the Bible as his naive reading had led him to believe, and the realities of church life in the present world. The more disappointed he became at the perversity of Christians he had come to know, the more he regretted his slavish and literal following of Bible teachings that had motivated him to separate himself from his blood family to become totally attached to the bond of the church. Tonight he felt separated from both home and church. He was indeed a man alone. Army life was changing or indeed had changed him.

He looked again at the brilliant moon. His uniform helped protect him from the wind and chill. But nothing screened his soul from the bare and raw sense of alienation that enveloped him. The pull to go home and enjoy his parents was strong. Somewhere he had heard the saying, "Home is that place where when you go there, they've got to take you in." He smiled briefly at the thought. "Okay, let's see." He said, making a conciliatory promise to himself by next summer I should have enough leave time built up, and enough savings put aside, then Jamaica, here I come!" He felt a tap on his shoulder.

"Hi there, soldier! Want some company?"

He turned to see a tall, slim, dark and attractive young woman smiling at him. Her jet-black hair streamed down in curls to her shoulders. The ends curved up in trained arcs that shimmied as she moved her head to look into his face. Her coffee skin was smooth and showed signs of care. Her thick lips were painted a bright red. Her sloe eyes sparkled in a dreaminess that matched the calmness of the night. Sammy felt soothed by her presence. He felt drawn to her. There was a self-confidence about her that was profoundly appealing. Hers was the extroversion he needed at the moment to pull him out of the doldrums that was enveloping him.

"Hello," he replied. "Sure, come on."

"And why are you standing out here all alone in the cold?"

"O, I just wanted to get some of the crisp evening air into my lungs. It reminds me very much of my home and the mountains where I was born."

"Oh, and where is that?"

"A long distance and many mountains away. I am a Jamaican."

"Jamaica! Aha! Harry Belafonte and 'Banana Boat'. So, what are you doing so far from home?"

"It's a long story. But I'm glad you know about Jamaica."

"Oh everyone here knows about the great Jamaican singer, Belafonte and about rum and cocoa cola."

"I see. As a matter of fact, although I am Jamaican, I am not as familiar as you are with those things."

"You are not? How come?"

"Well, I have been a Christian for many years. Christians in Jamaica don't spend much time listening to secular music. We may hear them on the radio, but the world of Calypso, and Soca, and Reggae is a different one from the church of which I was a part."

"You say was. Does that mean you are no longer a Christian?"

"Oh, I attend church and worship, but for many Jamaicans, being a Christian is a serious business. Christians don't mix too much with the world as do many American Christians I have met."

"I see. If that is so, what are you doing in that soldier's uniform? Conservative Christians don't usually join the military. They don't believe in fighting or going to war or that kind of thing."

"Well, as I said, it's a long story. But you tell me something about yourself. What is your name? What do you do?"

"My name is Doris Keezee. I am a senior, majoring in Elementary Education at Paul Quinn College, Waco, Texas. And what is your name, and what do you do?"

"My name is Corporal Septimus George Gordon, but my friends call me Sammy. As you can see, I am a soldier, and I am stationed at Fort Hood near Killeen, Texas."

"I can see that you are a soldier, but I mean, what is your specialization?"

"I specialize in weapons. I am in the infantry."

"And do you enjoy what you do?"

"Not really, when I was called, I answered. I do believe in loving and defending my country from all enemies, foreign or domestic; so that is the extent I am committed to knowing and using weapons within my command."

"Um Hm. So, why are you so lonely tonight? I could see you were not enjoying the party. I watched you walk outside and decided to allow you some time alone before I interrupted you. My responsibility is to make sure that all of you soldiers away from home enjoy yourselves tonight, so I couldn't permit you to stay alone too long." She smiled playfully at him.

"Well, thanks for your thoughtfulness," he said "Yes, I am a little homesick tonight."

"Your home must be a lovely place if it makes you so homesick. I can't imagine anyone being homesick when they are in the good ol' US of A. I believe there is no other country more lovely than America, with its lovely people, fine foods, and good times. Especially at Christmas."

"Lady, until you have experienced a Jamaican Christmas, you won't know what you are missing. Christmas in Jamaica is not just a family thing, it is a community thing and a nation thing. Not only that, but I was born in the mountains, so Christmas reminds me of fruits coming to ripeness, flowers in lush bloom, and people at their happiest. Christmas in Jamaica is our country at its best. To stand at night on a mountainside overlooking the sea, and watching Jupiter chase Venus so low across the heavens that you can almost reach up and touch them as they race before your very eyes, is to feel romance that cannot be equalled anywhere. Ma'am, Christmas reminds me of who I really am, and I want to dance and sing and join the laughter and vitality of my people. A Jamaican Christmas is magic!"

"So, you really are feeling separated from your people and your country, huh?"

"Ma'am, I would give anything to be home right now."

"Well, if that is how you feel why don't you go home?"

"It's not that simple. Besides the lack of money, I have not been in the service long enough to get the amount of leave I would need to go home and really enjoy myself. I was just now thinking that next summer, nothing will stop me from going home."

"Well in the meantime, come in and enjoy the party. There are some nice people here. Do you like to dance?"

"Well, I have not danced much, but I suppose I could move a little without doing much damage to your toes."

"Alright, soldier, let's get back inside and see what you can do". Doris took Sammy by the arm and led him inside. The room seemed much warmer, and the lights much brighter now than when he had left it. Doris slipped into his arms and they moved to the beat of the music. The movements were easy and graceful. Again he had reason to be grateful for his stint at Dentwood where among other things, he had learned some social graces.

Sammy felt alive. Connected. Perhaps it was the opportunity to express himself that brought the relief. Perhaps it was the magic of the sensitive and caring woman who sought him out, listened to him, and touched him where it mattered. Whatever the reason, he felt that a load had been lifted from him. His family and friends were again stowed in their special compartment of his heart. For the moment, he was no longer alone.

He became aware of the perfume that Doris was wearing. It reminded him of flowers, gardens, the outdoors. He became aware of her as a special person with a friendliness and openness that he truly needed at this time. He was wary to open up himself to anyone at this time because of the uncertainty of his future. He expected to be shipped out soon, and only God would know what would happen next. But he knew he wanted to extend this moment with this lovely person. He truly enjoyed her company.

His mood deepened as "Looking Back" a song sung by the golden throated Nat King Cole was played. The words transported Sammy on a journey that painted pictures of his entire life. No particular incident stood out, but he seemed to feel that he had missed a boat somewhere. The profound complaint of the song spoke to him of moorings missed; of roads not taken; of lost good. It painted pictures of covenants broken. Of mistakes made. Of uncertainty. Sammy wondered, as he danced, how with the best of intentions, he could have drifted so far from the journey he thought was the right one for him. How, always momentarily beguiled by what seemed to be good company and safe passage, he would always ultimately, be left alone to stumble around the next bend. Up the next hill. Where would his journey end? Cold, and broken and dead, on some distant battlefield?

"Soldier, I'm talking to you," said the bewildered girl.

"Oh, I beg your pardon. What did you say?"

"Am I that bad a company that you can't hear me talking to you?"

"I'm sorry. My mind was far away. Please forgive me. That's no way to compliment a lovely lady."

"Thank you, kind sir. I was asking you when you expected to ship out, and where you expect to be going from here."

"That's amazing. That was what I was thinking. The rumour is we will be going to Korea."

"Well, if you will be here through the weekend, will you come to my home for Sunday dinner?"

"I would be glad to come. You are very kind, Miss Keezee."

"You are very welcome, Corporal Gordon. My mother is the best cook in the world. If you can come early, we can go to church together."

"That would be great. I have been attending the Base Chapel since I've been here, but I would love to worship with you."

"Then I'll pick you up about nine o'clock on Sunday morning. I teach a Sunday School Class and you can sit in with my group or attend another adult class."

"Your group will be good enough for me. I will be happy to sit in with you."

Chapter Fourteen

Texas and the World, 1960-65

That Sunday he was picked up by Doris and they went to church together. Both worship and dinner were memorable for him. He met Doris' parents and they seemed impressed but hostile with him as a foreigner.

"So, what brought you to Texas so far from home?" quizzed Mrs. Kizzee at dinner.

"I came to America to attend college, Ma'am. But when I was invited to join the military, I decided to do so."

"And they don't have any military over.. Um.. Where you say you are from, Africa?"

"I am from Jamaica an island in the Caribbean Sea. Yes, they have military in Jamaica, I just did not think of being a soldier when I was there."

"Uh Huh. So, how do you like America?"

"I love it here. Very much."

"So, how come Doris said you are sad and lonely and homesick and want to go home?"

"Doris told the truth, Mrs. Kizzee. I have been gone away for three years, and this Christmas I really miss my family, especially my parents."

"Then why don't you go home? I keep meeting you foreigners who come over here and take away scholarships and jobs from our own people. If you are so smart, how come you all have to come over here to get ahead?"

"It is not easy to explain to you, Mrs. Kizzee. There are not many opportunities for the masses of people to get ahead in my country. Over there nothing is free, and there is no free education. Also, over there people are either rich or poor. There is not much of a middle class so people don't advance very far in life from where their family is placed socially, or economically. Here in America, education is accessible to anyone who wants it. With a good education come more opportunities for advancement."

Sammy was trying hard to be polite. He could not understand the hostility of the mother, nor the quiet calculating look of the father. He began to feel uncomfortable. He ate little and wished he could leave. He was relieved when Doris offered to take him back to the barracks. They were silent in the car for awhile.

"Sammy, I am very sorry my parents were so rough on you. They just don't understand foreigners. They believe Africans should stay in Africa, why I don't know. They have no idea where Jamaica is, so they just lumped you with all non-American blacks."

"Well, I do admit they made me feel very uncomfortable. I find it difficult to understand why they as black people are hostile to other blacks."

"I guess it's something they have heard or learned. Prejudice is strange like that. But I have a number of African and West Indian friends at college. We get along fine. Anyway, please don't let it bother you. I did enjoy your company and I want you to know that. You are my friend and as long as I live at home, you are welcome there."

"And I enjoyed your company immensely, Doris. Thanks for inviting me to church. The service and Sunday School class were both great."

"Again, you are welcome. If you want, I will be glad to write you while you are overseas. I have an admiration for young men who sacrifice their lives and their careers to respond to the call of our country. Even though it may be a chance to get ahead, the risks of losing your life is real."

"Doris, you are a very sensitive lady. Thanks for what you just said. Yes, I would love to hear from you. Because I have been moving about so much, I have not been getting any letters. Mail from you would mean a lot to me."

"That makes me feel very special, then. I hope we can see each other again before you leave. I look forward to hearing from you when you get my letters."

"Yes, it would be good to see you again. Maybe a movie one evening could be arranged. Meeting you has made my stay in Texas so far very special. Let me have your phone number and I will call you, if your parents don't mind."

"Oh, I'm not unduly concerned about my parents. I am impressed by you, Sammy. I am grown and I will do what I judge to be the right thing. Please call me whenever you wish."

Sammy looked at the resolute face of Doris. She sat rigidly holding the steering wheel as if to indicate that no one could sway her from her chosen course. Spontaneously, he leaned over to kiss her cheek. Impulsively, she turned her head to meet his lips fully with hers. The kiss began as a friendly salute. It became an impassioned and clinging expression of attraction and need. They held each other for long moments, then released each other.

"Please call me," she said.

"I will," he said.

Sammy exited the car and gently closed the door. Doris shifted into gear, waved, and drove away. Sammy watched the crimson tail light grow dim, then disappear. "That young lady could be good for me," he mused.

* * * * * * * * *

Sammy could scarcely contain his excitement. He was going home. He sat in the aisle seat of the Boeing 707. Doris sat in the window seat. Their lovely four year old daughter, Linda, sat in the middle. Outside the window, the airplane seemed to be gliding above a carpet of white and fluffy clouds. In the eastern distance, thunderheads reared their gray white peaks. Inside the plane, everyone was busy. The attendants were distributing immigration documents to the passengers. He looked over the documents, then at his family, and reflected on the contrasts of his experiences since he had left home. When he had travelled to the United States, some eight years before, he had flown up on a turboprop air-plane. He was returning home on a super jet. He flew up alone, with much anticipation and wonder. He was returning on vacation, but bring-ing with him a family. He had travelled up in the hope of becoming trained as a clergyman. He was returning trained as a soldier. So much had happened in those intervening years.

He remembered now his service in Korea and Viet Nam. That first letter from Doris was as much a surprise as a very pleasant experience. He had moved about so much that letters from his family had not yet caught up with him. She said she hoped he was adjusting to life at the battlefront. As she had told him, she admired men of commitment and direction who defended their country. She was looking forward to Stu-dent Teaching, and she would reply whenever he had a chance to write to her.

He had replied immediately. He expressed his appreciation for her thoughtfulness and shared that hers was the first letter he had received. He hoped she would write again. And she had. Soon their letters be-came a steady stream. He had completed his year of duty overseas and returned to Fort Hood. Their affection became a full blown romance. She was working as teacher. He had been promoted to Sergeant. Then he had been among the first contingent to be sent to Viet Nam. That experience was much more violent than had been his tour to Korea. The terrain was different. The enemy was different, the war was differ-ent. In Korea, he had primarily guarded the 38th parallel against incur-sion. In Viet Nam, the war was taken to the enemy who lived within the villages where the American soldiers patrolled. He had been wounded and sent to the rear on two occasions. Finally, he had been bitten by a monkey, and that had come at the end of his tour. After he was checked out and found to be unaffected by the bite, he had been shipped home.

He and Doris were married in the Base Chapel at Fort Hood. Mem-bers of his Company, and members of Doris' family had attended. They were very much in love, but could not afford a honeymoon at the moment. They had looked forward to the trip to Jamaica, but that had to wait until time and money made it possible. In the meantime, their daughter, Linda had been born. Sammy's parents awaited the sight of their new American daughter-in-law.

Sammy had expected to return home in the dark suit and clergy collar of an ordained minister. He was returning in the khaki uniform of a soldier. He had not earned a college degree, but he had earned the stripes that identified him as a non-commissioned officer in the Army, a man to be respected and obeyed. His broad shoulders and confident posture spoke volumes about his physical and emotional maturity.

He felt the plane begin to descend, and judged they were probably passing beyond the airspace over Cuba. His mind wandered as he thought of the reception he would receive.

Sammy examined the immigration form he had been given. He became tense when he looked at the line that asked about his citizenship. The year before he had taken the oath that made him a citizen of the United States. He had felt proud of his accomplishments at the time. He had been congratulated by a US congressman who had administered the oath, and welcomed him to the greatest nation on earth. Standing there in his dress uniform with all the medals for bravery and injury he had won in the military service of the country, he had felt that he had earned the privilege. Many of his friends in and out of service were there to cheer and congratulate him. He had felt then that he had settled once for all his sense of place in the world.

He had never voted in Jamaica. His one opportunity to do so was cancelled by a co-worker who had maliciously rubbed voter's ink on his finger thus disqualifying him. But he had exercised his rights of citizenship in America. He had voted for president, senators, congresspersons, and local officials. Those were his privileges and he had exercised them with pride. None of those actions had the impact on him as the small piece of paper that now rested on the table before him. "Citizenship" asked the form. Had he intended to desert his homeland? The answer was a resounding "NO". Then why had he sworn allegiance to another country? Many people had lived a lifetime in America, some never even returning to their native home for a visit, but never gave up their citizenship. He now faced some interesting facts. His sense of "place" in Jamaica had never been clear. Lack of sponsorship and opportunity had denied him the personal and career development he deeply desired.

In America, despite strong racial discrimination he had great opportunities for upward mobility. He could make his place. He was not locked in by narrowly defined strictures of class based on money, or colors of "white" or "light-skinned" with all the divisive apparatus appertaining to each grade. In America, there was power in numbers as the descendants of Africa coalesced to fight social and political problems. Jamaica would never rise above its poverty and provincialism as long as sophistry and clannishness combined to lock out and jeer those who were deprived of privilege. In America, all threats to the common good could be identified, and the powers and pressures of community solidarity brought to bear. Even the demon of racism could be defined and attacked. In Jamaica, even blacks denied their blackness and became enemies of the forces for social progress. Walls of denial of commonality were so thick that each small group crouched defensively behind their particular domain and suffered silently. To the detriment of themselves and everyone else.

There was more. There was his personal sense of misplacement caused by his floundering and constant movement. He lacked adhesion to any group. From childhood he had sensed this about himself. His decision to break out and be different made him a loner. He valued people highly, yet he felt constantly called to move onward to what he never fully found. That quality had required him to perform at levels of excellence beyond the expected. The urge was always there to move on; climb the next hill; to hasten beyond the next bend in the road.

So what was his citizenship? The aircraft dipped lower. He reached into his briefcase and took out his Jamaican Passport as well as the canceled British Passport with which he had departed the island. His picture on the latter seemed so young.. Boyish. He had matured in many ways since that picture was taken. He remembered his feelings when he had sent that British Passport to the Jamaican Embassy to be exchanged for a Jamaican one. He had wondered about Jamaica's isolation in some critical ways from far away Britain, and under the geographical and cultural heels of the United States. Jamaica's limited resources and international appetites made her vulnerable, and made him concerned for her future. Through radio and television and magazines, the United States was already reshaping Jamaica's view of the world. From comic books to cook books; from religion to movies; from clothing to food; from slang to slouch, the lifestyle of the people was changing. Some had even advocated that Jamaica become a state of the United States, but that was not only improbable, it also was not a true solution to Jamaica's complex problems.

He had looked at the new Jamaican Passport. The blue colour of its jacket was that of the native waters of home. The seal reminded him that the people and culture of his country had roots as old as the world. He felt pride in it. He felt himself a part of something fresh and grand and growing. He had never used that Passport since receiving it. He decided to do so now. Whatever else he was, he was born in Manchester and raised in Clarendon. He was first and foremost a Jamaican by blood and bearing. He had left home a Jamaican, he would return as one.

On the line of the immigration document requiring him to state his citizenship, he deliberately wrote "Jamaican".

The aircraft shuddered as it darted through cotton ball clouds, then it steadied as it broke through the cumulus into clear skies. "Sammy, look!" said Doris. He leaned across their daughter to look out the window. He saw small cottages perched on hillsides of red earth. Winding roads hid, then revealed themselves through the foliage. Green lakes of sugar cane and banana plantations eddied to the sea coast. Thrills of appreciation and pride coursed through him. He took Doris' hand and looked at Linda.

"Honey, we are home," he exulted. "Those places you see beneath us are towns and villages where I roamed as a boy. I rode my bicycle through them and travelled on them to school and work. They have never seemed more beautiful than now. Yes, we are home. We are looking at the parishes of Clarendon and St. Catherine that I told you so much about."

"Daddy, look. We are going out over the sea again. Did we pass Jamaica?"

"No, daughter, we have to turn to line up with the airport. You will see in a moment." As if in response to his words, the airplane banked gracefully to the left. It hovered low over the sea and was again over the land.

Sammy's face was still glued to the window when the lofty Blue Mountain came into view. It was unchanged from the way he left it, with gray peaks rising above the clouds, oblivious to the dust and drama always moving at their feet. He turned to Doris and said:

"I wonder how many ships those mountains have guided safely to harbour across the centuries. How many sails have found rest beyond the stormly waves in this great harbour at our feet."

"And I wonder," replied Doris, " how many people looking out the windows of this plane, have been gone away as long as you or longer, and areas bewitched by the majesty of these mountains as you are."

"I don't know," said Sammy, "but I can bet you that I'm not the only one. Jamaicans are naturally romantic and poetic. Anyone of them you see, even those who say they are unable to sing are ready to burst out in songs of praise of their country. They may be angry at the politics or disgusted with the economics, but the love of their land is spontaneous, and runs deep. Come to think of it, I cannot imagine anyone being a Jamaican and being unable to sing."

With a screech and a bounce, the Sunbird lowered its wings and glided to a stop on the tarmac near the entrance of the airport. Sammy guided his family through the aisles towards the exit of the airplane. He became aware of being surrounded by the singsong of patois. Jamaicans, who up to then had been speaking in subdued tones of their acquired alien twangs abroad, now lapsed into the lyrical accents of home. Linda giggled.

"Daddy, that's just how you talk to us when you get excited. But there is so much more of it here."

"Yes, darling," smiled Sammy, "welcome to my home. And it's your home too. You know that, don't you? Because you are my child, you are as much Jamaican as you are American."

"Wow! That's neat, Daddy!"

Sammy walked through the exit door of the airplane and stood at the top of the ramp. He was met by a draft of hot air so intense that it nearly took his breath away. He looked at the welcoming hills above the buildings of the airport. He drank deeply of the hot tropical air that was not unlike what he had left in Viet Nam. He took the steps to the ground in lightheaded joyfulness. Already he regretted that this would be a short visit. Within three weeks, he was expected back at his post in some as yet undisclosed assignment, barking orders, filing reports, and fighting America's wars.

But for now he was home. Beyond the barriers of customs and immigration officials, his family and friends were eagerly awaiting him. And yet, were there none other than the hills and skies, the clouds and rich musical rhythms of patois; and "scobeech" fish, and fruit punch, and curried goat and rice, it would still be home. He sighed in contentment and anticipation as he picked up his bags and followed his fast disappearing wife and daughter.

A serious and businesslike officer took and stamped his passport and documents. Sammy could not take his eyes off the man. Although he was a military man and had become accustomed to seeing blacks in positions of leadership in the military, his years in the American south had created in him a forgetfulness about the liberty of position and leadership in his own country. He had forgotten more than he realized. This black immigration officer shocked him into a present he had lost. Doris too was staring, as she too was unaccustomed to seeing blacks in positions of authority.

The man did his work with an air of quiet efficiency. Then, in an almost mysterious turn around from his grim demeanour, he smiled as he returned the documents and said "Welcome home to Jamaica, Mr. Gordon."

Sammy was surprised by the acknowledgment of his homecoming. It was as if all of Jamaica was embodied in that one man in that special word of greeting. It seemed a powerful extension of the muted greetings of the mountains, the clouds, and the peaceful Kingston harbour. The few simple words, and heartwarming smile caused a lump to settle in his throat. He braved a broad smile in return. He wanted to say so much to this man at the port of entry, but he was aware of the line behind him, and the recently smiling man had already turned his stern attention to the next person in line. With all the feeling he could muster, he said "Thank you, sir, it's good to be home."

He moved to collect the things he had checked through. Soon, he would be embracing his mother, father, sister and friends. But already he felt fully welcomed. It felt good.

Chapter Fifteen

May Pen, Jamaica, Late 1960

Birdy Gordon's breath came in short shallow sips. Even that was an effort she grew less and less able to bear. She accepted the fact of her impending death. Although she regretted leaving Septy, she took comfort in the thought that when necessary, he had left her to find a better life, even though he hated to do it.

Through the years, even though she had not attended church regularly, she held on to her faith in Jesus as her constant and best friend. Next to Septy. Now she knew that going to be with Jesus was the best way to be rid of the worn out body that no longer helped her spirit. It was becoming more and more a bother and embarrassment to her.

She lay propped up on pillows looking lovingly at Sammy. He sat on the bed holding her hands and smoothing her hair. In this second week of his vacation he had hardly left her side. He had arrived to see her standing weak and drawn beside his father, but he had no knowledge of the ravages of time on her. It seemed to him now that she had held on to life just to meet him on his return. She had taken to bed within two days of his presence home. Now they were inseparable. Sammy seemed to be making up for the years of neglect with these days of intense devotion.

The others busied themselves around the house. It was as though they considered her already dead, and were denying the reality that she was still alive though definitely declining. But Sammy had a full quota of watching men die in battle. He had sat or squatted by many comrades through their last moments, gently accompanying their final moments before they crossed to the beyond. He was aware that death was a process as mysterious and as natural as birth. It can be terrifying when done alone, but can be an easy passage when done in the company of loved ones. Now he and Birdie had been reclaiming the bond between them that had remained as strong as ever, despite the separation of the recent years.

He looked at her again and admired the shining silver hair that had been fixed so nicely by Girlie. He looked at the rheumy eyes and wrinkled features. The years had taken a cruel toll. Yet, beyond the ravages of time, the beauty and wonder of his beloved Mamma were still there. As if reading his mind, Birdie stirred and looked at him with unusually alert eyes. Despite her physical weakness, it seemed that her mental faculties had strengthened by his presence and affection.

"Yuh see mi gawn turn fool-fool," she said. "Mi cyan memba nutten nowadays. As soon as mi start to talk, me feget wha' me want fe say. Lawd, me turn fool-fool, an' me turn ugly in mi old age."

"Cho, Mamma, don't say that man, I understand everything you say. And you are still the prettiest woman I know. Birdie smiled.

"An' yuh did fin' a pretty wife tuh. I like har, Sammy, she is a lovely girl."

"Thanks, Mamma. She is kind, and she is a Christian. She has been very good to me."

"Well, Sammy, I jus' want fe tell yuh dat I did live a good life. I don' min' going to be wid de Lord at all. Jus' tell everybody for me dat I want to go back to Cocoa Walk an' be buried beside Mumaa. I miss har yuh see?. She was mi bes' friend' yuh know. Until ol' Septy come dance wid me and tek me away fram har. Yes, is Cocoa Walk me bawn, an' is dere me Pupa bury beside me Madda, an' mi sista an' bredda tuh. An' mi wan' fe res' beside dem. Lawd, mi tired yuh see!"

"Yes, Mamma, is a long life you live, and you took good care of all of us. We really thank you Mamma. Even though we never take the time to tell you, God will bless you for all you did and all the sacrifice you made for your family."

"Let me see, is how many of you, again?"

"Is eight of us, Mamma. Seven boys and Girlie, remember?"

"Uh Hm, an' yuh is de one that give me de hardes' time. Yuh was de breech birt' dat nearly kill me. Yuh did know dat?"

"Yes, Mamma, yuh tell me that over and over. And that's why you spoil me so much." Sammy laughed appreciatively. Birdie's face softened. It seemed to glow with tenderness. Sammy took her hands in both of his. For moments they were silent relishing the bond.

"Ah, but yuh was a good child. I did tell you dat yuh was born wid a veil ovah yuh face? Yuh is special, you know, Sammy. Yuh is a very special chile, and yuh can't forget dat. Das why I wasn't surprise when you start to be a parson. Ah thought God answered me prayers to save yuh because Miss Jane did tell mi dat you will either turn out very good or very bad, but yuh would nevah be just usual or ordinary. Neda Septy or me did know what tuh expec' but yuh is the seven son' and dem say that is a sign, yuh know."

"Yes, Mamma."

"Suh, which one is yuh now Sammy? Is you a devil or a angel? You not suppose tuh be jus' in de middle. Me know yuh is a good man, even if yuh nevah did turn out to be a parson. You know, me an' Septy did t'ink one time seh you would become a pries'? You was such a pretty little altar bwoy. When we did guh to church an hear yuh a talk inna Latin we was proud yuh see! But we would be satisfied even if you was jus' a good Christian man. Enny way, de Lawd knows bes'."

Birdie went quiet and apparently deep in thought for a moment. Sammy looked at her as in repose with her eyes closed. Their hands were still held tightly clasped. Then Birdie heaved a deep sigh. She opened her eyes and seemed to be looking at the ceiling.

"Is where Septy, deh?"

"Him out in de yard with Girlie, Mamma."

"Tell him come in ya fe me, nuh."

Sammy did not leave her. He knew the signs. He turned his head and called through the open door. "Dadda! Mamma calling you. Please come here!"

Septy came into the room apprehensively. He was followed by Girlie, and Tarzan who had come to visit that morning. They gathered around the bed. Birdie looked up at Septy and reached for his hand. The effort was feeble, but she accomplished it. Her breathing now came in swift shallow heavings.

"Septy, we didn' duh suh bad after all. Thanks to yuh an' your ambition we raise a good crop of children. Look 'pon Tarzan, 'im is a good farmer next door tuh 'im nephew Walford. An' poor Girlie is to me jus' like I was to me madda. She nevah did leave me even though all of the boys went away. Mek me see, we have two school teacha, one doctah, one farmer, de twin dem in business up a Canada, and Sammy is we soljah. Tenk Gad, we can be proud! I don' have no regrets on de life we live. But me body wear out and I know seh I'm goin' to a betta place. Suh Septy, hol' me han' and promise me seh yuh will tek me body back up to the mountains an lie me down beside Mummaa and Puppaa." She paused. The air in the room was still. None breathed. Septy's head was bowed. He seemed rigid as if nothing could move him from where he stood.

Birdie's body jerked as if she had just now awakened from sleep. She continued to speak as if she had not stopped.

"Septy, me thank yuh fe takin' good care of we all the long years. Even though sometimes we had it tough, you always tried to make a way. Even when you had to go away a foreign, yuh kep' yuh marriage promise. You never did leave me. An' I believe I will see yuh again on de odder side before we see de children dem. Suh, Septy, thank yuh." Sammy wondered at the clearness of the mind of Birdie whose memory had seemed to have failed. He watched her intently. She must have felt his stare because she turned to him.

"An' Sammy, yuh is de younges' but God mek you strong and smart. Tek care of yuh bredda an' sistah dem. I don' know what happen to Jamaica, but things change. Yuh all think seh me crazy, but me can see! Me can see that things bad, bad now. An' things gwine get worse. Ah don' kno' what tomorrow gwine bring to dis vile worl', suh Sammy ah beg yuh, protect yuh bredda dem an' yuh sista. Den Septy, a wan'.. a wan'..."

Her words died away in a gentle breath and a small sigh. Angels lifted the feather light soul of Birdie and escorted her to her rest. Septy continued to hold her limp hand.

There was silence in the room. None had responded to any of her commands or requests. All had been too busy listening to her. Sammy exchanged glances with Tarzan and Girlie. Then all three looked at Septy. He seemed to have aged and become smaller than any had recalled. His slight and veined hand still held Birdie. Long crystal tears flowed down Girlie's face, meeting and plaiting in a dripping bow under her chin, before falling like a ripe yellow jimbilin to the floor. Impulsively, all in the room intertwined arms to give support to each other as spasms of pain and loss engulfed them. Each had known the end would come for Birdie. Although they were prepared for it; each had thought she was being revived for a longer fight by the refreshing presence of Sammy. Each was devastated by her sudden departure. Tears came with wracking sobs and unabashed weeping. Sammy, who had seen so much of pain and death and had considered himself toughened by life, was surprised to find himself weeping with the rest.

All but Septy. He seemed beyond grief or belief. His bowed head was punctuated by an involuntary shaking as if denying the truth of Birdie's death. He held her hand as if imploring her to stay. Birdie. His friend, wife, and mother of his children. Birdie, his partner of a lifetime was gone, leaving only the worn out casing which now held a gentle smile on her thin and wrinkled lips, and a cooling warmth from perfectly limp and relaxing hands.

"What happened?" asked Doris breathlessly barging into the room and boring her way into the middle of the hand locked group.

"Mamma just died," said Sammy simply. Instinctively Doris put her arms comfortingly around her husband as their daughter, Linda, came in to join the close knit group.

"What happened?" asked Linda.

"Honey, your grandmother just died," replied Doris.

They gathered around Birdie's bed. Sammy began to pray.

Chapter Sixteen

Cocoa Walk, Manchester

The booth was erected by the large catchment tank. The sides and roof were covered with plaited palm fronds. It was a shelter from the cool night wind or rain. Inside, at the back was a table on which was placed a saucer with salt, an open Bible, and a small red covered booklet of hymns.

A gas lantern illuminated the inside and shone on the faces of the scores of people seated or standing. Many more people milled around in the yard. Some were renewing acquaintances. Others exchanged greetings after absences from each other. Birdie's children, some of whom had not seen each other for decades, all came together to arrange the funeral. Sammy yielded to the leadership of his older kin, some of whom were not really close to him since they had left home while he was still a youngster. But he respected them. The children, cousins of first and second generation, were introduced by parents or older members of the family.

Doris and Linda enjoyed meeting and being with Sammy's family. The mountains were magic. The simple and extroverted country people were kind and welcoming. Gifts of fruits and cooked foods kept pouring in as more neighbours and family members arrived. They moved among the crowd stopping to talk to everyone they could.

Two men and a woman sat at the table at the far end of the crowded booth. As Sammy and his family watched from the entrance, the worship leaders led songs, prayed and read scriptures from the Bible. As the long night of using their voices ravaged their throat, they would dip fingers in the salt and place it on their tongue to soothe the stressed vocal cords.

This was the "Set Up" event. Tonight, friends, neighbours and family assembled to keep company with the dead. Tomorrow would be the funeral. Nine days later, a smaller crowd would assemble for the "Nine Night".. the ceremony of final parting with the dead. Although the corpse was at the Mortuary in Mandeville, the spirit of Birdie was here. Some said they could still hear her infectious laughter across a lifetime. The wind carried it through the trees. Some said they could still see her walking from the shop at Buckup, or going to the market at Cross Keys. Somehow, the memories conjured this night were of the days when all were young and vital. Some had not even heard that she had been ill.

But Birdie's death accomplished what she could not have done in life. It brought all the family together. They ate, laughed, drank, sang, exchanged stories and addresses, and prayed until the chilly Manchester dawn drove them to catch quick naps as best they could. Many nestled against strangers who were not strangers. The strong bonds of family and the honourable ties of blood assured their safety.

The caravan of cars and vans slowly turned off the main road and up the track that led to the house. They were returning from Mandeville where the funeral services were conducted, and where the body had been stored. Now they were escorting Birdie's remains to its final resting place in the family burial ground. The house nestled among the many fruit trees and coffee copse, had been the family home for nearly a century. The burial plot was shaded by tall sapodillas and mango trees. Labourers had expertly cleared a path and levelled the ground to the tombs. Between two freshly whitewashed tombs, a hole, six feet deep, had been excavated.

Sammy was in the vehicle with his father Septy, and four brothers including Tarzan. In the car behind them were two brothers and their wives and Girlie, Doris and Linda. Behind them for nearly a mile, relatives and friends trailed in conveyances of every description and vintage. They came out of love and respect and family solidarity. The Sinclairs and Gordons had been bound by covenants of loyalty in life. In death the vows still held.

Up ahead of the family cars was the hearse. Birdie, who had not been able to come home for her beloved mother's funeral, was coming home to rest with her parents from whom she would never be parted again.

The cars stopped. The seven sons stood in two lines facing the bier. Following instructions, they took hold of the clasps of the casket and, followed by their father who led the procession, they bore Birdie to her last resting place under the shade of a naseberry tree. They laid her down gently and stepped back. A minister of the Gospel prayed, gave a blessing, and committed her remains to the ground. Tears of grief at parting and guilt streamed down Sammy's face. He was not alone. Fecund tears in tribute to a lost love and lost good, flowed copiously from children and family and friends.

Sammy remembered the words of the priest in Mandeville who had said it was okay to let go. Birdie's aged and paralyzed body had become a faulty shell incapable of bearing a spirit that was ready to soar. But for the moment he was inconsolable. There had been so many "If's" that could never be resolved. So many roads not taken. So many unkept promises. So many good intentions undone.

He had promised himself to get his aging parents to America for needed rest and medical care. He had promised himself to build them a new home as soon as he became financially able. He had planned to send them a big television set. Some nice clothes. A large amount of money, so they could shop and buy what they would enjoy. But circumstances had prevented him.

The fact that his older siblings had done their part did not console him. The fact that unlike those Jamaicans who went to America only to work, he had gone to study and had only limited access to money those first years, did not console him. The fact that he had joined the military, and as an enlisted man his pay was small, did not console him. The fact that his modest income had been spent on caring for his lovely wife and child did not console him. Before the open grave he shook in regret, remorse, self-pity, and helplessness. His life had been spent helping many others. His own mother had not been a beneficiary. Too late, he wished he had remained home and that his life had taken other turns.

He had given his best to others. He had failed to be there when his parents needed him.

What was clear to him was that he would never be able to do anything for his mother. It was also clear that he was still unable to do much for his father. It had taken years for him just to come home. Thank God he had come when he did. But he regretted the Christmas and birthday cards he thought of, but did not send. He regretted not sending the five or ten dollars because he could not send fifty or a hundred. He wished he had sent pictures for his mother to see. He wished he had written home to tell his mother of the accomplishments he had made. There were stories he would never now be able to share with her. Stories only she would have understood, and which would have eased his pain and removed the nightmares of the terrible battles with which he had struggled every night.

Now the workers began to shovel in the dirt and rocks. It seemed almost sacrilegious. There was something very final and even horrible about the sound of the heavy clods and stones thudding on and bouncing off the coffin. The final discarding of the body of his mother shook him profoundly. He looked with tear filled eyes at his father after whom he was named. Septy seemed in a daze. He was gazing at the grave as if he was being invited to a similar fate. Sammy moved to his father and put his arms on his shoulder. Septy kept nodding his head slowly as if to say "Yes, yes, I know. She is really gone."

They remained where they stood until the grave was filled and mounded. Many sang hymns as the grave diggers worked. A vast collection of flowers was strewn over the mound covering it with a thick quilt of green and red and pink and yellow and purple. Birdie was warmed with lavish affection where she reposed.

The crowd moved to the freshly whitewashed barbecue and the booth that served as a chapel the night before. A meal was served of curried goat and rice and boiled bananas and yams. This meal was taken in a more subdued manner than any before. Talk was muted. Older family members described how on this very spot, there had been the biggest wedding celebration when Septy and Birdie were married some fifty years before.

Septy talked with old friends. They had much to remember, before the sadness of the present again took hold and further tears were shed.

As night fell, the crowd reluctantly dispersed. Loads of passengers returned to Vere and Mandeville, Christiana and Four Paths, May Pen and Kingston, and other places where the scattered family now lived. Good-byes were sincere. Promises to write were profuse. They would keep in touch. They would not stay away from each other in the future. Soon the roaring engines faded, and all was quiet in the mountains as the "moonties" blinked their searchlights, and the night creatures began their nostalgic symphony.

Next day, Sammy, Doris and Linda bade farewell to Septy and Girlie. Doris and Linda would return to their lives in Texas. Sammy would return to report to his Army post in a matter of days. But he and Doris had talked about his shame at doing nothing worthwhile for his parents. He felt that the least he could do was to return to Jamaica at the end of his tour of duty and fulfil his promise made long ago to serve his homeland. He would also be fulfilling the promise he made to his dying mother to care for his brothers and sister who were trying to make a living among the rocks and plots of rich soil among the various mountain villages. He had seen more of the world than his father. He had been better educated. He had amassed enough experience and information to be able to make a contribution to his island home. Doris and Linda had fallen in love with the country and its people. Doris had been claimed and loved by the family like a sister. She felt that she belonged there. She was in love with Sammy and would be happy with him anywhere in the world.

Their future course now outlined, they boarded a plane. As it soared above and circled, they took long looks at the beautiful Blue Mountains and blue Caribbean Sea. This time Sammy had the window seat. The view below was clear and unobstructed. As the froth speckled sea receded, he looked and with a choked voice said, "Me soon come back."

CHAPTER SEVENTEEN

May Pen, Jamaica, Mid 1970s

The telephone rang with an urgency that somehow told Sammy that something unusual was happening. He was lying in bed reading even though it was only six in the morning. Doris picked up the phone and said "Hello." Sammy listened.

"Girlie! How are you? What's the matter?"

"Oh! I'm so sorry! Hold on, Sammy is right here. Sammy, its your sister Girlie in Jamaica."

Sammy took the phone. He held his breath in a steely calmness as he said:

"Hello, Sis. How are you?"

"Hi Sammy. I'm fine, but Dadda died a few minutes ago."

"Oh, what happened?"

"Well, you know he suffers from high blood pressure and has been taking medicine for it. Well, it seems he has been forgetting to take his medicine and he had a stroke. It seems like it took him suddenly. I heard some noises and went in his room. His eyes were staring and he was reaching out to me. I said "Dadda, what's the matter?" but he just made some sounds in his throat and never said anything. We rushed him to the hospital and the nurses tried to help, but by the time the doctor came and saw him, he was dead."

"Gee, Girlie, I am so sorry to hear that. Dadda was a fighter until the very end, henh?"

"Yes, Sammy, our father was one man who never gave up, no matter what. So, what you think we should do, you are the first one I call. Tarzan is here with me, and I am going to call the others as soon as I get through talking to you."

"Just hold everything until we get there. I know everybody will want to help plan the funeral. We will be down there by tomorrow or the next day. I will call you back."

"All right then, I will look for you soon."

"Yes. I'll be there as soon as possible. See you."

"Your father was a very nice man, I liked him," said Doris.

"Septimus George Gordon the First, was one of a kind." said Sammy. "He was devoted to his family and did not mind the personal sacrifices if it meant his children were well cared for. He can't be replaced." It was now almost three years since his mother died, and he had completed his military duties, having decided against making it a lifelong career. He and Doris had been saving their money towards a return to Jamaica to settle in the near future.

Now it seemed that their plans needed to be changed. His mind swept across the years of his relationship with his father. He thought of all he had learned from him, how he had disappointed him, and how his father had understood and forgiven him for refusing to become a tailor. Following his mother's death, he had kept his resolve to be more attentive to his family. He had visited more regularly, kept up with his relatives in the country, and he had provided more for their comfort. Now the question was what to do about his plans. He turned to Doris who had sat on the bed and was looking at him quietly.

"Well, the ol' man is gone, honey. I can't believe that my Dad is dead."

"In recent years you two have got very close. I know this must be hard for you," said Doris.

"It is hard, but you know, my father is eighty-six years old. In Bible terms, he has earned his 'three-score-years-and ten' with a few to spare. I guess I have much to be thankful for that he had lived long enough to see all his children grow up, and with a lot of grand children and great grandchildren too."

"So, when do we go?" asked Doris

"I have been thinking about that. I know all the family will be there, but we are planning to move to Jamaica permanently in a few months. I am thinking that we should pass up this funeral and send a warm message and some beautiful flowers. I will always treasure my father's memory and his wise counsel, but I believe that our desire to help my country should not be forgotten. I think we should decide to pack up and return to Jamaica within the next three or four months. I can then pay my respects to my father in an extended way by offering myself and my skills to the service of my home country. I think I will call my brothers and ask them to go without me. None of them are even thinking of moving back to Jamaica.

Sammy had called the twins, Henry and Lester in Canada and talked over the situation with them. They understood his position and agreed with him. "Sure, Sammy," said Lester, I think you are making the right decision, and I believe Dadda would understand. Since you were planning to be out there in a few months anyway, and since you had seen him only a few months ago, I think it's alright. We will explain to every one."

Sammy had then called back Girlie and they had talked about the funeral arrangements. Septy's body was taken to Manchester and laid to rest beside Birdie. "It was a lovely funeral," Lester, one of the twins had reported, when they talked later. "Everybody asked for you, and nobody could understand why you were not there. I did try to explain, but that did not do much good. They all said you carry your father's name and he and you were so close. Anyway, I am sure you know best. So, when will you move to Jamaica?"

"Within three months," Sammy said. "Thanks for telling me everything, man. I hope to see you soon when you come to Jamaica again."

He and Doris and Linda completed their plans and moved to Kingston. They rented a lovely house in Havendale, and Sammy began to look up his old friends and rebuild relationships he had before he left for America.

He made many trips to May Pen, but he did not revisit the church, nor did he explain to any why he was not a clergyman. He did discover his friend Myers on the police force. In the years since his absence, Myers had become a Detective Inspector and was widely known and loved in the island.

Sammy began to look around for opportunities that would provide him both an income and an avenue for helping his country. He had money saved, so he was in no hurry to work just for the sake of working. He made friends and he attended functions, and he began to meet other repatriates from England and Canada and the Unites States. They shared in common a burning love for Jamaica, and a deep concern for the economic stagnation that was suffocating the island. All shared the opinion that something had to be done to rescue the country from run-away inflation and bad management of scarce resources. Sammy continued to look for a niche through which he could serve. Nothing he saw appealed to him. The months rolled on, but nothing he saw daunted his spirits. "All it takes is time, Doris. I know that it is taking a bit longer than we had planned, but adjusting to this new nation takes time. Why don't you go back to Texas for a month, and relax while I stay here and keep on looking around."

"Yes, I am a bit homesick. I think I will take your suggestion," agreed Doris. "A month away will do me good, and it won't do you any harm, since you do stay gone for long periods during the days nowadays."

"Well, I will miss you, but we will talk on the phone and I will look forward to your return."

* * * * * * * * *

Doris had left to visit her family and had taken Linda with her. Sammy continued to look around and make connections with his friends. It was almost by accident that he attended the political rally in May Pen that would change his fortunes.

"Things can't go on like this much longer in Jamaica. All of you know it's a long time now that we Jamaicans have been clamouring for economic progress. There is only so much that any human can bear. It's time for a change!"

The speaker on the stage waxed warm in oratory as he spun out his fiery message. He held his audience at rapt attention and was reluctant to let them go. The audience too was caught up in his spellbinding delivery and was reluctant for him to end. He hammered home his points with a burst of energy.

"A better day is plainly in sight. All we have to do is reach for it and take it. It is time to stop skylarking and start doing something to change our situation right now. Election day is coming soon, and you can make the difference if you cast your vote like people with sense. Not only is it time for a change, it is time to rearrange the entire economic structure of this country. It is now full time for the little man to enjoy the fruits of his labour. This is the day that our parents dreamed about and slaved for, but never lived long enough to see happen. Go and vote and put us in power."

"Put us in power! We will give you quality education for every child in this country. We are not just talking about primary education. We intend to build a programme for every Jamaican boy and girl all the way until they finish college or get a technical education. Yes, college! We owe it to our children to make sure every one of them can make a contribution to the building of this country. It will be the obligation of our government to care for every citizen so that citizens can in turn love and care for their country."

"PUT US IN POWER! We will open up business opportunities for even the little man who has a vision and a plan. Put us in power! We will see to it that even the average Jamaicans will have splendid opportunities to exercise their abilities to become a part of the mainstream of the new Jamaica we plan to build. Put us in power. If you put us in power and you have a plan, we will provide the experts to help you reach your aims."

"PUT US IN POWER! We will guarantee health care for every Jamaican. For too long poor Jamaicans have had to die in pain without medicine because they could not afford to go to a doctor. It is their right and privilege as a citizen of this country to not have to suffer when they are sick. Your new government will provide clinics and we will renovate hospitals."

"PUT US IN POWER! Help us create solutions to our problems that are driving this country straight to the almshouse. Put us in power and you will see. As Winston Churchill said one time, this will be Jamaica's finest hour. Never! Never again, will the dreams of Jamaicans get sour!!"

The speaker sat down. The crowd went wild. The excitement was contagious. Children and youth clapped. Men and women waved and danced.

On stage, the speaker used a handkerchief to wipe streaming perspiration from his face and neck. A supporter came over and grabbed his hand. He had a broad grin on his face.

"Boss, bway, if dat speech didn' win you all de votes in this place, I will eat my hat. Boss, jus' look at dem. Dem gawn crazy! I wish election was tenight."

The candidate nodded his head in acknowledgment of the praise and assessment. He cast a calculating glance across the dancing, shouting, waving crowd who were shouting in glad hysteria "PUT US IN POWER!!" Yes, there was a movement that seemed positive, but in the game of politics, nothing was certain. Tides turn too quickly for any reasonable politician to relax. He would have to see the results on election day to be certain of anything. His party had come close and lost elections too many times for him to be satisfied just because one crowd at one place loved his speech and would probably make the effort to go to the polls and vote for him. He was still thoughtful as he listened to the local party leaders "mop up" any residue of energy still left in the crowd.

At last they broke out in a rally song. The candidate felt the fervour from the pitch of the voices and the joined hands of the throng. As they closed their eyes and sang, he concluded that at least at this place he had unquestioned support. He turned to the supporter who had spoken and said "You know, I think you are right. I strongly believe this crowd is with me?"

"I'm telling you, Boss, you have this place locked up. I talked to Mullings a few minutes ago and he said the same thing. You don't have to worry about May Pen. You have May Pen!" The candidate sighed with a show of guarded contentment.

Sammy was standing at the very front, where the crowd arched to the right of the stage. He had a clear view of all that was happening before him. His large "Afro" hairstyle had been freshly teased to a neat well-groomed coiffure. His full beard was trimmed to a square to match his full face. His dashiki was of green and black and red. His blue jeans were nicely pressed. The leather sandals on his feet were strong and freshly polished. His eyes glowed with excitement. This was the Jamaica of his childhood all over again. Once more he was at Water Lane or Lionel Town. Busta was on stage, and the crowds were wild and screaming "Chief! Chief!" His few detractors corrupted the words to say "Tief! Tief!", but that made no difference. Everyone present knew that this was "Busta country". He had the same feeling about the atmosphere here tonight in May Pen.

He was glad that he had finally given in to Tanya's invitation. He and Doris had met Tanya Dyer at the airport on their arrival back in Jamaica more than a year before. She was returning home from studies in America. Tanya soon became a welcome friend of the family. Doris was back in the States for a visit. Tanya had invited him to attend this political rally. He was reluctant to go anywhere without Doris. Tanya had told him that this candidate was progressive. He had his hands fully on the public pulse and if given an opportunity would serve the country well at this time in its history. After talking to Doris the night before, he decided to go. This would be the first time Sammy would have a chance to vote in Jamaica in his life. More than that, the speaker and the crowd charged him with a sense of reality that was similar to moods he had felt in the American South while a student.

In his days in Jackson, Mississippi, he had sat for hours in the office of Medgar Evers. Medgar had presented him with a copy of the book "We Charge Genocide," in which were outlined the atrocities of racists against Negroes in America. They shared similar passions for the uplift and franchisement of black people. He had told Medgar of the small efforts of the gasping fragments of the United Negro Improvement Association, that once formidable army of Marcus Moziah Garvey. Medgar had told him of the dangerous but necessary job of the National Association for the Advancement of Coloured People in Mississippi, trying to get Negroes to register to vote. Sammy had traveled with Medgar and other committed Negro citizens to big and small towns to rally the people. Although the opposition was fierce, the courage and commitment of the black people spawned the context for the Freedom Riders and the shouters of "Black Power" in the long broiling summers of the mid 60s. They had wanted liberation from racial oppression and economic injustice.

Here tonight, he felt something in the air that was similar to the cries of the American Negroes across the seas. These people sensed the need of a special something. They would never publicly say that their lack was caused by racism, but "something" was not right in their social, cultural, and economic lives, despite the fact that they had been voting for years. This speaker had given form to their longings in words that made sense to them. What he promised was not political "bread and butter "jobs, but an overturn of the social order to provide substantial opportunities for the traditionally ignored and overlooked classes. He had tasked about it so convincingly that the crowd could feel, taste, smell, and walk in the reality he conjured in their imagination.

Sammy linked his hand in that of his companion Tanya. As the speaker elaborated each point, he squeezed her hand tightly. As the speaker took his seat, he turned to the woman.

"Tanya, you think he's serious?"

"Then him nuh mus' serious!!" In her excitement, the Jamaican idiom dominated her years of formal education in the local university as well as in the States. "Jus' look around here since, Independence. What change you see? It's time for the man at the bottom to get a break. If that man don't get a chance to do it, nobody else will even try. The man is as serious as a heart attack. I believe him!"

Sammy felt good. He was convinced that his decision to return to Jamaica came at an opportune moment. He listened and watched the crowd. There was hope in their every move. Sammy felt that his job in Jamaica was not just to make a living, but to become a part of a process that could contribute to the development of his country. He felt joy. He was sure that very few could understand how a man with his humble beginnings, floundering for years in poverty and lack of opportunity in his native land, expelled as it were by financial insecurities to seek his fortune overseas, could return home filled with such patriotism and so eager to expend his gains for the benefit of a land that so mercilessly disgorged him. But there he was in the mingling crowd, in the luminous dark of a star-filled night, bursting with hope and charged with enthusiasm. If only this man and his party could be elected, he thought, things would certainly be different in the conditions of the common people. Tonight, in the electric contagion of this moment, he felt convinced that the man had a half a chance. But Sammy had come to know again his fellow Jamaicans. He was aware as well of the sagacity of the party in power. They could muster no new ideas to fire the imagination of the people, but they could still react with powerful agility to foil the efforts of the energetic upstarts.

He went home euphoric. His plans for the months ahead were clear. He would expend all the energy and money at his disposal to see that the promises he had heard the candidate make were given an opportunity to be tested for the good of the country.

Chapter Eighteen

Kingston, Jamaica, early 1980

Sammy sat in the waiting room. A dozen people were also waiting. Many made small talk with the receptionist in the game of "I'm a regular here. I'm no stranger to this place". The attractive young lady behind the desk shared her smiling glances with all in discreet proportions.

Sammy received his share of special glances and smiles. He became increasingly uncomfortable as each quarter passed and he was still not called. Try as he might, he could not adjust to having people arrive at eleven o'clock for a ten o'clock appointment, then act as though no offence had been committed. Wasted time spent in waiting was the normal course at every level of Jamaican life. Imposing the burden of waiting was on the one level an exercise in power and self-affirmation. Enduring waiting was the mark of affirmation of servility. This legacy from the days of laissez-faire colonialism has never been reconsidered by evolving Jamaica. Time as a commodity of value to be conserved or wisely expended, has never entered the imagination of those who exercise management or leadership. Its consequence for wasted human and capital resources had never been enumerated. Like their aristocratic forbears, the modern Jamaican elite prefer fiscal bankruptcy and abject organizational mismanagement, despite their ownership of the most fantastic time management technology, instead of the smooth efficiency with which progressive modem nations choose to do business.

Sammy ruminated in growing agitation as he shifted his weight. The Jamaican "soon come" mentality had been making him fearful of his ability to do business with the Jamaicans he had been meeting. They meant well and talked a good game, but level of production was far less than that to which he had become accustomed in his life abroad.

He was also nervous. He had been working on his proposal for more than a year. The election had been a landslide for the party he supported, and his admired "statesman" was now in power. It was now time to test if the campaign promises would be honoured. By now he was well known at the parish level. He had shared his plans with the people he hoped would channel his hopes and dreams up to the proper authorities. He had worked hard and established good connections, because he hoped for a chance to make a difference in the future of his country.

He hoped his work would pay off, but he was concerned about his ability to effectively convey his ideas to the Jamaican point of view. He recognized that his ways of organizing his thoughts had changed. He hoped he would be effective. He was still deep in thought when he heard his name called. He looked up to see the secretary beckoning him. She was standing smartly by a door that was slightly ajar. "The Minister will see you now, Mr. Gordon." Sammy went in.

The tall trim Minister rose from his chair and strode across the room. He was still the consummate politician with open smile and outstretched hand. "Sammy! Sammy Gordon!" he effused. "Come in, come in man! I have just been talking about you to some people down in May Pen. Yes, I heard a lot about all the hard work you did for us during the election. I want you to know that I am very grateful. Without support such as yours we could never have won the election." He placed his open hand on Sammy's shoulders and guided him to a chair. "Here", he said. "Have a seat. Now tell me, how can I help you?"

Sammy reached into his briefcase and withdrew two attractively bound documents. He handed one to the Minister and opened the other. "Minister, I was in the crowd in May Pen about two years ago when you made that powerful speech. That was what made me begin to think about ways to help my country. I had just returned from spending some years overseas. At first, I thought I would just come home and rest, but your speech made me believe that I could invest myself in the development of this country. "Good! Good!" prompted the Minister, palming the portfolio he was holding.

"Anyway, I have spent the last year working on a proposal which is spelled out in the manuscript I just gave you. I know you won't have the time to examine it now, but I can elaborate on as many details as you need. I know you are a busy man, but I would appreciate a few minutes to outline the plan I have."

Sammy was sitting on the edge of his chair. His eyes shone with an intense glow. His earnestness was contagious. "Okay, I can spare you a few minutes, Sammy. Let me see what you have here."

The Minister opened and began to scan the pages. His partly closed eyes and furrowed forehead showed his deep concentration as he read. He began to nod and slowly turn page after page. Then the pace quickened and Sammy got the impression that the man had found things of interest in the document. The nodding continued. At last he looked up, and returned the eyeglasses to his face that he had laid aside as he read.

"Mr. Gordon, you will never know how much I appreciate your presentation. Day after day my office is filled with supporters who come with ideas that are poorly conceived and inadequately developed. They want this government to back them, but the amount of work it would take to develop what they have in mind makes it impossible to give the support they are looking for. But your plans, now, I like them. You took the time to research your ideas and develop something that looks very feasible. You even anticipate problems and suggest solutions. I thank you for your hard work. More than that, your proposal is very much in line with the goals of my administration. I believe they can work.

"Thank you, Minister," mumbled Sammy gratefully.

"So, here is what I want to do. Give me a few weeks to pass this on to my planning people for their examination. Don't worry, I will see that your interests are protected. No one will steal your thunder. The planning people will give me their opinion, then I will consult the relevant ministries for their approval. Somebody will get back to you and inform you of the progress in a couple of months. Please don't worry if it seems that the time is passing slowly. That's how things work. But you will hear from us."

"Thank you, Minister."

The Minister stood up indicating that the meeting was over. "Mr. Gordon," he said extending his hand, "thanks for your offer of partnership with this government. We fully intend to go in the new directions I outlined in my campaign. I believe you can be a big help to us in the private sector as we try to create a new future for Jamaica. I pledge that we will work with you to develop a profitable endeavour. Sammy, thank you for coming to visit me. It was a pleasure."

Sammy shook his hand and left the office as if on a cloud. He felt cautious elation. The thing seemed too easy. He had studied and worked hard, but he expected more questions from the Minister. More inquiry about details. Maybe those would come later from the bureaucrats. He had doubts that his hard work would ever come to fruition, yet, the look of honest interest on the face of the Minister gave him hope. Just as he felt on that night two years before, he felt now that he was dealing with a man whose word could be trusted. He felt that his proposal had merit, and the expression of the Minister as he scanned was one of comprehension and agreement. If any politician could be trusted, he felt he had just been in the presence of such a man. Anyway, he thought, I have gained access. I have shared my plans.

I've done all I could to show I love my country and I'm avaiiable to work for its improvement.

His plan included three requests - monetary support, protected markets, and technical assistance. In return he would provide employment for over a thousand workers. He would manufacture goods to service needs in Jamaica as well as the larger Caribbean. He would provide a good quality product at competitive prices. He would create a work environment that would demonstrate his respect for the dignity of the common workers. He would dedicate a portion of his profits to support education through scholarships for the underprivileged. He would provide preventive health care for the workers and their families. He would provide hot nutritious meals in a company kitchen. He would provide uniforms for the workers. He would provide a pension scheme. Those were the touches that he felt would emphasize his commitment to the uplift of his fellow Jamaicans. There would be no effort on his part to hog profits and demonstrate overnight that he had become a "big man". He would develop gradually with the business, but his people would develop with him.

Now he would wait to see if his dream would find favour with the government. As he tooled his car through the busy streets of Kingston, he found himself doing what he had done so many times recently. He drove towards the harbour to a spot his proposal required to be the location of his establishment. It was overgrown with weeds. Broken down walls and rusted steel beams from the buildings of another time stared at him. A joy began to surge through him. Yes, it was possible. He could have a chance to help his people. "Please God, don't disappoint me now," he prayed. Somehow his mind rested comfortably on words that surged up to the top of his mind "Ask and ye shall receive." An embarrassment gave him pause for a moment. He had not prayed for years, nor had he asked God for help, even when under fire in Viet Nam. Then the unease passed. He felt that he was not asking for himself He felt his prayer was appropriate. Now, he would wait for the ponderous wheels of govermnent process to turn his vision into things that were tangible.

Chapter Nineteen

Kingston, Jamaica: Early 1980s

People moved in all directions in the large room of the plant. Some carried burdens on their shoulders. Others delivered messages. Still others shouted orders. Trucks backed up to loading dock, were taking on, or delivering goods. Busy clerks with lead pencils stuck behind their ears and note pads in their hands, lined up behind foremen to get signatures for documents. Telephones rang incessantly. Horns of motor vehicles cleared the roadways. Everywhere, there were eddying whirlpools of concentrated tasks that spun off from the complex flood of energy amassed and directed towards the fulfilment of one man's giant dream.

Sammy stood with both hands akimbo and gazed on the scene. From a vantage point on a raised platform at the centre of the floor, he sensed with satisfaction that all was well. Yet, his keen eyes studied in detail every movement and sound about him. He felt a depth of satisfaction that few could understand. It was not just that his dreams were being realized in a tangible way, it was more the conviction that all of his past life had conspired to locate him at this place and time. He felt fulfilled. Every hurt, disappointment, and twist and turn in his past had been knitted into the fabric of this perfectly full moment.

His glance singled out Doris. She was busily solving a problem with a worker at the far end of the building. Though a foreigner, she had taken to Jamaica as if she had been born in the country. What pleased him most was her adaptation to those aspects of Jamaican life that he would have been embarrassed to introduce to a foreigner. Like boiled green bananas with coconut rundown, fried fish, or cook up cod fish and callaloo, or roast breadfruit with mackerel. He had carefully instructed the cook to prepare American dishes like fried chicken and mashed potatoes. But Doris had countermanded those directions and skillfully provided the native dishes of his childhood. He had been proud and grateful. She was as easily at home with boiled dumplings and yellow yams, as she was with macaroni and cheese. His love for her deepened. He was proud of her. He felt good that he had been able to provide for her comfort as he had promised when they talked about the adventure of keeping his promise to return home. "We'll try it for three years," he had said, "if things don't work out, then I will at least have kept my promise. We can return and I can either re- up for another tour in the Army, or go back to college, or I can find some other kind of work."

But they never had to pinch pennies. They now lived in a comfortable home in the hills above Kingston. Now that the business was booming, they were building a dream home with every modern convenience. Yes, after years of hell in Korea and Viet Nam, he was grateful to just be alive, physically fit, and mentally healthy. The greatest miracle was that he had survived when so many had died.

Sammy felt a deep sense of accomplishment. Many called him "boas'y". A term corrupted from the word 'boaster'. It meant a show-off, but carried a weightier note of social disapproval, because the 'boas'y' one appeared to be leaving the social position to which his birth had assigned him. He disregarded his detractors. None of them knew or cared about his struggles. None could imagine the terrible price he had paid for every painful step he took up life's punishing ladder.

It was precisely his successes that irritated some who felt that his achievements diminished them, showed them up as less than enterprising, and were not to be permitted to a Jamaican with a black skin.

Interestingly, it was not only non-Black Jamaicans who called him boasy. In fact, more blacks were envious than others. But, threats to his position were more to be feared from the "brownies" and Jamaican whites with influence, than the blacks who could only mouth jealousy, but would do little to injure him.

Sammy was naturally kind. He shared generously with those who asked for help. He was good to his employees and their families. True to his word, he sponsored scholarships and health programmes for them. He cared deeply for people. He paid them the best wages possible without doing harm to the soundness of his enterprise.

Yet, the criticisms were not without basis. He carried himself with a certain flair. His walk was a combination of his military training and the sailor-like swagger he inherited from his father, Septy. That aura of savoir faire rubbed some the wrong way. Then, he lived in a plush neighborhood. The fact that he had spent years in vermin infested jungles, had laboured for years to improve himself, and had succeeded by sheer will and brain power was lost on his detractors. They saw that he drove a "Benz", wore a Rolex watch, dressed stylishly with shirt and tie, and had been appointed to directorships of important organizations.

His child went to an exclusive school. His wife shopped overseas or at expensive boutiques in New Kingston. They ate at exclusive restaurants. When they threw parties, those in attendance were the veritable "who's who" of the Jamaican social register. When he spoke, he demonstrated knowledge that others interpreted as arrogance. He meant well, he was eager to contribute. He considered himself a patriot and desired to play the part in both private and public life. In his enthusiasm, without intending to, he made enemies. Many striving businessmen without his insight and contacts, became jealous.

Now he stood in the centre of the assembly building and looked around. All told, more than a thousand people were working at jobs that provided good wages. The people were proud to be a part of an enterprise that they felt belonged to them. He was so content, he breathed a prayer "Thank You, God."

In the same breath it occurred to him that he had not attended a church worship in years. In that regard, he was like many Jamaicans who were basically religious people, some to the point of being superstitious, but who found it difficult to practise their faith in a systematic way. Many would not trifle with religion. Because they knew they would not abide by the teachings of the church, they refused to become members or even attend worship. Others had been stung by the hypocrisy of people who though far less than perfect, were destructively unforgiving of others.

In his case, so much had been going on, on so many levels of his life, he had simply given up relating to any religious group. Yet, his thoughts of God, and how God had been with him and answered his prayers, remained constant. He was profoundly grateful for God's blessings. But he had been very busy.

Then too, his memory of life in the church was filled with disgust at the contradictions at every level of religious life. It seems that the higher people climbed in the leadership of God's people, the lower were their estimate of themselves and others. The nearer they got to God, the more beastly they became. Church people he knew were filled with malice, revenge, cruelty, lust impatience, hypocrisy, and greed. True he had met and fellowshipped with some loving and wonderful people, but the many whose spiritual passions had been stirred, had no help in controlling their wicked ways.

His attitude of remaining aloof prevailed. In recent years the thought of going to worship had entered his mind. He began to promise himself that one Sunday he would get dressed and attend worship. But he had grown out of the habit. Sometimes Doris would go with a friend, but he would always find something else to do. He had grown wise. He could look behind faces. He understood people. The contrast between Sunday routine and Monday to Saturday behaviour was too sharp. He wanted no part of it.

Nor did he want to be called upon to be the leader of any reform movement. Many times in recent years when he had met friends from his former life, they had suggested that now that he had been trained, it was up to him to contribute to God and his church by leading people back to the right way. He was too aware of the people he had killed in wars, and the emptiness at the centre of his own life. In sober moments he realized that though he had been blessed by God with a loving wife, a darling daughter, and a successful business enterprise, there was an emptiness at the centre of his life that none of his achievements could fill.

There had been times in the middle of a party, or other get together with friends or associates when he would suddenly feel awkward, out of place, and unusually lonely. Sometimes he would withdraw for brief moments to catch up with himself. A short walk in the garden often helped. But he knew that the medicine for the malady he experienced would be a fully renewed relationship with God.

He would have to go to church to still the tumult of voices shouting deep in him that the way to peace was to worship God. Yes, he would get up early one Sunday and go to church.

His thoughts were interrupted by the loud blast of a truck's horn.

"James!" he called to a mechanic "tell that driver the truck needs a good washing. Anywhere it goes, that truck advertises this company. We have to give people a good impression. A clean truck is the best advertising we can give that we care about even small details. Tell him to keep the truck clean and stop racing the engine so much. A new engine costs a lot of money!"

"Yes, sah, Missa Gahd'n. An' by de way, sah, we need some hile filta an gas hile fe de two truck dem we fix ovah dere sah."

"Yes, well, James, you know who takes care of that matter, don't you?"

"Yes, sah, nuh de transportation foreman, sah. But is t'ree day now me tell 'im sah, and we still nuh get none. De truck dem ready fe run, sah, but de foreman a' hol' up we wuk, sah, and de driva dem want dem truck, sah."

"Alright, James, I will talk to Mr. Mac about it. You will get your oil filters and diesel fuel."

"Yes, sah. T'anks, Mr. Gahd'n. Ah will guh an talk to de driva right away sah."

Sammy sighed and moved to his desk. A pile of letters and several documents greeted him. Before attending to them, his eyes moved around the wall of the room. They rested on the oil painting he had commissioned. It was a tastefully done picture of the retreat he had built in the mountains. It had balance. The colours were striking and cheerful. It gave him a feeling of utter satisfaction. Yes. Life was good.

Sammy smiled as he moved a stack of papers to one side and made space for his work. He picked up a document requiring his signature. For a brief moment a cloud overshadowed his face as he thought about the second line of a song. "Eh! bear 'tell i' kill po Sammy" Could that be true of him? No, he thought, he had covered all the bases. He was on good terms with all whose favour he coveted. There was none, who wished him harm. "But a grudgeful naygar grudgeful mek dem kill him," declared the song. He looked towards the ceiling. What more could he do to hedge himself and guard his investments? He looked again at the ceiling. The rafters seemed to be shaking. It seemed for a moment that the building was caving in, coming down and closing in on him.

"No!" he said, denying the foreboding. He had not been aware of a premonition in years. Not since he had returned to Jamaica, anyway. There had been many which had warned him during his days in the trenches of war. There had even been many flashes during his years of growing up. But it had been years since he had seen a sign. He thought he had matured beyond the innate warnings which were like the appearance of a lifelong companion, whose presence always forebode imminent disaster to be avoided.

CHAPTER TWENTY

Kingston, Jamaica, late 1980s

The insistent noise of the ringing telephone finally bored through the deep sleep of the snoring man. He snorted his irritation like a bull in a pasture that has been disturbed by a rock stone thrown by a mischievous schoolboy. He reached for the instrument and pressed the horn against his ear.

"Hullo," he said in a resigned voice that carefully disguised his discomfort.

"I think we got that renkin boy now," said a voice that sounded mixed with both triumph and undisguised malice.

"Eh, Eh! So what happen?' asked the sleepy listener noncommittally.

"I can't tell you over the phone. Meet me somewhere so we can talk."

"Oh?"

"Yes, man. I know we have a way to get rid of him."

"So, what you want me to do?"

"I say let's meet and talk, man."

"Um hmm. What time? Where?"

"Lunch. The usual place."

"All right. See yuh, then, nuh."

"See yuh later, man."

The machine clicked as the caller broke connection. The listener slowly hung up his phone and laid on his back gazing into the dark.

* * * * * * * * * *

At mid-morning of the same day, a secretary approached the desk where Sammy sat. He held a telephone against his ear and was gazing at the ceiling as he talked.

"No man, unless we can get ten container loads it won't be worth my time. We have a whole heap of equipment to keep running ,you know. Yes, man. At least ten containers. And make sure they can get to our place in two weeks, or we will lose money on storage and that kind of thing. Yes, man, then do it, nuh? Alright. Get back to me as soon as you can. Thanks, man. Peace." He hung up and fixed his gaze on the secretary who had been waiting patiently.

"What happen? You look like you just see a ghost."

"Somebody outside to see you, sah. An' I notice that every time him cum here is bad luck him bring. Is not nutten me, kno', is jus' something me feel. Is Missa Myers, sah. 'im wan' know if him can come in an' talk to you, sah."

"Cho, man, is dat weh worry yuh?" chuckled Sammy, lapsing into the patois which he sometimes enjoyed using to show solidarity with the masses of average Jamaicans. Ralph is my good frien' from long time. 'im is alright. Tell him come in, nuh. An' Mirrie, get him some coffee, nuh man."

"Yes, Missa Gahden." She retreated. A look of resignation clouded her usually cheerful countenance.

As she left, her place at the door was filled with a carefully dressed man of medium height and build. His face was expressionless. One could never guess what he was thinking. He wore starched brown khaki pants, polished brown shoes outside ribbed brown socks, and a starched white shirt. His left wrist boasted a gold watch with gold band that smartly contrasted his smooth black skin.

He stood erect in the doorway and quickly appraised the office. He was a replica of the traditional technical school graduate who retained that bearing drilled into him from years of scouting that had given way to years of leading men in a cadet corps, and of course to added physical discipline of playing cricket and soccer at college. He closed the door behind him and strode across the room to Sammy's desk with outstretched hand. Sammy stood to greet him.

"But wait! How yuh do, Ralph. is a long time me nuh see yuh, man! Boy, yuh look well, yuh see!"

"Hi Sammy! yuh look well yuhself, man. How de wife an' daughter?"

"Everybody alright at home, man. Then have a seat, nuh. Mek yuhself comfortable, man."

They shook hands vigorously, and embraced. It was clear that they were glad to see each other. Ralph took the seat to which Sammy pointed, and looked around the room. His gaze took in the paintings, the large aquarium with colourful fish swimming among rocks and greenery, the polished desk with a picture of his wife and daughter in neat gold frames.

"Man, yuh look like you prospering in dis place," said Ralph.

"Me a gwan, man, me a gwan. Everything is beautiful, tenk Gad."

"Well, I don't really want anything important, I was jus' passing by and decided to drop in an' say hello to my old friend. I pass by here a lot, you know, but I am always too busy to stop. An' I know you are a busy man too."

"Yes, man, you know I am never too busy for you, Ralph. You can stop by anytime, man. Anytime. Anyway, what's going on with your business, nowadays. You get another promotion?"

"My business is cool man. Yes, I am a full Inspector now."

"Congratulations, man. I hope they know that they can't find a better Jamaican than you. You are loyal to your country, tough, and you know your job inside and out. It's a good move they made , Ralph. Both for them and for you. Congratulations, man."

"Yes, I work hard for it and I am proud for the promotion. But, by the way, when I was coming through the gate, I notice that one of your pretty dwarf coconut tree dem have something like rust pon de leaf; you did notice it?"

Every sense in Sammy became immediately alert. There was more to the casual comment than just rusting leaves, and he knew it. So, this visit was not as casual as had been stated. He became attuned to his friend.

"No, sah, me nevah did bother to look at those things. I leave that to the yard man. Yuh think is something I need to worry about?"

"Sammy, you can't be too careful nowadays you know. Even though you have good men working for you, you have to look after every little detail. Jus' one likkle problem lef' alone, in one likkle place, an' before you know it you lose every thing you plant."

"Eh, eh! Weh you a seh?" Sammy said softly. "Den mek we guh outside and look pon it nuh. Maybe we need to do something to protect the tree them."

"Yes, I think that would be a good idea."

The two friends got up and left the office. As they walked out into the reception area, Sammy called to tell the secretary that they would be back shortly. They descended a flight of steps and were out in the wide open yard of the busy establishment.

"Suh, wha' a gwan, Ralph?" asked Sammy, turning with concern to his friend. "Yuh have something to tell me?"

"Bway, I come across something that I think vuh need to know about. It may not be much, but when my ears prick up and I get a funny feeling, I just like to check things out."

"Uh huh. So what happen?"

"We buck up on a telephone conversation that kinda signal that something going down uptown. Wha' happen is that one of my men was running a check on some phone calls when we hear a strange piece of communication. Some man whom we won't identify was telling his friend quote "we got de likkle renkin bwoy now. I think we got him." Well, after I studied the message, is only three men I know fit the profile according to who make the statement. One of them is you. So, since we did pledge from way back to look out for one another, I feel like I had better give you an early warning. It may not be you, but the more time you have to look after yourself, the better off you will be."

"I see," said Sammy contemplatively. "Now, from what you hear, and from who did the talking, did you get the feeling that whatever they may mean would be personal violence, political, or business sabotage?"

"Hard to tell. The message did not register long, and the man who called was careful. There is supposed to be a meeting for further talks somewhere at lunch time today. I tell you what, I will have my men check out some places. If we find anything I will let you know. Remember what I said. You are not the only one who the situation fits. But I am concerned about your safety. In this present day Jamaica, you can't be too careful.

"Ralph, whichever way this situation goes, I am grateful to you."

"No problem, man, you would do the same for me. I know that. I didn't even wait to get everything before I came to you. As soon as I get anything else you will have it right away. But see your secretary coming here, let's change the subject. Yes, man, see that branch up there, is that one I'm talking about. I don't know all that much about coconut, but I believe you should get a good man to check it out."

"You know, it does look a little unusual. I think I know a man who can come and take a look at it and give me some good advice. If you can find one, send him over too. I wouldn't want to see an epidemic destroy all the healthy trees in this area."

"Well, I was just passing by, Sammy. I promise to stop by again soon. I have another meeting in half an hour an' you know about this Kingston traffic. It's murder this time of the day."

"Ralph, thanks for dropping by. Why don't you come up to the house one evening for a drink? It would be nice to see you. And bring the wife , is time we all get together again. We just have to take time to enjoy our families, you know. Life is so short!"

"Yes, man. We mus' do that. See you later. Bye, Miss Johnson."

"Bye, Missa Myers." Mirrie watched as the police officer retreated. Her gaze was speculative and hostile.

"I don't care what yuh seh, Missa Gahden, every time I see that man, I feel like him carry trouble 'roun' with him."

"Mirrie, Ralph an' I have been bosom friends from our days at Dentwood a long time ago. Ralph is a good man. How come yuh, can't like him. What him ever do to you?"

"Him nevah do me nutt'n sah, but ever since I was a little girl, I jus' can't stan' police. Me kno' seh dem necessary, but me jus' nuh like dem roun' me at all. Oh, Missa Gahden, is an important overseas call for you, sah. Dem still waiting on de line. You can come right away, sah?"

"Yes, I'm coming. Go and tell them I'll be right there."

He turned to see Ralph stopped at the gate and talking to a guard.

"By the way, Inspector!" he called. "Just a moment, please." Ralph walked back towards him.

"Listen, what are the chances you could get me a copy of that tape? Maybe I could get some helpful information from listening to it more than once. If you are right, a danger to any of the three you are thinking of, could directly or indirectly affect the lives of the other two. I could run some checks of my own and see what I can find."

"Let me think about it, Sammy. I will see what I can do." He turned, walked through the gate, around a corner of the protective wall along the roadway, and disappeared. There was a sound of a motor being started, a roar of finely tuned engine, a squealing of tires, then silence.

A chill ran through Sammy as he climbed the stairs to his office. He was aware that he had developed enemies. Unintentionally, but as he became successful there were those who envied him. For no other reason than that he had become successful where they had failed. They knew how he had developed from his years overseas, and the caring respect with which he treated his workers, yielded him dividends in loyalty and efficient production that others could not understand.

Yet, his naive goodwill had made him flash money carelessly in places and quantities that had embarrassed and disturbed many. There were those who had in the past had hoards of money but the new Jamaica had taxed them. Much of what they still owned was stashed overseas or given to their children as largesse. These now experienced cash deficit and were not benefiting from the new government as they had the old. Sammy had been flourishing where they had been in decline. Then his need to bolster his flagging ego had made him brag where he should have been reserved. The fact is that his years away had not helped to prepare him for dealing with the traditional aristocracy, with whom he had to associate on a daily basis.

Jamaicans hated braggarts. By the time he had learned the valuable lessons of quiet reserve and modest diplomacy, the damage had been done. Many big men were really very small and sensitive where their egos were concerned. Then ,if the whole truth were to be told, Sammy was a casualty of the reverse racism he had learned in America. He was home and associating with Jamaican white men, and light skin men who believed they were white. The chances he had to prosper as a black man in his homeland, made him feel the need to flaunt his skills and his successes. But he never intended to hurt anyone. Only to help his people survive.

Yes, he had made enemies. He wondered who could hate so strongly as to go to the trouble of plotting to do him harm. Faces and circumstances began to surface from the morass of congealed animosity he had concocted over the years. He took each step of the stairs deliberately as his mind unscrolled events and places across eight years of his life as a big time operator among the wealthiest and most powerful Jamaicans. He crossed the space of the plush carpet and picked up the telephone.

"Hello," he said.

Chapter Twenty-One

Kingston, Jamaica, late 1980s

The corner table in a secluded area of the dining room at Devon House was ideal. An animated conversation was taking place between the two men. They were fair skinned but deeply tanned. One had the straight brown hair of the pure blooded Jamaican white. The other was fair but his curly hair told the tale of a "dip of the tar brush". He was the more voluble as he waved a loaded fork in the general direction of his table partner.

"Frank, the study is clear. There will be a clean sweep in the next election. People are tired of scarce goods and empty shelves. They are tired of big talk and nothing to show for it. They are tired of borrowing money from every little barefoot, hurry come up nation. Frank, I'm telling you, Jamaica is an embarrassment to the whole world!"

"Yes, I know what you mean. So, how reliable is this study you talking about?"

"It has never failed yet. But even without the study, you can walk through Jamaica and talk to anybody and they will tell you the same. Things can't get any worse. Things must change or we will end up like Bangladesh, or Haiti. And I for one am glad that people are beginning to wake up. This government may have had some good ideas at the start, but we are in big trouble now. I personally told them that you can't get new people to take over the country and expect things to happen. We have failed. All our money is gone away, and all the people with the skills have absconded. Everybody, who is anybody has gone. Our friends are never coming back, Frank."

"Well, there is no doubt that what you are saying is true, Bobby, but the way out of this mess is not as clear to me as it is to you."

"Frank, the answer is a change of government. Another election. You know that we have always let the people of the country decide since we are considered to be the traditional trouble makers. For a long time now we have stood back and let the common people vote and decide. But we have to do something to save what we have left. All the old money is gone. Jamaica is bankrupt. As far as I am concerned, the lowest blow was when we had to go and borrow from little Trinidad. Boy, its going to take a long time for me to get over that humiliation. But for me, personally, when that little black dutty sore foot boy stood up at that trade conference and started talking about putting ten million dollars in an investment, I was ready to die and go home to my dead people them. I never did know that any black man in Jamaica could wield so much power and control so much liquid cash. I tell you, that boy is dangerous. If we let him survive, more like him will rise up, then is goodbye to everything our foreparents have cherished in this country. If we don't stop him now, he will buy and sell all of us and look in our faces and laugh. Like he is doing already."

"Bobby, I believe you are right in your assessment of the political and economic situation. But just why do you consider this man such a force to contend with? You know that one of the goals of my father was that the black Jamaican should rise to take over responsibility for himself. This is a new Jamaica. We are no longer slave-holders and slaves. I for one agree that economic franchise should be opened to every Jamaican who is able to responsibly manage power and influence. We have tried to identify the responsible ones and groom them for leadership, lowly of course. So, what is the danger you see in this maturing young man?"

"Frank, this particular man stands for everything that is wrong with giving privilege to people before they have learned how to be modest. The boy defies the very principle you have been talking about. He has come up too fast. He owes nothing to any of us in the establishment so he has no respect for us. He owes us no gratitude because we did not create him. If we let him flourish on his own, then he and those who admire him will believe they can just spring up and take over like they own this country. We must protect the avenues to success and permit only a groomed few to pass through, or we will lose control over our traditional way of life. If we let these eager new people who go away overseas for a few years and come back with new ideas take over, then new and careless ways of managing business will creep in. Credit will destroy hard currency, conservative ways of managing business will fly away. We will have to try to keep up instead of setting the pace. The boy is dangerous first of all because he is sure that he does not need us. Second, he will introduce the American mindset into Jamaica in which everything is hurry and big profits, and big credit. Soon, our economy will be so heated that we will lose everything. People will get big eye and try to buy and collect more than they can afford. And last of all, I just don't like him because he is facety. And I know just how to 'spoke' his wheel. I'm telling you, we have to do it, Frank!"

"Well, tell me what you have in mind."

"As I said, the polls show that our Party will win the next election. So, all we have to do is plan ahead. As you see, shelves in shops are empty. People with licences to buy goods are short of cash. In fact, they are not even allowed to take money out of the island. All we have to do is encourage the next government to help the poor people by permitting them to go where food, commodities, and haberdasheries are cheap, and bring them back and undercut the present market system."

"So, how is that going to hurt your friend?"

"Simple. He has his factory to produce goods, and a special franchise from the government protects him. If the new government opens up the market to all who can find cheap goods that the poor people need, several things will happen. Many more people will benefit by getting into the mercantile action. The things they bring in will be selling for cheaper than the boy can produce it. Within twelve months he will be a financial corpse. His business depends on protection. If the new government can be shown that they don't need him and in fact will get more from an open market, he will be dead. There is no way he can undersell the flood of cheap goods we will turn loose on the market," He chuckled happily. "The boasy naygar boy is as good as dead!"

"So," said Frank speculatively. "You will kill two birds with one stone. You will convince the government to help the little man in a broader way than your friend is now doing. Putting more people to work than the couple of thousand he employs, while at the same time get your revenge against this nasty little man whom you despise."

"That's it. I know that some poor people will lose their jobs as a result of this action. but any time there is progress, there is bound to be a reshuffling of the system. In time, new jobs will be created and the loyal employees of "Mr. Boasy man" will not even remember him in two years. People won't mind if an institution dies if they can get cheap stuff to meet their needs."

"Well, I hope you are not cutting off your nose to spite your face, Bobby. Long before the Gun Courts, we have seen an increase in the inclination of some Jamaicans to be violent. We have managed to control it with great effect. But Jamaicans are not easily fooled. An they easily follow sly leadership. Like Bro. Mongoose and Bro. Anancy, Jamaicans quickly discern tricks and they quickly employ them. It seems we will be turning loose some dogs in this country without knowing ahead of time what the consequences will be. I hope you have carefully thought through all the possible results and can live with them."

"Oh, it's been carefully thought through, Frank. Don't believe I am the only one who wants to get rid of that fellow."

"Yes, well, times have changed. We just can't be touchy and insanely protective of our prerogatives as in the old days. If we don't live and let live, we will lose everything. And let's face it. There's no use going to Britain, Europe, Canada, or even the United Sates to escape the new egalitarianism. It is sprouting up all over the world. I believe even South Africa and Australia will have to come in out of the cold and become a part of the new world that is breaking in upon us. I can't say I am not offended and disturbed by the freshness of some of these new black people, but we have to bend as we face new events or be swept away as so much foam off the surface of the thundering flood. I guess you will do what your mind tells you, Bobby, and I will not stand in the way of you and your friends. But I believe a note of caution is required. After all, if the new government moves too far in the direction you suggest, their strategy will become transparent and they will not last long in office. The fact that the present government made some terrible mistakes does not mean it is not admired by the masses for the fresh approach it took to solving massive third world problems. The people will vote for a change instead of starving, but they will hold deep inside them the memory of the noble and creative intentions of the very party they are booting out."

"You know, Frank, in all the years I have known you, this is the longest speech I ever heard you make. I didnt know you had it in you. You really sympathize with these bastards, don't you? If I didn't know better I would believe that after all these years you have got soft and would sacrifice all the centuries of labours of our foreparents to these lazy, idealistic 'hurry come up' peasants."

"Bobby, pardon what I am going to say. You know me better than to think me a mean spirited person. Pardon me, but look at your hands before you get too far removed from the realities of this country. Remember that if you are going to really choose sides, you can live only in Jamaica as a red man. Anywhere else in the world you go, they will have another name for you. You are more than a cousin to me, and a grown man free to do as you please. I will even back you as far as I can. But have some sense! Jamaica is too small to divide up in so many little pieces. It is not necessary any longer to assert your place by denying a place to others."

The fork dropped from Bobby's hand. His face reddened, and his shoulders drooped. He appeared to have been struck a mortal blow. Frank reached over and grabbed his best friend.

"Man, listen to me. 'Sticks and stones may break my bones'. Don't let my words to you go any further than I intended. I merely caution you to realize two things. First, as I said before, times have changed. This is not the Jamaica of our grandparents or even our parents. We have to decide whether this land is still our home or not. If we are to leave, we can leave. But if we are to stay we must realize that the old rigid lines we used to enjoy against other people can no longer exist. Second, for every action there is a reaction. You may get your pound of flesh out of this black boy whom you despise, but there could be disastrous consequences if you encourage the new government you foresee to institute economic policies that undermine the creative attempts of this present government to encourage indigenous self development. Our economic base must broaden itself to accommodate present economic realities. Whatever the future holds for Jamaica, it seems clear to me that dependence on traditional production of traditional raw materials for traditional markets is folly. To focus on supplying cheap goods to a hungry populace without addressing the question about the need for a constant flow of capital to drive our economy, is to dig a hole in the ground that will lead straight to hell for all of us. Please don't be hurt or offended by the stark piece of reality I introduced to jar you into our place in Jamaica and our world today. That's all I have to say on the subject."

The Jamaican white man stood up. His sharp angular face and regal nose spoke of British origins. His tanned features told of years beneath the tropical sun. His companion also stood. He was taller. Big boned. His golden yellow features identified him as of white and black blood lines. Fixed by generations of careful mulatto inter-breeding. His countenance was a study of fixed frustration and confusion. The white moved close to his friend, placed a fraternal hand around his shoulders and said something. A broad grin spread across the face of the larger man, erasing his self-absorption and relaxing the tension that had developed around them. Their bonding across several generations of family ties remained intact. Together, arm in arm, they walked away from the table.

Neither of them cast a second glance at the two stockily built black men seated at the nearby table. Dressed in Nehru style bush jackets, the black men seemed engrossed in business. As the two white and near white friends left the restaurant, with loud laughs the black businessmen concluded their lunch, pulled back their chairs, and moved towards the parking lot.

Chapter Twenty-Two

Kingston, 1992

The once busy showroom was now as silent as a cemetery. A single light bulb high in the ceiling shed a ghostly glow where once multiple globes of incandescent fire illuminated the place as bright as noonday.

Sammy sat on the steps in the shadows and listened as the ghosts of former voices filled the gloom. A skeleton crew shuffled about the vast space dutifully sweeping and cleaning.

Now, severely wounded again, though not physically this time, he shook his head to clear his mind of the vision. How could he pick up this sledge? He walked "woundedly" to his office, closed the door and dialed a phone number.

"Let me speak to Mr. Grant, please."

"Yes, sir. Is this Mr. Gordon?"

"Yes, hello, my dear, how are you?"

"Just fine, Mr. Gordon. One moment for Mr. Grant, Please."

"Sammy! How are you my friend?"

"Bway, you know more than I do what happen to me."

"Yes. We could see it coming, but still things happen too fast, didn't they?"

"Man, my back is against the ropes, you know. Anyway, my bills are paid up, right?"

"Sammy, you have always been a responsible man. We appreciate that. So, what you have in mind?"

"Well, people used to say, 'if you can't lick them, join them'. My business is dead, but I think I can get in this new game and meet the present market needs like all these new fellas are doing. I have some contacts and know how to get some cheap stuff at a good price. I want to get a few container loads of things in here and make some money to compensate for what I have lost from this new regime."

"Well, that may not be a bad idea."

"Yes, I used to sing "new occasions teach new duties." I have to try to get into this new game they are playing nowadays. I don't agree with it, but in this desperate situation I have to do what I can."

"Well, you have always been a good customer. I see no reason why we can't work with you in this situation. Let me know what you need and I will do all I can to help."

"Thanks a lot friend. I'll be in touch as soon as I have some details worked out. Take care."

"Okay, man. Check you later."

"Right Oh!"

Sammy hung up. He dialed another number and spoke briefly.

"Everything is settled. Release the containers and make sure they get here by Friday. I want my stuff on the market first thing Monday morning before other traffic flood the place."

"What?"

"Your money will leave here tomorrow by noon. Will I get the things?"

"Yes man. Good deal. I'll rush the things right away."

"Yes, I know what the new laws say about big shipments, but this is a one time deal. By the time they realize what happen, I will have made my deal and be out of the country. Jamaica is getting too hostile for me nowadays."

"Man, just do your part. I'll take care of my end over here."

"Good deal. I have a man over at Customs who will clear things for me. He is a good man. Okay , Eddie, we can't stay on the line too long. Talk to you later. Righty, Bye."

* * * * * * * * *

Sammy closed the office door behind him. The sound made an unusually loud noise in the empty space. He did not speak to anyone as he went to his car and started the engine. He waved at the guards at the gate in his usual warm manner. He turned into the traffic and headed east towards the centre of the city.

It was a sunny Sunday evening when the stiffly starched police officer with his shiny Sam Brown belt stretched across his muscular torso, paused to speak to a well dressed man at the entrance to a compound beyond which several office buildings could be seen. The officer's Land Rover contrasted with the shiny brown Volvo of his prosperous looking companion.

"So, he thinks he can escape us that easily, huh? He just doesn't realize that we have eyes on him and are watching his every move. Tear down the place and expose the contraband. Make sure that none of his goods escapes. Seize everything and hold it. Make sure the newspapers get a good look at the things. Then let's see how he's going to pay his bills. If he wants to run away he can, but we must teach him that he can't trifle with this new government."

The man drove away. His minions had their orders. Unmarked cars were dispatched. Soon, containers of contraband goods were pried open and seized. With the wrenching of crowbars and the belching of trucks pulling away trailers, the once bustling empire of a black Jamaican came rumbling, tumbling down.

In desperation, without first calling, Sammy speeded to the residence of the former Minister, now MP. Unlatching the gate, he bounded up the walk, climbed the scarlet steps, and punched the doorbell. Chained dogs barked furiously at the unwelcome stranger. In quick moments the door opened and there standing before him, clothes disheveled, face swollen, and eyes bloodshot, was the Minister. A fear seized Sammy as shades of an ancient memory crowded his mind. A day in Water Lane a lifetime ago came back in full force.

"What yuh want?" demanded the Minister new MP, no note of recognition in his voice.

"Minister, I need help" babbled Sammy. "Can I talk to you, sir?"

"Help? Help? Unnu help me enough when I lost the election, what more yuh want?"

"But, Minister, I am deep in debt. I mortgage everything I have to help you win, sir."

"Well, I win and our party lose. Now clear out of my yard. You hear me? I said clear out!"

"Minister, I beg you, please listen to me."

"Where the damn watchman? How did you get in here anyway? Watchie! Watchie! Turn the dogs loose on this man. His is trespassin' Turn the dogs loose and fasten the gate right now!" Sammy fled. Stunned, he drove in a daze and found himself back at his empty factory. He felt that he had no place else to go.

Sammy sat dejectedly on a stump behind the wire fence. He drew in quick and deep breaths and inhaled them in the typical Jamaican show of distress.

"Ayy, Sah!" he exclaimed.

He walked up the stairs and sat at his desk without really seeing anything. He toyed with a paper weight. The telephone rang.

"Hello?" he said with a kind of hopeful questioning in his voice.

"Bway, some cocanat a get ready fe drap. Mek sure seh none a dem nuh drap pon yuh head. Yuh don' have much time, suh look out fe yuh self."

"A wha' yuh a seh? Man, I thought they had hurt me badly enough as it is."

"Masta, I thought it was jus yuh business dem afta, but something change dem min', now dem afta blood."

"Fe true?"

"Is blood dem afta now. I don' know when, but I don' think you have much time. As a matter of fact, I can't talk to you any more right now. Too dangerous. Suh, take care of yuh self man, and good luck. Yuh are going to need it. I'll catch up wid you when I can." The caller hung up.

Tremors of shock wracked Sammy. He felt cornered. In all honesty, he wondered, what had he done to anyone to incur such malicious and personal violence? His mind raced to the days when in distant places he had wondered what he was doing endangering his life for causes that had little to do with where his home country nestled among the bays of the western Caribbean. He had endeavoured to keep himself alive, to have something of value to invest with his own people. He recalled how he could not wait to keep promises to his country that had been deeply ingrained in him in song and story long ago. And this moment of anxiety and cowering fear was the result of his devotion.

What he had not taken into account was that those Jamaicans who had not migrated were developing along separate lines. With totally different sets of experiences and formations than had been his. His memories had been frozen in time. Theirs had extended along lines he could never understand.

So much had happened in the years since independence. A new educational system had infused values that stressed the new without recalling the old. Years of economic depression had fostered keen drives to self help without much abiding love for others. Everyone was seen as possible sources of scarce commodities, but never as potential friends. Indeed, the once friendly Jamaica had become a land of grasping individuals who for the most part felt victimized, and held resentment to all who were party to their victimization. They were therefore not in a mood to welcome repatriates with open arms. Many saw those returning home as traitors and adventurers who left when things got tough and thought they could return with Yankee Dollar or British Pound to lord it over them.

He roused himself and shook his head. He pulled out a desk drawer and saw a New Testament lying where he had placed it some long time before. Mechanically, he lifted the booklet and began thumbing through the pages. He found himself reading from Psalm 23. "Yea, though I walk through the valley of death I will fear no evil." He read the words again as if he had discovered them for the first time. "I will fear no evil." His mind began to race. Lessons learned from soldiering returned. The best defence is a strong offence. Think.

He became methodical. Calm. He was again the fighting man in charge of defending his perimeter. He went into a back room and opened a carton box which lay on the floor under a stack of others. He lifted out the box and opened it. There beneath a number of wrenches, pliers, and tubes of lubricant, wrapped in oilskin, was a pair of service automatic weapons of heavy calibre. He removed the wrapping and observed their clean, oiled, and well preserved condition. He held them like long last friends and hefted them to feel their balance and weight. Expertly, he pulled back the safety and checked magazines. He removed the clips and replaced them with new ones. He carefully wiped every vestige of the oil from them, then placed one in his pants pocket. He carried the other in his hand. He returned to his desk and began to read again. This time, words from the Gospel of John held his attention "Let not your heart be troubled, ye believe in God, believe also in me". His mind wandered.

Let's see. If danger is to come, and soon, how would it happen. It could be an automobile accident. It could be an attack at his home. It could be a chance encounter at one of his frequent meeting places. He could be waylaid on a visit to his farm. Or, it could be an encounter here at the store. But that would have to be very soon. The place was closing down. It could be an employee that has been laid off, or one that was disgruntled about something. Or one bought out by an enemy who paid high wages for special services rendered. Well, it would be coming. And as best he could, he would be ready. Now, he had that sharp quick mental picture of foreboding .He saw a brown rumpled heap in a corner. But the image did not remain long enough for him to concentrate on it. He had seen it before. He shelved it for now. He had to think. The telephone rang. He picked it up carefully as if it were a poisonous spider.

"Yes?" It was the guard at the front gate. Sammy exhaled slowly in relief.

"Mr. Gahden, is a man out here sah, seh him cum tuh talk to yuh 'bout cocanat tree, sah."

"I'm by himself?"

"No, sah, two odder man dem in de Jeep wid him, sah."

"Alright, let dem in nuh. But Busta, nuh let in nobody else until I tell you. You hear? Nobody, not even my family. Keep everyone off the premises until I tell you is alright." He hung up the phone. Then instinct lifted him from the chair and drove him to the window. He peered out and watched as the three men parked the vehicle. It took only a moment for him to appraise them and reclose the blinds.

Once more he was the warrior. He felt every sense in his body responding to his alert mind at fever pitch of efficient performance. He was defending his territory. His office was specially built for personal security. The walls, ten inches thick, were constructed of concrete reinforced with steel. Anyone in that room was virtually his prisoner. There was no escape except by the door through which they entered, or by a back door, unknown to everyone, behind his desk. He was still enough a soldier to handle any three men especially with the element of surprise.

He waited for his visitors with a steely calm. He knew what would come later. He heard the men laughing and talking as they climbed the stairs. Sammy focused all his attention on the door before him. The knock came.

"The door is open. Come in! Come in!!" he said.

The knob turned and a tall black man in khaki pants and shirt ,with shined black shoes entered the room.

"Good afternoon, Mr. Gordon. You must remember me, sah."

"Oh, yes, I remember you, man. What happen? What brings you here today?" As he asked the question, he studied the man before him. How smart of his enemies to send a man who had access to him. So, the planned execution was to be in his office. He smiled. Poor Myers, he thought. Even the inner circles of the detective force were not secure from traitors in the new Jamaica. There were some men of honour left, he knew. Especially among the older ones of his generation. Hunger and absence of values had made the new breed susceptible to purchase by the highest bidder. Every skill in Jamaica was now for sale. The new political axiom, "No permanent friends; no permanent enemies," was sweeping across the landscape of interpersonal relations in every quarter. Perhaps the new axiom was "No friends; no enemies. Just conveniences to achieve personal goals." Not even blood family could really be trusted anymore. A deep sadness enveloped Sammy. He concluded that the weapon was in the small of the back as no telltale bulges were evident. Or maybe the colleagues who were still hidden from view would do the killing. This one may just be the Judas goat to set his mind at ease and make him careless.

"Yes, sah. Is me Detective Lambert. Inspector Myers did send me to talk to you about some coconut trees some months ago."

So, he was uneasy about the deed he had been paid to do. Or, did he know enough about Sammy to be cautious? This amateurish sign of nervousness should not be part of a man trained by Myers. Some steps had been missed. More the pity. But it is never easy to betray members of one s own select group. It is done. It is never easy.

"Yes, Mr. Lambert. I said I remember you. Myers didn't tell me you were coming. How can I help you today?" That should heighten his unease. I am signaling that he is not here as per our prescribed arrangement.

"Well sah, I did go home to St. Thomas and buck up on two of my friends from Agriculture. I told them about your problem and did promise that the next time they were in town they would come and check out your trees. They had to be at a conference this morning so I decided that it would be a good time to bring them by. I hope you don't mind."

Excellent, thought Sammy. So they were in the outer office awaiting an invitation to enter. He wanted them all in the room where no concrete wall would protect anyone or allow them to escape.

"Good man. Tell them to come in, nuh."

"Yes, sah." Lambert turned his head towards the door and called. "Tony! Alfred! Come in here!"

The men came through the door into the room. As they moved towards the desk, Lambert seemed to casually move his hand as if to reach for a handkerchief in his back pocket. As quickly as a striking snake, Sammy shot him twice in the stomach. Even as the gargantuan man collapsed, Sammy dropped to the floor and before the frightened men could clumsily reach for their concealed weapons, they were dispatched by the deadly coughing of the silenced automatic guns in his steady hands.

Once more he was grateful for the prescience that had finally bored through his mind and helped him prepare a surprise for his death angels. The call from Myers had helped. The images in his mind had clinched the warning. What now agitated him was his elimination of these men who were of the kind he had sworn long ago to protect with his very life. How could these renegades have given up the high privilege and honour of service to their country as to cavalierly deceive their superiors and settle for mere money as reward? True, he now needed what he had forgotten, that, it had been only a few weeks that he had spent in the force with Myers after he had left a job in Clarendon, but the oaths of loyalty they had taken were intended for a lifetime and were supposed to be transferable to all who ever wore the red seam or the private garb of detectives. In the vicious war against the criminal elements they were to stand back to back, and be the wall of defence of each other against a hostile world.

There on the floor, oozing out their life at his feet, were comrades who came to him as agents of death. He had no choice. It had come to this. Jamaica was now an armed camp with every man's hand at the throat of his brother. All in the name of getting rich. Escaping hunger.

Escaping disrespect. Buying prestige at any cost. The future, if there was one, was bleak. The sickly smell of hot human blood reached his nose and he began the familiar trembling that always accompanied every kill. He was nauseated. He sat as a weakness overcame him. He wiped cold sweat as tears streamed down his face. A self-pity blanketed him. After moments of sobbing, he pulled himself together and blew his nose in a handkerchief, he picked up the telephone.

"Yes sah, Missa Gahden."

"Ummm, uhm." He cleared his throat and removed the last vestige of tension from his voice. "Busta?"

"Yes, sah?"

"Um, who out there on that front gate with you?"

"Nuh me an' Willie, sah."

"Uh hmm. An' who is at the two gate them down there?"

"Well, is Shorty and Bulla at de warehouse, an' Jahnny an' Brendan down at de back dere sah."

"Alright, I need you to do me a special favour, you see, so here is what you do. Tell Johnny to chain and fasten the back gate, padlock it and put the key in his pocket, then tell Brendon to look sharp and make sure that nobody come over the fence or crash the gate. You hear? Then tell Johnny to come up front and stay with Willie. Tell them to let nobody through the front gate until I tell them. Tell them I get some news that some prisoners escape and may be coming this way, so they must look sharp and don't let anyone on the premises. If they see even a fly crawling over the walls they must call me right away. Okay? Then you hurry and come up here Busta. We have a little problem here and I need you right now. Hurry!"

In brief minutes there was a knock at the door. Sammy could tell from the familiar footsteps that it was his trained and trusted guard. He crossed to the door and let him in. Busta's eyes went wide and his lips parted. But his training stood him in good stead. Sammy placed a finger on his lips to indicate silence. He no longer trusted the integrity of his office. He would check again for any compromise to his safety in the room.

"Well as you can see, we have some soiled carpet here. I don't know how this garbage got in my office while I was outside, but we have to clean up the place. Look in that back room and you will see some bolt ends of material. Bring out some of the dark brown one and help me wrap up this trash."

"Yes, sah," said Busta, wrinkling his face as he stepped over the bodies.

He returned dragging two rolls of fabric which he began to unroll on the floor beside the inert bodies. Sammy bent beside him.

"Examine them good, first, Busta. Whatever you find is yours to keep. I mean everything you find is yours. These men came in here to kill me. I got them first because you were smart enough to do your job and call me. I can't thank you enough. Now, let's pack them up."

He helped Busta roll the corpse into mummies, tucking in both ends of the bolts. Then they dragged the three bundles into the darkened back room.

They then returned to the office and carefully rolled up the stained carpet and underlining. These were used to cover the bodies. They formed a large crumpled heap in a corner of the storage room. Sammy looked and shook his head in astonishment.

From among standing bolts of materials, a large roll of padding was lifted and moved into the office. With grunts and pulling, a new covering was installed, followed by carpeting of the exact colour as that removed. The floor looked as if nothing unusual had happened. The two of them sat down, weary from their efforts. A mere hour had passed since Busta had made his appearance.

Sammy opened a closet and removed two glasses and a bottle of brandy. From a small refrigerator he retrieved a tray ice. He poured generous portions of liquid in the glasses and dropped in the pieces of ice. He handed a glass to his helper.

"You know these men came in here to kill me, Busta?" he said conversationally.

"Yes sah, I did see the gun dem pon de body dem sah. But wha" mek enny baddy wan' fe hurt a nice man like you, Missa Gahden? Yuh treat every baddy fair. Yuh is a nice an' decent man. Suh, wha' mek dem wan' fe kill yuh, sah?"

"Busta, I really don't know. But I have to get away from here for awhile. You know if they try once and fail they have to try again. So, I will have to go under cover for awhile."

"Yes sah, ah t'ink yuh right sah."

"So here is what we going to do. First thing is we have to get rid of the vehicle. Here are my keys. You drive my car like you are going on an errand for me. Then I will go and get the Land Rover and park it round the back of the building. Just tell Willie that you soon come back. He don't need to know anything else. Come back in about fifteen minutes. Park the car, come in, then go back to the front gate. Send Willie to cover the back gate and tell him he is in charge back there until further notice. When it gets dark, tell Johnny to take care of the front while you come talk to me. Then you come up here and we will load the bodies and the carpet in the van."

"We will dispose of them. Then I will have to go somewhere, but I will keep in touch with you. After Friday, this place will close anyway. Mass George will pay everybody on Friday, but I will keep you on the payroll for one full year until I know what I am going to do. Your job will be to come and look over the place every once in awhile. Okay. Go back to the gate now and I will see you in a little while."

Sammy was alone. His mind was cool and functioning like a tuned machine. Somehow, his movements were being monitored and relayed. Information from his office was getting to his enemies. His monthly security sweep of his office had been negative when done two weeks before. He had been too trusting. He examined every stitch of his office carefully. Then he saw something that he had not seen before. It was small and apparently insignificant. But it had with deadly accuracy relayed his every word to his enemies. An anger flashed through him.

He picked up his telephone and dialed a number.

"Hallo?" said a cautious voice

"The boys you sent can't pick coconut, man. Nex't time, send some men that know how to climb tall trees." He slammed down the phone. A look of extreme fury was on his face. He reached for his glass and downed the drink. It relaxed him. He knew that somewhere in this city telephones were ringing. There would be heavy discussions before another operation would be attempted against him. He figured that he had at least a few hours to relax. He would need all his energy later. He left the building quickly, got into his Isuzu sports utility vehicle and disappeared into the night.

* * * * * * * * *

It was three months later when he considered it safe enough to make contact with his home. He found a public telephone and dialed his home number.

"Hello" said the familiar soprano voice.

"Maggie, let me speak to Mrs. Gordon."

"Oh Lawd, Missa Gahden! Is which part yuh stay suh lang, sah? Me seh we wurried to deat' 'bout yuh, yuh kno', sah!"

"Yes, then quick, Maggie, let me talk to Mrs. Gordon. I don't have much time on the telephone."

"Den Lawd, sah, is nuh dat me a try fe tell yuh ,sah. Miz Gahden an' Miss Linda gone weh since las' week, sah."

"What you mean, gone away? Where did they go?"

"Back a 'Merica, sah. When she did get de news fram Missa Myas seh yuh naw cum back fe a long time, and yuh inna heap a trouble, and w'en she did try fe guh inna de factory an' some police man dem try fe arres' har, she did come back yah an' call har madda. Har madda start fe quarrel an' seh 'bout de firs' time she set yeye pon yuh, she did kno' seh yuh was trubble and don' mean har dawta no good. Suh a whole heap a dem come dung yah las' week an' help har pack up har sinting dem, an' she gawn sah. She tell me fe tell yuh, if yuh call, dat she took as much sufferin fram yuh as ennybaddy suppos' fe tek in dis life. Suh yuh nuh fe badda try fe contac har, sah. She tell me an' Joe fe stay here an' keep up de place till we hear from yuh, ar until police seize it. She seh nutten in dis worl' will evah bring har back ovah ya, she is t'rough wid Jamaica an' Jamaicans. Dem too crabbit, sah."

"Uh huh. So, anybody else call or leave any message for me?"

"O yes sah, one man call, seh fi tell yuh seh jelly cocanat can' mek rice an'peas, an dem nah guh have no dry cocanat roun' Kingston fe a long, long time. But me see plenty a good cocanat inna de market suh me nuh know what dat man a talk 'bout, sah."

"Ah hah."

"Suh when yuh a come home, sah, wha' yuh want me an' Joe fe duh?"

"Maggie, thanks for everything. Just stay there till you get a message from me. I wont call you again for awhile. Keep the house and water the plants. Feed the fish, the birds, the fowl and the animals. You will get your salary every month, just as usual. Thanks, you hear. If Mrs. Gordon should call, just tell her I said:

"A nuh tief, Sammy tief, mek dem kill him,"

"But a grudgeful, naygar grudgeful mek dem kill him."

Can you remember that?"

"Yes sar, we use fe sing dat sang long time ago, when I was in school."

"All right then, take care, Maggie."

"Yes sah, Missa Gahden, an' before..."

The line went dead.

Chapter Twenty-Three

South Manchester, March, 1995

After awhile, none of the people who lived around him had paid much attention to the man everybody called "Captain". He had moved in mysteriously some three years before. He wore the dreadlocks and tam of a Rasta man and his clothing was always old and worn but clean. He kept much to himself but was polite to anyone he met with his standard greeting of "Peace and Love". In present day Jamaica few things or people were as they appeared, so everyone kept his or her own counsel. Rumour had it that he was running from the law, but no police ever came to ask anything about him, so he was left alone. Yet, there was something about him that demanded a second look and required respect.

And Sammy preferred it that way. He remembered his last hurried talk with Ralph Myers. It was in his Land Rover parked on a side street off Spanish Town Road. He had apologized for calling him despite his warning that further contact could mean trouble, and had quickly briefed him on the incident in his office.

"Ralph, I saw the guns bulging on them when the men came into my office. There were three of them and I couldn't allow them to catch me in a crossfire. I had to use the element of surprise."

"Well, as I have been telling you, Sammy, you have made some enemies. You can't help that, but you can be sure they will try again. There is no report of any missing persons and I don't want to hear anymore about anything that suggests your breaking any laws. I believe your friends want to play this thing very close to their chests. I think you did a brash thing when you called them and pointed a finger at yourself, but that can't be helped now."

"So what do I do now, Ralph? Man, my life in Kingston is over."

"One thing for sure, you can't leave the island right now. Your enemies will be checking for you at every port. The best thing is to go underground. You know this island like the back of your hand. I would say go where you have friends, but not where your enemies will look for you. They have to be careful too, since they have been breaking the law. Why don't you try Manchester? Go to someplace like Prattville, or Warwick or Alligator Pond. I'll pass the word around for people to leave you alone. If you begin to feel uncomfortable, or if you need anything special, leave me a message with Miss Sylvia Heron, a teacher at the Newport Elementary School. But don't hang around Newport too long. It's too close to Mandeville and even Cross Keys, and I don't have total influence over those places.

"Well, thanks for everything, Ralph. I hope I get out of this alive, and I hope I won't cause you too much trouble." Sammy said gloomily.

"Don't worry, man, just stay low. This thing will blow over. As I said, your enemies are too smart to raise a stink when they have no legitimate reasons. As soon as I see how things are going, I will send you a message by my cousin. And that is the only way you are to ever contact me. OK?"

They had shaken hands. Sammy had donned his Rasta disguise, walked quickly to his Isuzu sports utility vehicle and headed east towards the parish of St. Thomas. He would take the scenic route around the island to his hideout on the southwestern part of the island.

He settled in Plowden, near the border with the parish of St. Elizabeth. He was supposed to have relatives there, but he had never visited that part of the country, and knew no relative personally. As he had examined the face of some of the people he met, he thought he saw family resemblances, but he kept to himself.

****

A year later he lay in his crude but comfortable thatched hut, and read an old copy of the GLEANER. The words of an article jumped at him like a vicious wasp flying to the attack straight from the nest:

COLEYVILLE FARMER SHOT TO DEATH

David Gordon, cattle farmer from Coleyville, was shot to death by robbers last night. Report of the Christiana police is that Mr. Gordon had been the victim of praedial thieves for months, and had lost several prized calves to robbers. After keeping watch for several nights, Mr. Gordon had seen and confronted the thieves. He was shot and killed on the spot. Up to press time, no arrests have been made in this vicious homicide. When asked, the police reply that they are no match for the thieves in the area. They are without adequate transportation or weapons. It is reported that the death of Mr. Gordon brings to five farmers who have been violently attacked and killed in as many months by robbers working in the area.

Sammy had folded the newspaper and turned on his back to look up at the thatched ceiling as anger seethed him. At the same time, his mind recalled the image of his dying mother "Sammy, you is de younges', but God did mek yuh strang an' smart. Tek care of yuh brother an' sistah dem. I don' kno' what happen to Jamaica, but t'ings change. Yuh all t'ink me crazy, but I can see! An' t'ings gwine get worse." Shame, guilt, and regret flooded Sammy. He had been too concerned about his own affairs in the past few years to give much thought to the rest of his family. He had not seen David for years even though he lived just a few miles away from Mandeville. The years between their ages had prevented them from being close, but they held family affection, and they were together for family events. They had a good chat, for instance, when they had gathered for their mother's funeral. Now he felt that he had to do something to avenge his brother. He found pencil and paper and scribbled a note:

Dear Ralph:

The David Gordon who was murdered recently in Coleyville by cattle thieves was my brother. I hear that the police have neither weapons nor transportation to do their jobs well, I have both. The paper says that four besides my brother were killed in the past several months. Somebody has to stop these crazy fools before they kill any more of my family. Leave me a message if you think I am wrong. Maybe what I am about to do is what my life has been shaping me for. Maybe God wants me to be an instrument to help my country in this way.

He had cranked up his van and hurried up the mountains towards Newport. He had found Ralph's cousin and left the message for him. Then he had traveled up to Coleyville to begin his own investigations. He was sure the fearless thieves would strike again. They did, and they met the justice that Sammy had been trained to mete out by his trusty weapons with silencers attached. Three days after he had despatched the thieves, he had received a reply form Ralph.

Dear Sammy:

I mourn your brother's violent death. I remember meeting him at your mother's funeral. He was a warm and friendly man. I can't advise you on any course of action in this situation. You know that I must stand on the side of law and order despite the fact that we police take the blame for every thing that goes wrong in this country. We do work under extremely trying circumstances with our people often living in squalor at the stations and often without tyres for cars, or bullets for guns because of the economic situation of our nation. Criminals have us over a barrel and yet we are expected to work miracles. Whatever you do, please exercise extreme caution. I am your friend.

* * * * * * * * *

Sammy remembered all these things now, as the Isuzu hummed smoothly with the long shadows of the late morning sun racing before him. As he steered the vehicle careening through Four Paths and Porus, he realized that the newspaper story was warning him that at least the police were giving thought to the crimes and making connections. He had been stupid to leave the tools of the robbers beside their corpses. But at the time he had felt that it was important to send a message so that they could no longer attack and destroy people with impunity.

The two whom he had killed the night before was the result of rumours he had heard that his Cousin Walford was being slowly ruined by persistent thieves. His hunch had proven correct when he had stopped by the bar at the crossroads. It had been a perfect night for a crime, and he had struck another blow for defence of the helpless.

But he wondered how much the police really knew. Had any word of his activities got to the wrong people? If things were getting out of hand, it was almost certain that he would have been warned. But then, it had been several months since he had visited the teacher in Newport. That last time, he had brought the lady a basket of fruits to show his appreciation. She had smiled in appreciation, but she had been very tentative in her reactions to him. He had cut his visit quite short.

It was time to pay her another visit. So much had happened since he last saw her, it was possible that a message could be awaiting him. The newspaper had been full of the election that took place two years ago, and of the changes taking place as a result across the country. He had never told Ralph of his vendetta against the Minister who had so cruelly treated him. It had been too embarrassing. Nor had he mentioned his suicidal decision to wipe out his enemies and then allow himself to be captured by the police and gunned down. With his business ruined, his family deserting him, and all his friends shunning him, there had been no reason to live. Only his pledge to his mother had kept him going. He would take out just a few more bad men to hammer home the lesson, then the final showdown would come. First, the offending Minister, then his other detractors, then the police shootout. He had it all planned. He was only sorry that Myers would have to grieve the loss of a lifetime friendship in which he had invested so much.

He stopped and bought her a bottle of wine. He parked near the schoolyard and waited until he saw her on the playground. When she separated herself from the children and some other teachers, he walked over to her.

"Hello Miss Heron,"

"Hello, Captain. I've had a message for you for several months now. Why did you stay away so long?"

"Well, the last time I came you were not too friendly, so I thought I had better stay away."

"Oh, please don't let my expressions fool you. I think you are a very special man, and so does my cousin."

"Well thank you very much. I too think you are a very nice person. You say you have a message for me?"

"Yes, a letter has been waiting for you for the past three months. It's in my purse, but I don't want to give it to you in public. Why don't you wait until school is over and follow me as I drive away. I will slow down and you can overtake me and I will hand it to you."

"I have a better proposal. Why don't you meet me at a restaurant in Mandeville for dinner this evening. I haven't had a social event in my life for years. I would just like to talk to a human being."

"I could meet you at six o'clock at the restaurant of the Versalles Hotel in May Pen. I have to be there on business later."

"OK, I'll meet you at six at the Versalles Hotel."

Sammy looked at his watch. It was two-thirty p.m. He had time to go to his retreat and change clothes. His black sweat suit, even without the hood or Rasta beard and tam was still a formidable attire in the rural Manchester environment.

Dinner with Miss Heron was pleasant. She was a good conversationalist. But he was distracted. He wondered what the message said. He gave her the wine, collected the message, and excused himself. She too was pleased at his hurry as she had business elsewhere. Sammy hurried to the men's room and ripped the envelope open. The scrawl was familiar and the message cryptic.

> Your favourite Minister wishes to see you ASAP. No need to contact me, call 929-0000. His Secretary will advise you.

He had wondered what to make of the message. He decided not to call the Minister, but to send a message through Ralph Myers instead. He hurried to find Miss Heron and caught her as she was departing the hotel lobby.

"Miss Heron!" he called. He hurried to her side and spoke in a much lower voice. "I am sorry we were both in a hurry. I did enjoy dinner with you. The next time you see Mr. Myers, please tell him I will not call the Parson, but his Secretary can call me any day for the next three days beginning three days from now, at two o'clock each day at the Astor Hotel in Mandeville."

Sammy drove back to his retreat with much to think about. What could the Minister, who was again in power want with him? He had insulted and degraded him. What did he now want? He was surprised he had even remembered him. His memory of their last encounter still stuck with particular pain and bitterness in his stomach.

Chapter Twenty-Four

Sammy lingered in the shower savouring the scent of the soap and the stinging freshness of the cool water. After years of spartan sponges in places where water was scarce, he luxuriated in his return to the city where piped water afforded him a complete bath. Stepping from the shower, he towelled himself dry and walked the few steps to the dresser.

He looked at himself carefully in the mirror. He had aged. It showed at the corners of his eyes and in the deep furrows that lined his face. His sad eyes told of a life that was mirthless and near depression. There was a grayness in his hair and beard that was not there five years ago, the last time he had seen the Minister. Before that he had been a happy man. Then he had a family and a business and was committed to his country.

But he had been betrayed, his life's work wrecked by jealous men. It was the callous way in which he had been undermined that shocked him. Nothing had prepared him for such savagery. At first, he refused to believe the warnings, but soon enough he started to face the reality of the nightmares - the threats on his life, the creditors suing him, his name published in the papers, - the unrelenting humiliation of it all! He who once rubbed shoulders with the elite was now snubbed socially. Those who cautiously spoke to him, did so only to tell him that he should lay low, or better yet, leave the country. The hired assassins had not succeeded in murdering him, but something of profound value deep inside him had been killed.

Since that day when he escaped the attempt on his life, he had seen clearly that many whom he had counted as friends were proven to be enemies, and many with whom he had done business had proven to be conspiring traitors. But along with the men who ruined him, he held a grudge against those who had insulted him when he was down. He knew the names of those and had taken an oath to get his pound of flesh. Everyone would pay, and a certain Minister of Government headed the list. Now it seemed his luck had turned and God had delivered the man into his hands.

The call had come on the second day of his stay at the Astor Hotel.

"Mr. Gordon?" said a familiar musical voice.

"Yes?" he had replied cautiously. The years since the last time he heard that voice had been sad and difficult ones. It seemed that he was speaking into a cave of the distant past.

"Please hold for the Minister, Mr. Gordon. He would like to talk to you."

"Yes, I will." He had not participated in the recent election which had returned his party to power, so he wondered what the call was about. Politicians only repaid debts.. Some of the times. As far as he was concerned, he was owed nothing.

"But, who are you again?" he questioned the woman on the phone.

"Mr. Gordon, I am Linette, secretary to the Hon. Vincent Parchment, Member of Parliament with portfolio. Have you forgotten us already, sir?" The voice was slightly mocking.

"Lawd, Jesus, how you do, Linette? It's nice to hear your voice again. So, why are you all calling me?"

"It's nice to hear your voice too, Mr. Gordon. The Minister will be with you in a moment. I'm sure he will have answers to your questions in time. Please hold for him."

Sammy took a seat as he prepared himself to listen to what his nemesis had to say. The man had come on the line and greeted him as though nothing had happened between them. He was being invited to meet with him in his office at ten o'clock the next day. It was a matter of some urgency. Would he be kind enough to come? He was very busy at the moment, but would have more time to explain everything when they met. Sammy had sat back in his chair angrily remembering all he had done for the man, who in his need had turned his back on him.

He thought of the day when in an act of desperate loyalty, he had mortgaged his land to make sure that lack of money was no hindrance to Vincent's reelection. But the election had failed and the party had lost all. He had lost all as well his land, his business with the loss of the election. He remembered how the politician had turned on him and blamed him for the party's defeat. He flushed at the memory of how he was dismissed from the man's house like a yardboy. The thought of seeing him again filled him with disgust, but he would be there all right with a little something special. It was payback time. A little earlier than he had planned, but nevertheless on schedule.

"Yes, I'll be there at 10:00," Sammy said into the phone.

Now Sammy looked at himself and frowned. How would he seem to Linnette and the Minister? He had lived in the rural areas subsisting off the food of the poor. He was thinner almost to the point of being gaunt. A sadness swept over him.

Now he sat in his underwear cleaning his guns and checking the clips to make sure the magazine was fully loaded. He placed one of the guns in his overnight bag and got dressed. Then he put a silencer in his jacket pocket, and the other gun in the sheath he wore under his arm. He combed and brushed his hair, and wiped his face carefully, placing the handkerchief in his pocket. He checked himself one last time in the mirror, then walked out the door. He left early to be well ahead of the rush hour.

Sammy planned to breakfast in New Kingston and then go on to the Minister's office. He would arrive early and find his way to the Minister's chambers by the back entrance. He would quickly deliver his "message" and be long gone before anyone discovered the body. The chase would then be on, but he intended to elude his pursuers long enough to dispose of the three other wretches. He would allow himself to be found only when he had completed his mission.

He drove easily through an awakening Kingston, and made his way through Halfway Tree in good time. He found a place to park and had a true Jamaican breakfast at the, Pegasus Hotel consisting of Johnny Cakes, Callaloo, Ackee and Saltfish, and strong hot coffee of which he drank several cups. Then he bought a newspaper and slowly read all that could be absorbed since his mind was not on the news.

At nine o'clock he left the restaurant and within minutes arrived at his destination and parked. Alert guards watched his approach and asked him to state his business. The guard checked a schedule.

"O yes, Missa Gordon. You can go straight in. You are a little early, but you can have a seat and the secretary will come for you when it is time."

The layout of the office was different than he had remembered. From the lobby, there was no way in but past the secretary who was seated at the reception desk.

"Mr. Gordon!" she said. "It's been a long time! I am glad to see you. How have you been?"

"Hi Linnette. It's good to see you too. You look wonderful."

"Thank you. How about some coffee? You are a few minutes early."

"No thanks, I just had breakfast a few minutes ago."

"Very well, let me see if the Minister can see you before the other appointment gets here. Just hold on a little bit. Let me check things out."

"That's fine." Sammy said.

She was gone for only moments.

"Good! you may go in. Please follow me."

He was grim as he stood. Tense. He felt a pounding in his temples and his right hand itched. He tried to relax. The door opened and he walked past the secretary as she announced:

"Sir, Mr. Gordon to see you." Sammy stepped across the threshold of the room. The door closed behind him.

The Hon. Vincent Parchment, Member of Parliament was facing a credenza with his back turned as Sammy entered. He had no way of knowing the metamorphosis that had occurred in the life of the man since they last met. Vincent Parchment had lived in his own private hell of lost friendships, broken promises, and political misfortunes when his party lost the election. He had been returned to office a chastened and cautious man, no longer as sure of himself. But he had listened intently to the talks of the Queen's Minister. He had always admired the man. Above and beyond credentials and competence, he seemed to wield an easy confidence in his office that had been lost on most.

The man looked well, thought Sammy. Even from the back. Trim. Not the raging, rumpled, tyrant that chased him away from his yard. The "bang gut" was missing. Obviously, the return to office had done him much good. The suit was expensive, and of a continental cut with sleek lines that were tailored to fit his elegant form. Yes, man, Sammy thought, while your supporters sacrificed for you, you never ceased prospering. While they were starving, you ate well. Well, I'll add just a few ounces of lead to your weight. I hope you will like it.

For a full minute he stood and waited, gazing at the broad back while the man finished some task. Then the man turned.

The face was different. Something had changed. The eyes seemed more at peace. This was not the bloated face Sammy was used to seeing on television, or in the newspapers during the last year of the last regime. The forehead seemed smoother than he remembered, and he got the impression that the man had stopped indulging in harsh alcoholic drinks for some time. There was a calm to his demeanour , a poised sobriety, that Sammy did not expect. The Minister standing before him seemed to be one who had come to terms with his life. He had discovered his place in the world, and was dispensing his duties with caring commitment as should a mature minister and responsible statesman. He commanded Sammy's respect.

"Sammy! Welcome! Welcome, my friend," he gushed as if they had never been any hard feelings between them.

Sammy hesitated for a moment, then clasped the extended hand.

"Then how yuh duh, man? Let me look at you. Boy, it seems you have lost some weight."

"Good morning, Mr. Parchment. Yes, I guess you could say I am a little thinner these days than when you used to know me."

The politician seemed to wince but otherwise ignored the note of accusation in Sammy's reply.

"Then sit down, nuh, man. And tell me what you have been doing. Wait a minute, would you like some coffee?" Without waiting for a reply, he punched a button and the secretary appeared.

"Linette, please bring us some refreshments, would you. Thanks." He turned again to Sammy.

"Yes, man, so, tell me what you have been doing."

"Not much sir, just roaming the country. You know how it is when your business mash up and your creditors swoop down on you like parry hawk chasing John Crow," he replied, unable to suppress the bitterness.

Sammy watched as another wave of emotion clouded the Minister's face. It seemed to be a complex mixture of gentleness and sorrow that gave the man an aura of spirituality that is rare in a seasoned politician. He appeared to be wrestling with a deep sadness.

"I wonder," thought Sammy, "if this man too has been struggling with God."

The door opened and a man entered carrying a tray with an assortment of drinks, sugar, cream, crackers, and cheese. He placed the tray on a credenza and slipped away as silently as he had entered. The diversion eased the tension in the room.

"Here," said the Member of Parliament. "Have some coffee."

Sammy accepted and the two sat, sipping their beverage in thoughtful silence. Then the Minister put down his cup.

"Yes. Sammy, before you even ask, let me tell you that I have never forgotten you or all the sacrifices you made for me. I want you to know that I remember my disservice to you in your time of need. Man, I was hurt and frustrated. I took out my anger and disappointment on you. I chased you from my house."

Sammy shifted uneasily in his chair and put down his cup. Anger boiled in him afresh. He said nothing.

"My friend, I was wrong. I have lived with the image of you walking away from me for all these years. I have not forgotten for even one day. I was wrong. I apologize for insulting you Sammy, please say you forgive me. Sammy, none of what happened was your fault. All the money in the world could not have won that election for us and I knew it. I did a terrible thing. Please forgive me, Sammy."

Sammy had entered the room with bitter vengeance in his heart. He now sat staring at the floor and trembling. He felt the pressure of the gun heavy in his armpit. A terrible load that no man should carry. He felt the burning in his eyes and watched as heavy drops of tears fell to the carpeted floor. For a moment, the only sound in the room was that of his heaving sigh.

"Ayy Sah!" he heaved. "Ayy Sah!" he repeated.

This Minister was not the hardened politician he thought he knew. The man he knew would never have admitted to being wrong, and definitely would never ever ask anyone's forgiveness. The lump in his throat became a pain that was almost unbearable. This man before him had changed, and he couldn't but admire and respect the person he had become.

"It's all right, Minister. Thanks for telling me how you feel."

"Sammy, not every leader is fortunate enough to have supporters like you. I appreciate you, Sammy, for being both a man of sound principles and a stalwart patriot as well. I could never let any harm come to you."

"What you mean, sir?"

"Come on man, you remember somebody told you that you may run, but you can't hide? You think intelligence only work one way in this country? Power is a strange thing, Sammy. Sometimes it can only react, and can't act. Sometimes it can only protect, even if it can't prevent. You have never been totally alone, Sammy. You always had friends. You think, Myers was working alone to save your skin?"

Sammy leaned forward in his chair. The minister took his hands and looked him in the eye.

"We've known almost every move you made, Sammy. Except the ones we didn't want to know, We were sure you could take care of yourself underground. We were very sorry about your family situation, but we couldn't do anything about that. We can't interfere in domestic situations. But you know, it's been only two years since we were returned to office. We had to take our time and move slowly. As people say " Stan' pon crooked and cut straight". You understand. So, although we were thinking about you, we had to wait for the right moment to show our appreciation. As a matter of fact, that's why I sent for you."

"Yes, sir?" the question was filled with alert interest.

"I wanted to see you to express my gratitude and apology. But I wanted to do so in a substantial way. You understand me so far?"

"Yes, I think so."

"Sammy, how would you like to go back into business? There are no charges against you anywhere. Your name is fully cleared. I know you are good at business."

"What do you have in mind?"

"It won't be anything like you did before. Hold on, let me show you something."

He got up from his chair, went to his desk and returned with a brown paper sack. He brought it over and handed it to Sammy.

"Go on, open the bag and take out what's in it."

Sammy had to put some effort into removing a pockmarked green object. It was a fruit that was about the size of a basketball and just as round, with a long stem on one end.

"Now, that is a breadfruit!" exclaimed the Minister.

"Yes, sir?" said Sammy, quizzically.

"That is just one of the products of my constituency, my friend, a Yellow Heart Breadfruit!"

"I see."

"Uh huh, let me tell you at least three things about this fruit. First, there are millions of Jamaicans all over the world who are waiting and willing to pay ten dollars for a plate of good roast bread fruit, fried golden brown , if they could get it. Second, not even the best hotels in Jamaica carry breadfruit on their menu as part of the tourist trade, even though more and more Jamaicans return home by the thousands wishing to enjoy their native cuisine. Third, the same way God gave cereal to the northern climates, God gave banana, breadfruit and tubers to the tropics. Yet, the same Jamaica that is so inventive and creative in other ways, lags behind in the technical development of its homegrown resources.

"Are we only to excel where the European mind has led the way? Think about it, Sammy. What part of the world population is expanding? And what are the exotic foods that are now claiming giant shares of the market? Island people are now rapidly populating the first world countries. The same way Americans need hamburgers wherever they go, island people need their own food. But they must be prepared in novel ways, utilizing modern technology."

"Sammy, our breadfruit has a rightful place on the tables around the world. But it must be creatively developed. We need research into dwarf trees and accessible lands to facilitate easy and safe reaping, regulated seasons of bearing, and many other related projects. You see what I'm saying?"

Sammy shifted in his seat. Mere moments remained in his allotted time. The Minister's enthusiasm was contagious, yet he held back. What the man was saying held merit. The trend all around the world was towards exotic cuisine. Even the military was serving Chinese, Italian, Spanish food and everyone enjoyed them. If introduced into the hotels to tourists here, it could easily be exported, if properly prepared. The businessman in him was reactivated, but he was still reeling from the turn of events. Besides, how serious was the Minister anyway? What kind of support could he expect? There was only one way to find out.

"Go on, sir, I'm listening."

"The problems with commercially developing breadfruit have to do with husbanding, harvesting, storing, processing, marketing and shipping. Everyone of these has to be researched and developed. I have spent some time looking into these matters and I have some sketches of plans already. That's where you would come in, Sammy. You are my first choice for leading an enterprise of this magnitude. What do you think?"

"What you say sounds very interesting so far, sir."

"Good. In my view, refrigeration is the key. Quick transport is the lock. I have been talking to some people in North America and the UK, as well as hoteliers here in Jamaica. What we need to do is find a company that will produce the fruit in quantity. We could regulate breadfruit harvests in Portland, St. Mary, St. Thomas and other parishes. It would be your job to plan, produce, and market the commodity, utilizing ports where air transport is easily available."

"That is possible, sir. I could do that."

"Well, many are waiting anxiously for this latest addition to their menu of ethnic foods. Somebody is going to capitalize on breadfruit and make a killing. It may as well be you. I invite you to get back in business with a new product that has no present competition. It will repay the debt I owe you, provide work for thousands of Jamaicans, and will benefit the poor people in my constituency. I have already secured a grant and a sizable loan to get you started. I believe you will be able to bring this product on stream in just one year for an initial outlay of five million dollars US. It will be a good beginning and I know you will know how to expand. You will have free rein to work as you see fit. I have full confidence in your planning and management skills, and I know you to be an honest man. The sponsors will not be disappointed and I will have no reason to be embarrassed with you at the controls. So, come on man. Say something. I have another appointment in a few minutes."

"Minister, I am at a loss for words. I don't know what to say but thanks. And yes, I will work with you. The project has excellent chances to succeed.. Yes, I will head up the project."

"Excellent. I was hoping you would say that. I have lined up a list of experts from all over the world to help you, and have instructed my secretary to give you a folder with details of what I have been telling you. See that you guard that folder, it should not fall into unsafe hands. I have also had her put together a list of local experts to serve as consultants. Use them well in their areas of competency, but do not abuse them or permit them to abuse you. That five million will go far but it is not infinite. Our investment needs to show a substantial return. Be prepared to travel extensively so that you will learn every aspect of the project. There will be a major presentation on breadfruit culture in Malaysia and I expect you to be there. Take a couple of good local agronomists who know breadfruit with you."

"Yes, sir. I will get started right away."

"Well, take your time and get properly grounded. And by the way, you will probably not see me to talk to about this project any time soon. But be sure that I will know your progress and will be kept fully briefed. Thanks for coming. If you need any help, about anything at all, just call my secretary. You two have worked together before. Good luck, Sammy. If you work the way I know you can work, you will be a rich and powerful man again in a few years. Here, take this one with you. It's from my own tree, and I can assure you there is no finer specimen anywhere in Jamaica."

The Minister stood up and extended his hand.

"Okay, Mr. Gordon. Thanks for coming. My secretary is waiting to brief you."

Sammy stood and shook hands. He clutched the ponderous paper bag as he turned and left the office.

He was still in a daze as he walked to his car. He held the files with all the necessary information carefully as he balanced the brown bag while fiddling for his keys. He started the engine and drove slowly in the caravan of traffic. At Half-Way-Tree he turned north. He would head for the hills and find a quiet spot where he could think in peace.

Chapter Twenty-Five

Mandeville, 1998

The yard of the St. Peter and Paul Catholic Church seemed strange to him. It had been years since he attended his mother's funeral there, and a lifetime since he had been confirmed there. Yet, it was still holy ground to him.

He sat in his van and watched the worshippers go in, asking himelf what in the world he was doing there. The world of any formal worship, especially a Catholic Mass, was now alien to him. He wondered if his name was even still on the records of this church. Since those innocent and idyllic days of childhood, he had roamed far and wide. He had not even returned for the funeral of his father.

Life's ventures had taken him from the Manchester Mountains to the plains of Vere and Liguanea; from the rurals of south Manchester to the metropolis of Kingston; from the rustic hills of upper Clarendon to the shores of the Gulf of Mexico. From the cities and military forts of the United States of America, to the swamps and camps of Southeast Asia. From poverty and aimlessness to wealth and ambition; from preaching the Gospel of Christ offering eternal life, to the extinguishing of human life. He had gained much, lost all he had won, and was in the winning streak again.

He had come full circle. The journey to this churchyard on this Sunday morning had been an imperative. He was now satisfied with his life, but was hungry for that inner-self he once knew and cherished. Somehow, he felt that he would find it here. Wherever he had gone, whatever he had become, he had always claimed this church as his spiritual home. Although none here knew him, it was here that he considered his sacred shrine, and from here that he hoped to be buried at the end of his life. If they would have him. He hoped his desire to return home would be respected.

He remembered the day of his confirmation. The bishop, dressed in elegant vestments and holding his shepherd's staff, had annointed him with oil on the forehead, while the Choir sang:

> *"Before us at the altar the holy shepherd stands*
> *And over us he raises his consecrated hands."*

and

> *"Come Holy Ghost, Creator blest, and in our hearts take*
> *   up thy rest*
> *Come with thy grace and heavenly aid to fill the hearts*
> *   that thou hast made."*

He wondered now how those invocations had been answered. In what ways had God's Spirit, in response to the prayers of the church as the sacrament was administered, influenced his life? He did not pursue the thought for long.

* * * * * * * * *

His business was doing well. His dignity and pride were being restored. He was again being accepted in some of the old circles. He had learned tact and humility in his dealing with others. Now, he would think things through carefully and was more reticient in his responses to others. Yes, maturation was a never-ending process. Yes, his life was bouncing back. And his love for Tanya, even through she was more than a decade his junior in years, was growing steadily.

He hadn't intended to stay in Mandeville overnight, but a voice within him had urged him to stay. So he had!

He had retired early because tomorrow he would be off on one of those necessary trips to the United States, Canada, and England. He would be leaving his second wife, Tanya again. He hated that, but this trip was necessary. Since their recent marriage he never wanted to be separated from her, but she couldn't always travel with him, as she was needed to manage some details at home.

Since operations began, production was only now beginning to keep up with demands. The start up problems had been solved and markets were responding well to the addition of breadfruit. Sammy was now contemplating the addition of other venues for the delicacy as well as expanding production to other Caribbean islands. The ringing of the private phone by his bed cut into his thoughts.

"Sammy! How are you my friend?"

"Hello. Who's this? Oh, good evening sir, this is a surprise!"

"Yes. Well, how are you? How goes your enterprise?"

"I really can't complain. We are meeting our projections. As a matter of fact, there is such a demand for breadfruit that we have to be stepping up our production. I can't complain at all, sir Fine! Fine!

"Good work, Sammy. I always knew you were the man for the job. Now, Sammy, I need a little favour. As you know, we will be gearing up for another election beginning next year. You know what that means. Yes, we have to search high and low to find funds to fight for our lives. I know you will want to help."

"O yes, I'll do the best I can."

"Fine, fine! Please make a reservation to take my secretary to lunch as soon as you come back from your trip. I know you are just getting on your feet so I won't look for a lot from you right now. See if you can, hand her about half a million for a start. I would deeply appreciate your help, and I won't forget your kindness."

"OK, I will make the reservation and I will send a package."

"Thanks, Sammy. Have a nice trip. Do give my best regards to Tanya."

"I'll do that, sir. Thanks for calling."

"Goodnight, Sammy."

"Goodnight, sir."

His wife turned to face him as they lay on the bed. She looked at him intently, questioningly. "You don't plan go back through that again, do you?"

"Go back through what?" he asked.

"O come on, Sammy, you know exactly what I mean. You know I know who you were talking to. I honestly thought that man would leave you alone now after all the hell he put you through the last time."

"Tanya, it's not all that simple, you know. If he does not get support from people like me, where is he going to get it? Remember. I am what I am today because of his sponsorship. That's the name of the game."

"But he ruined you last time because of his excessive demands. You told me that!"

"Well, I was right up to a point, but what happened was not entirely his fault."

"So, whose fault was it that you lost your business and had to go underground to escape creditors and other people who wanted to kill you?"

"Well, he was not the one who started it. I told you that I started to support him even before I knew he could win an election. You were there the night it all happened. You remember that night in May Pen, when I had just moved back here from America? I just believed in the man's message and his programme for Jamaica. In some ways, he is as much a victim as I am."

"Then how come you had plans to kill him and went to his office to blow his brains out?"

"Tanya, as I said. It's not that simple. Long before he let me down because he was upset and could not think straight, other selfish and vicious people had set traps to destroy me. In some ways they succeeded, but thanks to Mr. Parchment and other friends who worked behind the scenes, they did not succeed in taking my life."

"Like Myers?"

"Well, it's not wise to start calling names. People are not even safe in their homes nowadays. But, to finish answering your question, when I went to the man in desperation for help and he drove me out of his yard with those awful curse words, I was humiliated. The same way he took things out on me, I focused my anger on him. He did not have to lose his temper and drive me away as if I was some little barefooted boy, but what happened was not all his fault."

Well, I still insist that he should leave you alone now and give you a chance to catch your breath. You are just now getting back on your feet. Let him go and ask those dope dealers for money."

"Well, if he knows any of them, and if they have any money, I don't doubt that he will take it if they offer it. Remember the old saying "politics make strange bedfellows." But I doubt that he will go to them. The man has pride and character. I know that."

"Lawd, those people who call themselves politicians. They don't have a heart? So, what going to happen to you when you go back in politics this time? Henh? Tell me that!"

"Tanya, face it. I entered politics as soon as I said yes to the man's proposal nearly four years ago. I was expecting that call long before now. An important part of politics is that whoever makes the king, controls the politics. So, if responsible people don't support a candidate, what do you think will happen to the fortunes of the country? Would you want the future of Jamaica left in the hands of people who don't come from here, who may only be passing through and have no investment in the country?"

"Well, I see what you mean, but what happens when you give away everything you have and when you need help there is none to help you? Does that make sense?"

"You see, whether you want to accept it or not, we can't exist in a society without politics. All we can do is exercise the power to choose the kind of politics and politicians we will have. Like any other profession, politicians come in all shapes. None are any greater than their character, training and experience. Politics is not bad in itself. It is its effects on the individual, and the effect of the individual on the system that make changes either helpful or a disaster. Whether you believe it or not, just as not all doctors or lawyers or preachers are corrupt; there are sound politicians with integrity who genuinely care for people and our system of government. There are good politicians, Tanya. Granted, in Jamaica right now it may not seem to be so. Many good people have followed bad examples. Some become disillusioned by a system that puts them down when they try to assert themselves."

"Lawd Jesus, so why you preaching to me, Sammy? I only say leave the man alone and get away from a hurtful situation. You telling me you want to run for office? I will personally kill you if I ever see you sink that low!"

Sammy chuckled. "All right, just before you throw acid 'pon me, or use ice pick tuh stab me, mek me finish what me start tuh seh."

His lapse into jocularity and a familiar patois scored a hit in the soul of the lovely girl. Her intense features softened. She smiled briefly.

"All right. Talk. But I still don't want any politicians in this house."

"What I was saying is this. Some of the men and women who run this country are good people. They have had to learn the skills of a vicious game to survive. They have developed the knack for dealing with the devil and emerging with benefits for the little people they know, love, and belong to. That's where they came from and they are determined not to let them down even when others don't care. True, many of them entered politics as poor as a church mouse. True, they don't want their personal poverty to be embarrassing, so, they have interests like all of us. But they still have consciences and they still go to church, and they still believe in God, and they do their best to do the right thing. They don't always succeed at everything they try. They take their licks, but they wheel and deal to keep prices down, keep food, shelter, clothes, medical services and water available. Yes, there are some good politicians left."

"Well, Rev. Mr. Gordon, you will have to show me one. When I look at the pot holes they call streets; and when I can't get water; and when they turn around and even tax the air I breathe, I wonder where the good politicians gone. Sammy, all I see and hear people talk about are a bunch of hungry crooks and incompetents who can't wait for some money to come down here from anywhere before they dig their hands in it and rake off the lion's share. They all live in big houses and drive big cars and eat in big restaurants and we down here are starving and have to box bone out of dog's mouth. Boy, you better walk off from me with your politics and politicians. You just making me angry now. I don't want to hear anymore. You hear me? I think we have talked too much already about this dirty subject. I want a cup of coffee. You want some? Blossom! Blossom! Where's that gal when you want her? Blossom! Come here!"

A sleepy eyed and plainly dressed young woman appeared at the door of the bedroom.

"Yes, Miz Gordon?"

"Blossom, fix Mr. Gordon and me some coffee, please. Do we have any of that nice sweet potato pudding left?"

"Yes, ma'am."

"Okay, then bring a piece of the pudding too."

CHAPTER TWENTY-SIX

"Tanya, that girl looks intelligent. Who is she?"

"Come on! Sammy, you remember that you helped me interview her for the housekeeper position. She comes from Manchester. She finished high school, but can't find a job. She works hard. She is cheerful and respectful. Reads a lot. You don't have to tell her every little thing. She can think for herself. I can depend on her. Help like her is hard to find nowadays."

"You say she reads all the time?"

"Every chance she gets. And not just comics and romances either. That girl is ambitious."

"Then Tanya, we must help the child if we can. That's another thing. This damn class system is ruining this country. Don't people realize that every time we help one of these bright young people up the ladder we are helping to strengthen this country? We can afford it. If we help her go to the university, she may even come and work in our company in a job that gives her dignity and self- respect. People helped us. We must pass on the favour."

"So, you are saying that being a helper to us is not dignified or respectful."

"No, I'm not saying that. I'm saying there are too many maids and servants in this country right now. And most of us treat our house helpers like slaves. We don't respect them."

"So, if there are that many of them, how come it took us six months to find her? Sammy, you can't be nice to these people. They don't appreciate it. They will turn around and attack you if you are too soft."

"Uh, huh. But what if you are too hard? What if they become disillusioned and come to think of themselves as being of no worth. What happens to a person who stops dreaming of a bright future and is left with no recourse but to begin scheming? Whom do you believe they come to see as the enemy? And they have access to your very bedroom?"

"Well you can talk all you want. I'm not going to help any good maid get away, then have to turn around and start all over again looking for help."

"But darling, don't you see? If she is any good, she could not possibly be content to stay here for the rest of her life. You said she is a serious person and a good reader. That means her world is expanding. We who have seen the world can help make her dreams come true. Point her the way forward. We may lose a good maid, but we could also gain an excellent and loyal manager or accountant who will never forget our kindness. That's the best protection money can buy."

"Here's you coffee, Miz Gordon. I warmed up the pudding for you, ma'am."

"Initiative, see what I am talking about?" said Sammy.

"Thanks, Blossom. By the way, where did you say you come from, and where did you go to school?"

"I come from Pratville, ma'am. I finished two years at Buxton College before I stopped."

"What made you stop?"

"Well, my father died, and my mother couldn't help me any longer. I am the oldest one, so I had to find work to help the family."

"You know she goes home every time she gets her leave and I am always helping her buy things for her family," said Tanya.

"So, what is your goal in life, Blossom? What do you want to be?"

"I was planning to study accountancy, Mr. Gordon, but I forget about all that now. I'll just have to stay here and work and see what I can save until better comes."

"OK Blossom, thank you for the coffee. The pudding is very nice," said Tanya.

"Now. You see what I mean? Should we help a person like that uplift herself, or keep her down like so many others do?"

"Sammy, you may be right about someone like Blossom. I am still not sure. But you can't go around helping everybody. They won't appreciate it. I am telling you. Especially politicians."

"So we are back on your pet peeve. What do you want me to do?"

"I want you to leave Mr. Parchment and people like him to his own kind of life. I don't want to see you hurt again. If I had my way, every one of those incompetents who are out to line their pockets with people's money and can't even get a road fixed would be voted out of office. A few years ago some of them were walking barefoot and riding bicycles. Now all of them are driving big cars and living in big houses, and don't do anything but tell lies to the rest of us."

"Tanya, there is some merit to what you say. But our form of government requires the participation of all the people. Part of our problem is that we are not always able to hold our candidates accountable. We become so dependent on them for the spoils of office that they are left free to exercise power without restraint. The correct way would be for the people to have the say in the country, with the politicians acting as instruments to bring about the will of the people."

"So, what are you going to do?"

"I'm going to give him what he asks. It will strain me a little, but I can afford it. This time though, I intend to do more than just give money to the party. I am going to have a meeting with other major contributors to the party along with the politicians and talk candidly about the cancers that are destroying our land. We must insist that our party develop think tanks to address the pressing local and international issues facing our country. We have good minds here that must be used to help turn things around and direct the future course of action. I alone may not be able to wield control over a candidate, but together, I believe a group of us can hold our Ministers accountable."

"Well, with all the work you have to do both here and abroad, how are you going to find the time to do all this other stuff you are talking about?"

"We have no option. Leaders of the private sector have to take the time. Clergy, professionals, business people, the military, and police must face up to their public responsibilities and live by standards on which civility and public decorum are based."

"So, how did we jump from you meeting with business people to start talking about civility and public decorum?"

"They all hang together, Tanya. Have you seen how clerks and civil service workers treat people nowadays? Things have changed in the past few years. People no longer honour and value others. We must insist on respect again. We can't succeed in business if we send the message that our customers don't matter. It has to begin in schools. Our basic institutions must be permitted to thrive."

"Sammy, you can talk all you want, but you can't turn back the clock. What gone bad a morning can't turn good in the evening'. You know that!"

"Lady, if you are right, then God help us. It's all over for our country! We may as well run away."

"Well, Sammy Gordon, I know that nobody can stop you when you get an idea in your head. All I have to say is: remember they stripped you of everything you had one time and they will do it again."

Sammy had been holding the coffee cup and sipping as he talked. He carefully put the cup in a saucer and reached for the hands of his wife and clasped them. He looked deeply into her eyes. She was lovely and loving. His Jamaican wife had filled the void left by his first family. His pleading calls to Doris had met with hostility and even his daughter Linda had become cool when he called to talk to her. Finally, he had stopped calling and had wished her well in whatever course she would take. In Tanya, he had found a sympathetic and grounded companion. She was his friend long before she became his wife, and was his constant source of comfort. Life without her was unthinkable. He was grateful that he had found a Jamaican woman who embodied every virtue a man could wish. In her mid forties, she was several years his junior. Her mature beauty and serious demeanour were balanced by a gracious smile, Christian commitment, and educated mind. Like him she had travelled to the United States and attended college. She had earned a graduate degree in business. Her travels had broadened her outlook and given her a modified egalitarian view of things that the untravelled Jamaican lacked. She had returned home after graduation to serve her country, and had worked for a major corporation until she married Sammy. Their admiration for each other when they first met was instantaneous. It had been as though they had always known each other. They shared a profound love for Jamaica, and mutual concern for the way in which the country was suffering from archaic views, greed, mismanagement, and abuse of power. Their genuine friendship had blossomed into love after Sammy resurfaced from hiding and sought her out. He drew her close to him.

"Tanya, I know you love me. And I know of your concern for me. Nobody knows more than me about the hell I have been through. I have known a lot of suffering. But what is my life if I cannot serve my country? How can I stand by and let our land be ravaged and our future thrown away by those who have no idea that we are creating a legacy for our children?"

She returned his gaze with tenderness.

"But what can we do, Sammy? Already this country seemed to be owned and bossed by people who neither fear God nor regard man. People nowadays will as soon kill you as look at you. If you want to know, I was thinking we should just pack up and leave and go back to America or Canada. You could still direct your business down here from up there. Then you wouldn't have to bother meeting and dealing with all the criminal elements."

"So, cut and run, henh? As so many others have done. You make it sound so easy. Many have left, and many more will leave. But for many of us, Tanya, America is not home. England is not home, Canada is not home. Anywhere we go, we need a place to return to that belongs to us. For me, and you, and others like us, Jamaica is it. No group or individual is going to run me away, so help me, God!"

"Boy, you really love this piece of dirty rockstone, don't you?"

"Well, maybe God has fixed it so that it is up to our generation to make the decision to fight to save it. To risk our lives to protect and preserve it. To prove that at last it is finally ours, and nobody can take it away. Up to now, it was not really ours, you know."

"What you mean?"

"Well, it's not the first time in history that a nation found itself dominated by foreigners. We are in lawlessness and rebellion partly because of foreign influences. If any outside influence wins, then Jamaica, as we have known it, is lost. We will become, as one cynic said, 'a marina for the United States'... or some other nation. We who know and love this land enough to stake our very lives and property for it, must struggle to safeguard its future. Maybe this is what I have been getting ready for all my life. This time, our problem is much more than just getting one man reelected to office. You see, as I said before, some of these politicians are good people with backbone and sound judgment. They stayed on and guided the country through its many hardships at a time when many others were running away and migrating. These people know the country through and through."

"Well you are right about that," agreed Tanya. "Yes. While we were preparing our minds and refreshing our souls, things were happening to the minds and spirits of these people that we couldn't even begin to imagine. They watched while their treasured institutions and vital infrastructure crumbled. Even now, when we look at our scavenged railway, our dilapidated hospitals and schools, and our damaged roadway system, we often forget that it is not just politicians who got away with the money, but foreign banking powers who had no mercy."

"That's part of the reason for the proliferation of drugs, you know. Not only that, but also many leaders could not imagine the choking effect of the demon drug trade on our world. True, it is not only Jamaica that is in a mess these days, but we can't spend time looking at other nations, or guess what they have to do to save themselves. Jamaicans have to concentrate on Jamaica first. We have to build integrity from the inside, then look around at others. After all, it wouldn't be the first time we set good examples for the rest of the world to follow."

"So, first you going to lead community improvement and enter politics. Now you sound like you are going to save the whole world!" Tanya exclaimed.

"Oh no, I am not anybody's saviour. But committed citizens must take part in building a vision. And you know, even now I feel a wind of change blowing across the island. The call for moral rectitude is coming from everywhere. Some can't see it, some won't believe it; some will even kill to prevent it, but I feel that a new Jamaica is being born even as we speak. There are many that still hold to a sense of optimism and have not forgotten how to invest material resources for the benefit of good causes. The will to survive is here, once we can get beyond the mistrust, jealousy, suspicion, and bad-mindedness, and once we can come to see that all Jamaicans put together are too few to be divided into so many small and destructive social castes based on shades of skin colour, then we can begin together to tackle the larger problems we face. The survival of our nation."

"So, now you are calling Jamaicans racists. Sammy, stop! I am a fair skinned Jamaican. It never entered my mind to be prejudiced against you. I don't even know what you are beginning to talk about. Boy, I think you have gone too far!"

"Tanya, nothing I have said is to be taken simply. The issue of race has a place in what's wrong with Jamaica and how we are to face a committed future. Skin colour by itself is not the problem. It is skin colour plus a choice to employ the historic desire to dominate that creates a mind set that divides and distorts. We can go deeper into that at another time. It is a ticklish topic anywhere. It is a ticklish topic here in Jamaica too. Anyway, let me rush on to finish answering the question you asked that got me started on what you call my sermon. No sensible man should oversubscribe in supporting a party to the detriment of his family or himself. We should all give generously and sacrificially, but not to the point of being foolhardy. I learned that the hard way. But far more valuable than giving money must be input that makes sure that the aims of politicians are in the best interest of the nation. I believe that a few lives banded together for patriotic good will be vested in honour and will make a great deal of difference. Maybe, just maybe, others seeing a few dedicated souls believing their land is worth saving and sticking their necks out to make their point, will join in the struggle and do what they can in their circles of influence to make the changes we all need so desperately."

A glow came over Sammy's face. His eyes gleamed. Still holding Tanya's hand, he jumped from the bed and pulled her to a window.

"Look out there," he said, pointing. "Tell me, what do you see?"

"You know, it's interesting you should ask that. I have looked out this window almost every night, but it has never been more than a glare of lights to me."

"Well, now, look. What do you see?"

"I see the haze of the city under a cloud. I see some bare spots, which must be water or undeveloped land. And, I see lights of different colours."

"Uh huh."

"Now that you mention it, I do see some twinkling lights. It must be an airplane or something. And I see what looks like a stream of traffic along some roads. So, what do you see? What should I see when I look?"

"I see the same things you do. The harbour, the airport, the streets filled with traffic. I see movement. I see the results of thought, planning, and hard work. I see gifts given for our enjoyment and convenience; and I see the responsibility to maintain what has been given to us to improve it before we pass it on to those coming after us. You know, one year at college, a speaker addressed a graduating class. He quoted some advice that King David in the Bible gave to his son. I have not forgotten the advice. You know how Jamaicans of our generation were taught to learn by rote. Well I treasured the lines and can still quote them:"

"He who rules over men in justice, who rules in the fear of God, is like the light of morning at sunrise; a morning that is cloudless after rain, and makes the grass sparkle from the earth."

"Tanya, show me a well run organization. One where the leadership knows what is to be done, directs effort with competence, and respects employees as thinking persons, rather than mere dumb children; then I will show you an organization that will not only produce efficiently and profitably, but will also enjoy a reputation for justice and humanity. Such an organization will be a credit to the present and an asset for posterity. By the same token, show me a country whose leaders fully understand their reason for existence; and their responsibility to all citizens, and I will show you a country that will survive no matter what forces impact it."

"So what are you saying about what you see outside this window?"

"I am saying that the same way I took bullets and shed my blood for other people with their own set of noble causes, I must be willing to give all I have left to save my country. But the idea is not to work harder. We are required to apply the same mental energy we employed to make money, coupled with spiritual power, to rebuild our institutions. Any future my country is to have, must begin with me."

"I agree with that," said Tanya.

"Just look at our Jamaica. We are a mere speck on any map. Yet, across the centuries, we have been known for producing and offering to the world brilliant men and women. Wherever they went they have been a credit both to their homeland as well as the places they settled. But in recent years, Jamaicans have been feared more than admired. We are regarded more for being dope peddlers and gangsters than for being Olympians, scholars, artists and statesmen. And you know, it's not by accident that even Jamaican bad men are the baddest of all. From when we were children it was hammered into us that whatever you do, do it well!"

As if mesmerized by his own speech, Sammy's face grew intense as he looked down on the glowing city.

"No, it's not over. We are not through. We are becoming more and more disgusted with the slow wrecking of our nation. We are even now turning away from the brink of disaster. The deeply treasured values that have been there with us all along are now breaking to the surface. We are affirming our character of honesty, toughness, self-sacrifice, industry, and love and respect for one another. You know Tanya, years ago, when I came home for a visit, one of my cousins lifted up one of his little boys and said to me. "Den Sammy, tek dis one back wid yuh, nuh?" I got angry and began to think he was giving away his child like a little puppy or a goat kid. Only recently did I come to realize that the man was tearing away a piece of himself to see that it had the best chance for development. Jamaicans have been like that. Sacrificing for the good of the future. Yes. We will again be known to the world. But this time we will be admired for the strength of our resilience. Our ability to bounce back from death and live again with integrity. The day will come when the higgler on the street and the common labourer will be honoured as citizens and patriots. Their children will be educated to love and respect their country and countrymen. Jamaica will be Jamaica again."

Tanya looked at her husband. He was staring straight ahead. His lips were parted as if in mid speech. Then his body shuddered. He grasped her hand with a new pressure.

"Come," he said. "Let's go to bed. We have a lot of work to do tomorrow." He lay on the bed and held his wife whose light breathing told that she was in fresh sleep. He held her as if to pour his strength into her and to draw from her the reassurance he needed. Her head shifted and rested easily on his muscled forearm. He settled down.

Epilogue

The eminence of Coke Methodist Church rose above the northeastern square of East Parade in downtown Kingston. It stood as a solitary witness of ongoing activity against the now silent core of the bustling heart of the city.

Chief Inspector Ralph Myers wore a broad grin as he wheeled the polished Black Isuzu sports utility vehicle into an available parking space, got out on the driver's side, and walked briskly around to the front door on the passenger side. He opened it with a flourish, and Sammy got out. The morning sun reflected off their silver hair, tinged with black in some places. They were still erect though well over sixty years of age, these friends of a lifetime; still trim from exercise, hard work, and disciplined living. Their mutual affection was apparent for all to see.

Sammy opened the rear door of the van, reached in, and took a pale blue bundle from Tanya. Ralph reached in and helped Tanya to exit the car. A cheerful breeze cooled the morning even as the sun rose higher on the cloudless Sunday. Tanya emerged, dressed in a lovely powder blue dress trimmed with white lace. She took the baby from Sammy and handed him the bag holding the obvious accessories for a newborn child. Together, the three of them moved away from the parking lot and walked to the side entrance of the church.

They took seats on the front row. Sammy looked at his watch and noticed that the time was ten o'clock. The sanctuary was filling with worshipers. As the service began, Sammy's mind wandered. He thought of the many rich stories of faith he had heard about this church. He had only become a member in the past year at the invitation of business friends, but his affection for the grand old church far predated his membership. He thought of the story of the venerable Rev. Mr. Nuttall who served as Pastor at the dawn of the twentieth century. During a religious meeting, a severe earthquake had shaken the building. Those who had gathered inside were terrified and wanted to run. The good Reverend had pleaded with his flock to remain inside and continue the Lord's business while nature ravaged the world outside. "If the Lord decides to claim us," he had said, "what better place to find us than in his church doing his business?"

All but one had stayed, and that one had been killed by the electricity from a fallen power line pole. His thoughts moved to the days when as a leader of the Boys Brigade in May Pen, he would visit the small book store to buy supplies for the Company. He wondered if any of the fellow worshippers, caught in the confusing maelstrom of present day Jamaica, could think with appreciation on their spiritual heritage.

And, of course, what one could say of Coke, could with the same thrill of pride be said of much of historical Jamaica. Have we become so foreign minded that we have lost all appreciation for the wealth of our island home that has given so much inspiration to so many? True, a lot has changed. Time, the inexorable upheaver of institutions and cultures had been steadily at work on this land. Yet, memory and values remain strong. Some in the present could only hold on and hope for the better future.

Those members of the generation who survived the holocaust of the seventies, were still alive and struggling. What did one of their poets say? "An see I ya; I still deh ya!" But they had bought time for the children. Jamaica shall be as strong as the will of its loyal children to survive. Those who remain within its ancient and hard won traditions, committed by love to the hills and valleys; to its hurricanes and its sunshine; to its past, but much more to its future: these will form the bridge across which the victors of the future will march.

"Will the candidates for Baptism please come forward," said the Parson.

Tanya nudged Sammy. They stood together and along with Ralph joined a number of other parents and sponsors at the altar.

"What is the name to be given to this child?" asked the clergyman.

For the briefest of moments Sammy felt a twinge of pain and regret. He wished he was the pastor caring for a spiritual flock. That should have been him in the clerical robes administering the rituals of the church. The twinge passed.

"Ralph Septimus George Gordon," he said, handing the child to the minister.

"Ralph Septimus George, I baptize thee....."

www.ingramcontent.com/pod-product-compliance
Lightning Source LLC
Chambersburg PA
CBHW030515020726
47494CB00004B/1107